A GHOST OF
A CHANCE

PETER GUTTRIDGE

speck press
denver

First published in the United States by *speck press* 2005, speckpress.com
Printed and bound in Canada
Book layout and design by *Magpie*, magpiecreativedesign.com

Published in Great Britain by Headline Book Publishing 1998
Copyright © 1998 Peter Guttridge

Library of Congress Cataloging-in-Publication Data
Guttridge, Peter.
A ghost of a chance / by Peter Guttridge.
p. cm.
ISBN 0-9725776-8-8
1. Journalists--Fiction. 2. Haunted houses--Fiction. 3. Sussex (England)-
-Fiction. 4. New age movement--Fiction. 5. Motion picture industry--
Fiction. I. Title.

PR6107.U88G48 2005
823'.914--dc22

2004021720

10 9 8 7 6 5 4 3 2 1

Praise for the Nick Madrid Series by Peter Guttridge

" … Peter Guttridge is off to a rousing start … a serious contender in the mystery genre."
—*Chicago Tribune*

"Original and highly readable … but a word of warning: never let this man house-sit if you value your pets."
—Lynne Truss, author of *Eats, Shoots & Leaves*

"Peter Guttridge has … the kind of mordant wit and cold-eyed social observation to make his Nick Madrid mysteries de rigueur reading."
—*Good Book Guide*

"Jokes are delivered with the speed and accuracy of a Gatling gun."
—*Daily Telegraph*

"… a near laugh-riot."
—*Library Journal*

"Few British crime writers can match the outrageousness of their American counterparts but Peter Guttridge is well on his way … the satire is spot on."
—*The Guardian*

"Wacky … Hilarious … A great read."
—Minette Walters, author of *The Sculptress* and *Fox Evil*

"Brilliant … Peter Guttridge is a fresh, stimulating new talent."
—Peter James, author of *Faith*, *Host,* and *Possession*

"Guttridge's series is among the funniest and sharpest in the genre, with a level of intelligence often lacking in better-known fare."
—*Balitmore Sun*

"Brilliant one-liners, lightning action, lots of suspense and very funny—self-deprecating Madrid is fast becoming my favorite crime hero."
—*Good Housekeeping*

"A plot that engages and amuses to the end."
—*Crime Time*

"A fast moving, laugh-a-line frolic."
—Reginald Hill, author of the *Dalziel and Pascoe Series*

"Sharp and sassy."
—*Birmingham Post*

"Peppy plotting is Guttridge's stock-in-trade."
—*The Times*

"An extremely likeable hero ... Agatha Christie on laughing gas."
—*Colchester Evening Gazette*

"The funniest crime novel of the year."
—*Publishing News*

Other Nick Madrid Mysteries
Now Available or Coming Soon

No Laughing Matter
Two to Tango
The Once and Future Con
Foiled Again

For Deborah

ONE

I screamed when my mobile phone rang. I would have preferred a more *manly* response—a bellow or a roar, perhaps—but at five in the morning, in a dark, deserted graveyard, a scream somehow came naturally. Especially with the company I was keeping. I jerked the phone free of my pocket and looked round warily. My scream had been loud enough to wake the dead. It didn't appear to have done so. Yet.

"Hello?" I whispered.

"Your wake-up call," a familiar voice said, loud despite the poor reception.

"Bridget, I wasn't exactly asleep."

"Pleased to hear it," replied my best friend in journalism—make that my only friend in journalism. "Why are you whispering?"

"I'm in a graveyard. And I'm not alone."

Bridget was silent for a moment—a new record for her. Then she said stiffly:

"The whole point of this article is that you're in a haunted place *on your own.*" She sighed. "Who is she? That long-legged PR from the film festival? I hope you were a gentleman and let her go on top. Doing it on gravestones at this time of year is just asking for piles."

"It's not like that," I said. I looked at the man in front of me. "I'm with a dead man, actually."

She barked a quick laugh.

"I've had dates like that. Put him on, then."

"What?"

"I'm pleased you're taking your brief to communicate with the dead so seriously, although I didn't actually specify gay necrophilia. But let me hear what he has to say."

"Not a lot," I said, ignoring the rest of her—frankly rather cheap—remarks. "I must say you don't seem very surprised."

"A dead man in a graveyard—that should surprise me, should it, sweetheart?"

"You don't believe me, do you?' I said indignantly. "That's because you're missing the point. This man isn't a corpse."

"What's the difference between a corpse and a dead man?"

She had me there. I shone my torch on my companion again.

"Don't distract me," I said eventually. "What I mean is he's not dead and buried. Well, not buried. He's not in a grave or a coffin."

"More council cutbacks, I suppose. Okay, I'll go along with this. Where is he, Nick?"

"He's hanging upside down from a tree by his right leg."

"Tory MP is he? Bin liner over his head, drug-impregnated orange stuck in his mouth?"

"Ha ha. He's hanging by his ankle, not his neck."

"Maybe he's a beginner. Or just incompetent. You're sure he's dead? Have you tried the kiss of life?"

"Yuk. You must be joking. Even supposing I knew how to do it there's some gunge on his face."

"So cut him down and wipe it off."

"And disturb evidence of a crime?"

"Nick, what was your drug of choice last night? The guy

has hanged himself. There's no crime in that. What are you up to?"

"I'm not up to anything. I'm being serious, Bridget."

There was another silence down the line.

"You really are sitting there with a dead man," she said in a puzzled tone. "Are you okay?"

"I'm being very brave."

"Doubtless. Well, you really should try and see if he's dead."

"He's dead, believe me. I touched his face earlier. It was very cold."

"So what do you think killed him?"

"Strangulation. The rope goes down his back and round his neck. He's trussed up with a really complicated series of knots."

"So the police should start looking for a deranged Boy Scout. Have you called them yet?"

"I'm going over to Ashcombe Manor to phone them now."

"Why don't you just use your mobile?"

"Because, dear heart, my battery is about done—I can hardly hear you. Plus, I'm not hanging around here any longer than I need to. This has been a very strange night."

"Nick, I understand how upset you must be. But try to take the long view."

"Which is?"

"You could be on to a great story."

I'd reached Ashcombe Manor originally by a more circuitous route than the one I took now. My chum, Bridget Frost, the 'Bitch of the Broadsheets,' had recently switched from poacher to gamekeeper and taken a job as editor of a Saturday magazine for one of the nationals.

The publishers didn't care whether she took it downmarket to compete with the *Mirror* and the *Sun* or upmarket to compete with *The Guardian, The Times,* and *The Telegraph* just so long as she didn't leave it in the middle market, where it was being trounced by *The Mail* and *The Express.*

She'd told them it would take two years and an extra £2 million on the budget to turn it around. They offered her a six-month contract and whatever money she could save by sacking people. She didn't intend to sack anybody, but she accepted the offer for the hell of it and to see how much of their money she could pass on to her freelance friends in commissions before she was fired, as she inevitably would be.

Within a matter of days she was sending her mates on freebies to posh restaurants and upmarket health spas and on travel jaunts all over the world. Not all her mates, mind. She invited this mate to spend a night in a haunted place and live to tell the tale. And she didn't even make living to tell the tale an urgent priority.

"Perhaps you could make notes all the time you're there," she said when she gave me the commission. "In case anything, you know, happens to you."

Bridget smirked as I looked sourly at the lavish travel brochures scattered across her desk. She picked up a book called *The Haunted Houses of Britain* and pitched enthusiastically into the task of finding somewhere really gruesome for me to go. A smoking cigarette clamped in the corner of her mouth, she riffed the pages, telling me the history of each place with gleeful relish: who went mad in this one, who had a seizure in that.

I interrupted her: "Bridget, have I offended you in some way?"

She tilted back her chair and stuck her feet up on the desk, her skirt riding somewhere up around her hips. She had good legs—a good figure all the way round, come to that—but I hardly glanced at them. We'd been friends for years and I was probably closer to her than almost anyone else but we never thought of each other sexually. Or if we did, we never did anything about it.

She exhaled smoke.

"Here's one. Ashcombe Manor, an Elizabethan great house in Sussex."

I groaned.

"I hate Elizabethan ghosts. Guys in tights with their heads under their arms, white ladies floating through walls looking droopy. If I'm going to do this I want a ghost with a bit of spirit, you know? Isn't there a medieval ghost clanking around in full armour anywhere, gore dripping off his cuirass—if you'll pardon the expression?"

"Queer ass?"

"*Cuirass*. Skip it."

She scanned the page. "Ashcombe Manor has a lot going for it. Haunted neolithic graves nearby. John Dee, the Elizabethan astrologer and black magician, performed scrying—whatever that is—there. Then, in the twenties, Aleister Crowley, The Great Beast, lived in the house and performed black masses there. It's even got a lake where they presumably disposed of all the sacrificed virgins."

"Crystal balls."

"Same to you with knobs on."

"Scrying is seeing things in crystal balls. Dee's crystal ball is in the British Museum. And Aleister Crowley—I've heard of him. He was a member of the Golden Dawn with W. B. Yeats."

"That old cricketer?"

"That was W. G. Grace. Even you must have heard of Yeats. He's a great poet."

"A poet?" she said, in a tone of voice she usually reserved for paedophiles, white slave traders, or boyfriends who'd done her wrong. She sniffed. "Says here Crowley was a demonologist, necromancer, drug fiend, and sexual pervert—sounds right up your street, Nick. He and his friends tried to raise the devil on the South Downs near Ditchling Beacon."

"D*ae*monologist," I corrected her. "On The Downs? I thought that was all National Trust. Couldn't he find anywhere less prosaic?"

She gave me one of her looks, the kind that make grown men quiver. I quivered.

"D*ae*monologist?" she said. "Anywhere less *prosaic*? You talk like a real poncy pillock sometimes, Nick." She threw the book on the desk. "Do you want this commission or not?"

"Of course I do. I'm perfect for it. I know all about this stuff. I grew up not far from Pendle Hill."

"I'm thrilled for you."

"It's witch country. It's where 500 years ago the Lancashire witches lived, turned their neighbors into toads, and died. Every Halloween as teenagers my mates and I camped out all night on Pendle in the hope of seeing witches fly by on broomsticks. Mad, I know, but we were going through puberty—it's a tricky time for a lad. Years later I took part in the Bloksberg Tryst, a 15th century magical ceremony for turning a goat into a hand-some young man. It wasn't altogether successful. It's a real prob-lem getting shoes to fit me."

Bridget laughed. Politely. Then: "Don't witches have orgies at their Sabbats? You'll probably like that."

I blushed. I frequently do, which is a bit embarrassing for a man in his early thirties. Quivering and blushing all in one morning.

"No, thanks," I said. "The devil always wants to join in and he's well known for having really bad breath and ice-cold hands. Plus, everybody has to kiss his bum."

Bridget snorted.

"I didn't realize the devil was just another bloody editor."

The people at Ashcombe Manor had turned me down. It was some kind of New Age conference center these days and the administrator, a woman called Moira Cassidy, was worried that I was going to take the piss out of the place.

"Trust me, I'm a journalist," I said.

Cassidy laughed.

"Does that line usually work?"

"Never," I said. "I can't think why." I grinned sheepishly—a total waste of time, since I was speaking to her on the telephone, unless I was turning into one of those radio DJs you can actually hear smile. She harrumphed, a sound I always associate with Margaret Rutherford. Worryingly, I found it quite sexy.

"So can I come down to Ashcombe Manor to be haunted?" I said again.

"I admire your persistence, but I think not," she said. "You may, however, visit in the daytime whenever you wish. Goodbye, Mr. Madrid."

I thought that would be the end of it. Bridget thought otherwise.

"What's a tumulus?" she said when I called her.

"Roman name for a burial mound or barrow," I said. "Why?"

"There's a tumulus on the Downs above the manor that's supposed to be even more haunted than the house."

I groaned.

"You want me to spend the night on top of the Downs?"

"The weather's warm enough. You can practice those skills you learned as a Boy Scout."

"What—competitive farting and mutual masturbation? I wasn't in the Scouts, actually."

"Weren't you, *actually*? The ones you learned as a Girl Guide then. Says here witches and warlocks have been making use of this tumulus for centuries. When it was excavated in the 1880s a dozen children's skeletons were discovered, bound hand and foot. Been there a couple of thousand years. Probably been buried alive. Crowley and his gang did sexual magic up there in an attempt to raise their spirits."

"Sounds like they needed cheering up."

Bridget ignored me.

"What's sexual magic?" she said.

"Supposed to be a potent way to summon demons and the devil. An excuse for perves to dress up in weird clothes and have sex on altars."

"I told you this article was right up your street."

Which is why, six hours before I found the hanging man, I'd been sitting beside a haunted prehistoric burial chamber, looking mournfully down on the Manor. I'd come up at dusk by taxi from Brighton to the Ditchling Beacon then walked a mile or so along the top of the Downs to the tumulus. It was in a place with the unlikely name of Faulkner's Bottom.

The Manor was a big, gloomy pile set among woods, beside a road that ran beneath the Downs connecting the village of Ditchling with the market town of Lewes. I knew Lewes—it was Islington in the Country, with a bedrock of hippies who moved down in the seventies from Portobello Road and Camden Lock. Folk music was popular—from the first time round.

The old house was in darkness now, although the pub beside it was still brightly lit.

I could hear the occasional car zip along the road, engine noise disproportionately loud in the silence. My attention had just been drawn to the squealing tires of a car leaving the pub car park. I heard a throaty roar as it revved round a bend heading towards Ditchling.

The moon was full, its cold light illuminating the Downs, silvering the flint paths and giving a spectral look to the slice of sea at Birling Gap. I could see the pale shapes of cows in the fields to my right.

Although I don't believe in ghosts and the supernatural, there was something undoubtedly spooky about sitting up here beside a burial chamber. I looked doubtfully at the tent I'd miraculously managed to erect. It didn't seem like much protection against demons from Hell—and not just because it was leaning at a drunken angle.

I thought I might cope better if I too were leaning at a drunken angle so I cracked the bottle of beaujolais I'd brought with me.

I'd chosen to be here on the night of April 30/May 1, a night known to witch covens everywhere as Walpurgis Night. Or *Nacht* if you want to be pedantic. Like me. The conjunction of Walpurgis Night and a full moon augured some heavy joo-joo among the satanically inclined this night.

Indeed, given the number of crank cults the approach of the Millennium had brought into existence; Sussex's age old reputation for dabbling in what we childhood readers of Dennis Wheatley call The Dark Arts; and nearby Brighton's interest in all things New Age; the Downs were probably crawling with satanists, pagans, and those UFO freaks who hope to be abducted by passing alien craft.

Me, I was gearing up for midnight, when the Wild Hunt was supposed to come by. A terrifying spectacle, the Hunt is a band of spectral riders running with black hounds led by a wild huntsman.

The huntsman is the devil, the hounds are the body spirits of unbaptized children, and the hunt careers across the sky and the open fields accompanied by rustling winds, shouts, the blowing of horns, and the infernal baying of the hell hounds. Yes, sounds like the Tory party conference to me, too.

By twelve thirty I had sadly concluded that the Hunt had either been banned under new legislation or found a new venue. By now clouds had dimmed the stars and the moon. I lit a fire outside the tent. A pathetic flame but it sufficed. I shared humanity's dread of the dark. A primitive fear, stemming in my case from the fact that I didn't want to put my hand on a slug.

By two the moon had disappeared completely and the lights of the towns I could see spread out towards the north had for the most part gone out. It was *very* dark.

I needed a toilet. I'd downed most of the bottle of wine to go with my favorite sandwiches—cheese and picallili on currant teacake, I'm embarrassed to admit—and nature was more shrieking than calling. I made my way towards what I had designated as the toilet—a sad looking bush on which I should probably have taken more pity.

I saw the lights as I was standing there, a wavering procession of them in the grounds of the Manor. My attention had been attracted by the noise of car engines. A small convoy of caravans, headed by a dark-colored, sporty looking car, turned onto the main road from the road junction by the pub. A four-track of some sort brought up the rear.

As I followed the convoy's progress along the road, I saw the lights.

I would have paid more attention but a man is at his most vulnerable when emptying his bladder in the middle of the night in a haunted place, especially when he thinks he can hear footsteps somewhere behind him. I had my torch but it was pretty feeble and both hands were, well, occupied.

There were some fifteen seconds or so when I was totally at the mercy of any passing ghoul. I looked over my shoulder just as the cloud across the moon cleared for a moment. I was startled to see silhouetted against the sky some quarter of a mile away a tall figure with a stag's head on its shoulders. The antlers glittered in the moonlight. Other figures with animals' heads were standing in a line beside the stag.

I gulped. Either I'd stumbled upon the Royal Ballet recreating *The Tales of Beatrix Potter* or I was in deep shit. I dashed back to the relative safety of the tent. I was sure my trouser leg would dry quickly.

I could see the line of creatures from the entrance to the tent. I didn't know how long they had been standing there. They remained for a further five minutes, their heads tilted up to the sky, then, one by one, they moved off across the Downs to the south.

I decided they must be part of some pagan cult from Brighton and that, therefore, I was quite safe. Pagans prefer peace and love and nature to human sacrifice. On the whole.

I went to sleep with surprising ease, though the empty bottle of wine might have had something to do with it. At around five, something woke me. I was aware of movement outside the tent. I lay stiff in my sleeping bag, my eyes straining in the dark, hardly daring to breathe. Shuffling footsteps near the entrance flap. And a moaning. A low moaning.

"Get a grip, Madrid," I whispered aloud when I realized the moaning was me. I tried to calm myself. Maybe whatever was out there didn't know I was here. Then again, maybe It did. Maybe It was even now homing in on my tom-tom heartbeat, fangs bared.

For what seemed an eternity I huddled in my sleeping bag, too frightened to move. Eventually the sounds ceased. Very reluctantly I decided to leave the tent to see what might have caused them.

Had it been the pagans? A supernatural being? A denizen of Hell? I didn't know. All I knew was that when I crawled out of the flap, I put my hand in a brown, steaming mess *that had not been there before.*

Damned cows. I cleaned my hand and looked down towards the Manor. It was in darkness but in the churchyard of the old Norman church, just outside its grounds, I could see a single, unwavering light.

I knew that a lot of people in Sussex would be up early to celebrate the dawning of May Day on certain high places. Chanctonbury Ring was one venue; a hill outside Ditchling another. But a single light in a churchyard? There was something ominous about it. As a journalist who thrived on danger—so long as it was relative, the expenses were good, and I could stay in a five-star hotel—I decided to investigate.

It took me about twenty minutes to get off the Downs. I cut through a plantation of trees in the form of a large V. I had read in my local guide book that it had been planted last century to celebrate Queen Victoria's Jubilee.

Call me intuitive, call me paranoid, but I had the distinct feeling I wasn't alone in the plantation. Glancing quickly from side to side, I hurried down to the church.

I entered the churchyard through a low wooden gate. Soon I was close enough to the light to see that it was a torch beam. The torch itself was in an odd-looking holder. I looked more closely then dropped my own torch in horror. The holder was a human hand, sticking out of the ground.

Only when I retrieved my torch did I see the man hanging upside down from a branch of an ancient oak tree.

I stepped back and looked nervously around. Then I looked back at the man. Hanging there, dressed in black, his jacket bunched round his chest and shoulders, he looked like some strange, giant bat. He was elderly, with a full head of white hair hanging down like a badly made halo. His eyes were open, staring and quite lifeless.

His right foot was tied to the tree branch by several loops of rope. The rope then ran to his left leg, which was bent at the knee and crossed behind his right knee. His elbows stuck out on either side of his body. When I walked cautiously round him I could see that his hands were tied together behind his back. The length of rope was wrapped tightly round his neck.

I approached and reached out a hand. My fingers grazed his cold face. I sat on my haunches and looked at him for a few moments more. I was contemplating him when Bridget rang.

There was access to the Manor grounds by a lich gate from the churchyard. I walked across the gravel drive and stopped in front of a massive, ironbound door. I tried the handle. It was locked. Since dawn was arriving by the second, I hoped a caretaker or cleaner might be up. I tugged on a bell pull and heard a clang somewhere far within.

Whilst I was waiting, I stepped back and looked up at the crenellated walls of the Manor. After a few moments, I heard the sound of huge bolts being drawn. The door swung open.

"May I help you?" a tall, bearded man in jeans and a fluffy pullover said, in a tone of voice which indicated he hoped he wouldn't have to.

"I've just found a dead man in the churchyard."

He looked at me without interest.

"You think that unusual, do you, a dead man in a grave-yard?"

Everyone's a bloody comedian these days.

"He's hanging from a tree. I think we need to call the police."

"*You* need to call the police. I need to finish my dinner. It's nothing to do with me."

"Can you let me use a telephone?"

"Unwillingly."

He led the way down a short passage, which opened out

into an Elizabethan great hall. High ceiling, massive wooden rafters, stone slab floor. A minstrels' gallery at the far end. A wide staircase with an ornate wooden balustrade at the near end. All that was missing were suits of armour and pikes and battleaxes up on the walls.

"A bit early for dinner, isn't it?" I said conversationally.

"Not if you're living on a rota of twenty-seven-hour days," the man said, without slowing his step.

"Of course," I said. "Silly me."

He took me to the right of the staircase into a small office overcrowded with furniture and filing cabinets. Almost filling one wall was a large chart headed Weekly Courses. On another wall were abstract photographs. I looked at the chart.

"Which course are you taking?"

"None of your business," he said. He indicated the phone on the cluttered desk and gave me a sour look.

"I'll tell Ms. Cassidy you're here."

I watched him go, wondering where he'd learned his interpersonal skills. Then I sat down behind the desk. A fan heater blew hot air on to my feet. I dialled 999 and told the police briefly what I'd found. They asked me to stay at the manor until they arrived.

I put the phone down and looked round the office. I walked across to examine the photographs more closely. They looked polarized in some way—flashes of color, nimbuses of light.

"Kirlian photography," a woman's voice said.

I turned towards an attractive red-haired woman in her mid-thirties, standing in the doorway with a short, self-important looking man at her side. It seemed they were early risers at Ashcombe Manor. She came forward, her hand held out. I shook it lightly and smiled.

"Moira Cassidy," she said. She looked puzzled. "And you're the man who wishes to use our phone so early in the day. You know there's a public one down by the church?"

"I didn't actually. But I've already used your phone. The police will be along shortly."

Her expression changed.

"The police?"

"About the hanged man. Didn't your colleague tell you?"

"Henry simply said you wished to use the telephone."

"He was probably eager to get back to his, er, dinner. He said something about a twenty-seven hour day."

"A hanged man?" her companion said in a lightly accented voice.

"This is Mr. Stassinopolos, one of our course leaders."

The man was in his fifties, good looking, olive complexioned with a full head of Pynchon hair and blue tinted spectacles that obscured his eyes. He was a well built man, though little more than five feet tall.

I couldn't help noticing he gave himself a lift by wearing cuban heels. I was impressed he could find them, even given the fashion for retro sixties stuff. I'd only ever seen them on the covers of old Beatles' albums.

Wearing the heels meant he stood with his bum sticking out. As if to compensate he puffed out his chest. The overall effect was to make him look like the figurehead on the prow of a ship. My rule of thumb has always been 'Beware of Greeks Wearing Lifts,' but for the moment I was willing to give him the benefit of the doubt.

"Henry doesn't see why he should operate by a time system imposed on him by a society he despises," Cassidy said. "He rejects the twenty-four hour day as a bourgeois conceit."

"A bourgeois conceit," I repeated. 'Yes, I see that. I'm Nick Madrid. We've spoken on the phone, Ms. Cassidy.'

Her eyes narrowed.

"The journalist."

"You said I could visit in the daytime at any time."

She looked at her watch and frowned.

"I didn't really anticipate it would be at six in the morning."

"Yeah, well. I came down to spend Walpurgis Night up on the Downs and I found a dead man hanging from a tree in the graveyard of your church."

Ms Cassidy put a hand to her throat.

"St. Michael's is the village's church, not ours. Is it someone from the Manor?"

"I have no idea. The police are on their way. They'll identify the person. They've asked me to wait here until they arrive. I hope that's okay."

"Okay?" said Cassidy tartly. 'I refuse you permission to spend the night here for a newspaper article—"

"Magazine article—"

"But you come down anyway bringing scandal and bad publicity with you." Cassidy sat down heavily in the chair behind the desk.

"I didn't actually bring the dead man with me. And there's no reason why it should reflect badly on Ashcombe Manor. I've told you before, I'm an honest journalist."

"An honest journalist?" Stassinopolos said, with a curl of his lip. "Isn't that oxymoronic?"

The smile disappeared from my face. Not because of the sarcasm—I was used to that—but because of the word. I know *oxymoron* isn't the kind of word you expect to cause trauma but it has bad resonances for me. A few months earlier, I had used it in an art gallery in Edinburgh and had been immediately set upon by a bunch of yobs. Not artists, real yobs. They weren't averse to the word. They were averse to me.

"And what do you do to earn a crust?" I responded sharply to Stassinopolos.

"*Earning a crust,*" he repeated disdainfully, "is not a priority in my life." He pulled himself up to his full height. He wanted to look me in the eye, I could see, but being a good sixteen inches shorter than me this was difficult. "I am more interested in the spiritual than the earthly."

"Bully for you. What do you do around here?"

"I teach a course in personal magnetism." I frowned. "To help people maximize their innate powers." He indicated the photographs. "I took those photographs."

Personal magnetism—I could go for that. He had my interest. "What is this Kirlian photography?"

"The means by which we can photograph a person's aura."

He had lost my interest. I've got friends who believe in auras, crystals, and all that New Age shit. They tell me we each have an aura some twelve inches thick right round our bodies. Maybe. I've never seen one, but then I'm a cynic. As far as I'm concerned, an aura has to be believed to be seen.

"Mr. Stassinopolos, perhaps you'd like to show Mr. Madrid to the lounge?' Cassidy interrupted from the desk. "There are hot drinks and biscuits there, Mr. Madrid."

Head thrown back and bum stuck out, Stassinopolos led me back across the great hall and into a corridor. He indicated a couple of doors at the far end and with an imperious nod left me there. I opened one of the doors and found myself in a library, the walls lined from floor to ceiling with books of all shapes and sizes.

Most of those on the higher shelves were leatherbound, probably bought by the yard by some previous Manor owner. I worked as a librarian for a couple of years before I turned to journalism—and what's so funny about that? I love musty old libraries.

I ran my eyes over the spines of the books—collected essays by long forgotten philosophers, travel books, volumes of poetry by minor poets, the classics.

The lower shelves were a mish-mash of novels, science,

folklore, and some recent New Age books—the collected works of Deepak Chopra, for example. I went back to scanning the higher shelves. I couldn't help noticing a number of volumes were irritatingly out of place.

A Wodehouse novel in among Kingslake's five volume history of the Crimean War. A topographical tour of Sussex wedged between the volumes of Dennis's cities and cemeteries of Etruria. And, most glaringly, among the twelve volumes of Needham's *Science and Civilisation in China,* in brown leather, a single volume with a red spine. Curiously, rather than a title the book had only a motif on its spine, in the shape of a upside down letter T.

There was no coffee here, so after some more minutes mooching around I stepped across the corridor and entered a large room that had a spectacular view over the lake through a set of long windows.

The rising sun flooded the window bay with golden light. I'd read that Luytens had worked on this house in the twenties. In fact, that he'd created the lake. And that whilst the earliest part of the house dated back to 1586, the windows were either Georgian or his. The long window looked like some of his handiwork.

I admired the view for a moment, then helped myself to a cup of herb tea from a table by the door. Instead of chairs or sofas, large cushions covered with throws were scattered around the floor. Only when I had sprawled on a pile of cushions by the far wall did I notice that I was not alone. A woman was sitting in the lotus position on the floor over by the window. I couldn't make out her face. Bathed in sunlight, she was form without features.

I didn't want to interrupt her meditation. I picked up a Tarot pack from a low table. Several of the cards were laid out, face up: the Ace of Cups, the Knight of Pentacles, the King of Swords.

Four others were turned face down. I flipped one of them over. Looked at it for a moment. Looked more intently.

The woman in the window stirred as Moira Cassidy walked in.

"Mr. Madrid, the police have arrived to speak with you," Cassidy said stiffly.

On impulse I slipped the Tarot card I'd turned over into my pocket. It was a card called the Hanged Man. It showed a man hanging upside down from a tree, his left leg bent at the knee and tucked behind his right leg, his hands clasped behind his back. Just like the man I'd discovered at dawn.

TWO

Moira Cassidy flashed an angry look at me when I told the policeman about the lights I'd seen in the grounds of the Manor in the night.

"What about these lights, Miss Cassidy?" he said, his voice unpleasantly nasal.

His name was Bradley and he was altogether an unprepossessing man. Tall, very thin, with thick eyebrows and the hairiest ears I'd ever seen. It looked like two bushy-tailed creatures were burrowing into them. He also had a weeping eye, which he kept dabbing with a large checked handkerchief.

"*Ms.* Cassidy," she said sharply. She folded her arms in front of her bosom. "I presume the lights belonged to our 'Moon Goddess Within' students."

Bradley tilted his head to examine Cassidy with his good eye.

"It's a course we run," she said, meeting his eye determinedly. "It was a full moon last night, Mr. Bradley. A cause of celebration for women."

Bradley dabbed his eye, then pondered his handkerchief for a moment.

"Frankly the fairer sex has always been a bit of a mystery to me," he said. "You're going to have to explain."

Cassidy sighed. "The course acknowledges and celebrates the moon's sway over us."

"Tides and such?"

"The tug of the menstrual tides, yes. The things that make women goddesses."

"You lose me on goddesses, Ms. Cassidy," Bradley said. He showed surprisingly white teeth in a nervy, ingratiating smile. "Don't get me wrong. I think women are bloomin' marvellous, I do really. But goddesses and, er, ladies' matters—I'm not following."

Cassidy smiled thinly.

"It is our belief that our menstrual blood ebbs and flows with the waxing and waning of the moon," she said, in the manner of a teacher addressing a particularly slow child. "Ovulation tends to occur when the light is brightest, at the full moon. We believe our menstruation begins at the new moon."

Bradley nodded. "With you."

"Hence in ancient cultures," Cassidy continued, "the moon was considered the source of fertility and birth. Cultures who focused their worship on a goddess, the Great Mother Goddess, existed for thousands of years in Asia and Europe. The Great Mother was also the Moon Goddess, with the many faces of the moon."

"With you," Bradley repeated. "Most interesting. And how exactly do your students celebrate the full moon?"

I could tell by his expression that he was having tabloid fantasies of some kind of orgiastic rite.

"I imagine they went round the lake in procession, told stories, sang, danced in rings, built a fire and jumped over it, hugged ..."

Bradley looked bemused.

"Men as well as women, was it?" he said after a moment.

"Men would be most unwelcome," Cassidy said curtly.

"Of course," Bradley said. "But at any rate it's likely the lights Mr. Madrid saw were your students in procession."

"I have no idea what lights Mr. Madrid imagines he saw but it seems possible."

"We'll need statements from these women. Are they available?"

"Not at the moment. Most of the college has gone to Lodge Hill in Ditchling to see the sun rise. It's May Day, you know. I would be there myself had not Mr. Madrid turned up so unexpectedly."

"Ah yes," Bradley said. "It's quite an occasion, I believe. Morris dancing at dawn. With *wassailing* on the cards later, I have no doubt." He showed his teeth again. "You see, I do know a little about all this. You can't go to Lewes Folk Club for as long as I have without picking something up."

He suddenly clapped a hand over his ear and began to open and close his mouth very rapidly. I thought for a moment the furry creature had burrowed into his brain, then I realized he was doing a mime of the stereotypical folk singer.

I smiled and nodded. Cassidy looked at him as if he had pissed in the punch. Bradley turned to me.

"And you, Mr. Madrid, were spending the night alone on top of the Downs."

"For an article. I'm a journalist."

Bradley's eyes narrowed. He tutted. "A journalist? That's unfortunate."

"For me or you?"

"Journalists finding bodies is never a good thing. They go rushing off into print with all sorts of half-baked theories, make our job much more difficult." He favored me with his ingratiating smile. "Wait a while before you put pen to paper, there's a good journalist."

"I'm very happy to cooperate with the police," I said. "As a matter of fact I have something to show you."

I handed him the tarot card. He looked at it for a moment.

"Where did you come across this, might I ask?"

"Not at the scene of the crime," I said, "if that's what you're thinking. I took it from a tarot pack here but only for the purposes of comparison."

"May I see what's causing such interest?" Cassidy said, stepping over to Bradley. He proffered the card.

"This looks like more than coincidence to me, Ms. Cassidy, since this is how Miles Lyttle was found by Mr. Madrid."

"Miles Lyttle?" I said. "You've identified him then."

"Oh yes. I came along with Constable Chadwick, the community policeman for the area. Knows Lyttle well. A literary type, Chadwick says." Bradley looked puzzled. "Made his living *writing book reviews* apparently."

"Killed for giving someone a bad review?" I mused. "Seems a little extreme. Even John Osborne would have drawn the line at that. Or at least hesitated for a moment."

"There's no reason to presume he was murdered, Mr. Madrid, unless there's something you're not telling us."

"Only that he seemed to make it an extraordinarily complicated death for himself."

"You'd be amazed what one person can do with a good slip knot or two," Bradley said sagely. He glanced at Cassidy. "So what about it, Ms. Cassidy?"

She shrugged her shoulders.

"Why do you assume I would know?"

"Isn't this kind of thing what you go in for here? Mr. Madrid says this card is yours."

"This card may very well have come from here," she said patiently. "But these cards are used in a great many other places by a great many other people. There's a gypsy on the pier at Brighton who tells fortunes with Tarot cards. A number of shops in the North Laines sell them. And no, this is not what we *go in for*.

We are a center for serious spiritual learning. I'm surprised the police share the standards of journalists. I expect Mr. Madrid to use the coincidence as an excuse to smear our center but I thought more highly of the local constabulary."

"Why would I want to smear you?" I said.

"Journalists find it easier to laugh at things that are a little out of the ordinary rather than genuinely attempting to understand them. Why should you be an exception?"

Tricky question.

"No one is trying to smear your center," Bradley said, in what he probably imagined to be a soothing voice. "I'm asking for your assistance. From your knowledge of these things, can you shed light on this? Could Lyttle's death be some kind of ritual?"

"The Hanged Man is the twelfth card in the Tarot pack. The number twelve might connect it to the twelfth house of the zodiac—the house of karma, where the sins of life are stored in preparation for the cleansing fire of the after death experience— a cleansing which makes a new life possible."

"So he might have believed that if he killed himself like this he was heading for a new life?"

"The card has a lot of contradictory meanings. The awkward posture may reflect awkwardness inside him. Some people think his isolation represents a fundamental loneliness. He doesn't seem to be in pain—but then how many of us do realize our own inner chaos?"

"How many indeed?" Bradley said briskly, glancing at me as he spoke. Bloody cheek.

Moira shrugged. "Other people say it means triumph over the flesh, still others that it means selfishness."

"And what does that tell us?"

"I haven't the foggiest idea."

"You are forgetting two other interpretations, Moira," a deep bass voice said from the doorway. We all looked as a tall, broad shouldered man in cossack boots and baggy trousers strode into the room. Probably in his early fifties, he had a shaved head and was wearing a cloak, which he held across his body with his left hand.

"Gentlemen, Oscar Savage. Excuse my intruding." He planted a big kiss on Cassidy's lips and turned to face Bradley and me.

"The gentlemen in blue, I presume." He eyed us quizzically. "One further meaning of the card is 'voluntary sacrifice.' A second is 'death by violence.'"

Bradley raised his handkerchief but stopped before it reached his eye. "Murder or suicide," he said.

Savage nodded.

"You are aware, I am sure, that there are different versions of the Tarot," he continued. "Your colleague here—" he indicated me "—is holding a card from the A. E. Waite set. A very inferior pack that manages to lose the esoteric content of the original Tarot sets.

"In the Charles V pack, however, the links with suicide are clear. The Hanged Man has two bags in his hand. They are presumed to contain the thirty pieces of silver Judas received for betraying Jesus. There is a medieval tradition that Judas hanged himself, weighed down with the guilt of his betrayal."

"So Miles Lyttle betrayed somebody?" I said. "Who?"

"Undoubtedly he betrayed Aleister Crowley."

"Aleister Crowley?" Bradley said.

"Aleister Crowley, officer. The Great Beast of the Revelation, whose number is 666. The mage. The black magician. The wickedest man in the world, if you are to believe the yellow press."

"With you. And does this gentleman also live in the neighborhood, sir?"

"Aleister Crowley, inspector, died in poverty in a Hastings boarding house."

"So …"

"He was cremated in Brighton."

"But …"

"In 1947."

"I'm not sure I understand."

"Then I shall attempt to explain."

Bradley looked at Cassidy and me.

"Perhaps somewhere a little more—"

"*Intime?*" Savage said.

"Private. Mr. Madrid, CID will need a statement from you shortly. Can you hold yourself ready. And Miss Cassidy, I'd like to speak to the ladies who were out last night as soon as they return from their dawn revels."

"Can I just ask about the torch?" I said.

"The torch holder, I suspect you mean. Yes, curious thing that."

I glanced at Cassidy then back at Bradley.

"Was it a real …"

"A real hand? Lifelike, but no."

"A hand?" Cassidy said.

"A light held in a severed hand?" Savage said.

Bradley looked at him, nodded.

"You know something about it?"

"Not this particular hand, but I know about the Hand of Glory, yes."

"The Hand of Glory?"

"The dried and pickled hand of a man who has died on the gallows," Delarent explained. "If a candle, made from the fat of a malefactor who has also died on the gallows, is placed in the Hand of Glory, as in a candlestick, it renders motionless anybody to whom it is presented. Such a person cannot move so much as a finger. It is as if they are dead."

Bradley put his handkerchief to his eye.

"It was an electric torch and, I can assure you, Mr. Lyttle is genuinely dead."

"I don't doubt it. Sometimes the dead man's hand itself is the candle or rather bunch of candles, all his withered fingers being set on fire."

Bradley led Savage out into the Great Hall. Cassidy sat down behind her desk and glared at me.

"What?" I said.

"A black magician. That's all we need."

"You can't blame me for that," I said. "Crowley lived here, didn't he?"

"That's not the kind of thing we want to draw attention to. People come here for serious spiritual research. We're not interested in black magic or the sexual shenanigans Crowley went in for. That's so much negative energy."

"But this house has been linked with black magic for centuries, hasn't it? When John Dee lived here—"

"Two people in a 400 year history. It was precisely that approach that made me unwilling to let you come and stay overnight here for your stupid ghost story. We discourage any associations with black magic. The black magic room doesn't exist anymore."

"Black magic room?"

"It doesn't exist anymore. It was destroyed just after the war."

I hadn't known one ever had existed.

"Do you get many people enquiring about Crowley?" I said.

"Too many. A film company wanted to film here recently but we wouldn't let them. They were quite persistent."

"Film what?"

"Don't you read the papers, Mr. Madrid?"

"Why should I want to read something somebody like me has written?"

"I see your point. A Hollywood producer—a man called Zane Pynchon—is making a film biography of Aleister Crowley. He was very miffed when we turned him down, but we don't want this house to become a shrine to a self-publicising mad man, thanks very much."

"That's no way to talk about the producer of six of the biggest box office hits of the 20th century," I said.

Zane Pynchon was the loudmouthed, macho producer of "more bangs for your buck" event movies, noted, among other things, for their extreme misogyny. However, of late he had been linked to a couple of lower budget, "quality" films—Hollywood's idea of quality, that is.

"I was talking about Crowley," Cassidy said icily.

She soon made it clear she had no more time for chit-chat.

"Would you mind leaving as soon as the CID have finished with you, Mr. Madrid? You're not really welcome here."

"Don't mince your words," I said. "Just give it to me straight."

I loitered down by the lake waiting for the cops to get back to me. It was some 400 yards across and looked gloomy and forbidding. As I watched a couple of swans busying themselves in the middle of the dark water I was startled to see something large, black, and glistening emerge from the lake on the far bank.

It took me a moment to realize it was a diver in a wetsuit, wearing a face mask and oxygen tank. The person looked back at me then flip-flopped his way into the woods beyond, between mounds of earth that looked as if giant moles had been busily at work.

CID took a brief statement from me. I told them about the animal-headed figures I'd seen, and asked if they knew yet how the man had died. They weren't saying. The coroner had just arrived. The post mortem would probably take place later in the day.

When they had finished with me I thought I'd take the opportunity to pack up my tent. I walked across the road and made my way back up the track to the brow of the Downs.

It was only seven thirty, but the sun was already hot on my shoulders as I followed a diagonal path that probably dated back to Neolithic times. I crossed a steep field of pungent wild thyme. Summer had come early again this year. Butterflies flittered around me, birds sang in the trees. In the fields below, newborn lambs stayed close to their mums. You want bucolic, I got it.

Bridget phoned as I was nearing the burial mound.

"Who's the stiff?" she said without preamble.

"Don't overdo the sympathy, Bridget. Some local guy called Miles Lyttle. A bald-headed bloke at the Manor—guy called Savage—thinks it was either ritual murder or ritual suicide because Miles had done old Aleister Crowley wrong. You know Crowley—that black magician at the start of the century?"

"Makes no sense to me. Why are you puffing? Or is it your flat battery? Where are you?"

"I'm just going up Faulkner's Bottom. Don't say it—"

"Well, when you've finished with his why don't you shift yours back up here and pack some overnight things?"

"Why would I want to do that?"

"Because this could be an interesting story. Remember a couple of years ago there was all that stuff in the paper about witchcraft in Sussex? People just over the border in Tunbridge Wells afraid to let their cats out in case they're nicked by satanists to sacrifice at the summer solstice? And in Lewes, some school-boy sacrificing cats on church porches, rigging up a black magic room in his mum's outside loo. You say there might be an Aleister Crowley link? Cozy up to this bloke Savage to find out more."

"Bridget, he wears a *cloak*. He makes Roy Strong look like a nineties man. He probably has a wardrobe full of floppy brimmed velvet fedoras and long silk scarves. He's one of those guys who wants to be thought a *dandy*, not twigging that it's just another word for Very Sad Indeed."

"I gather you don't like him."

"Correctamundo. Plus he's got a bad case of the Donald Sindens."

"Even so, hang out there for a couple of days."

"Bridget, I've got a date tonight."

"With?"

"That PR from the film festival."

"I knew it, you randy sod. Break it—you'd never be able to keep up with her anyway. She'll eat you for breakfast."

"That's what I was hoping," I said glumly.

"Stop into the office when you come up and we'll go to Gravity's Rainbow."

"I thought you'd been banned from there."

"On the contrary, it's one of the few places I haven't disgraced myself. In any case, people can be remarkably forgiving if they know you have an expense account."

In the months before she got the editorial job, Bridget had been going through a period of—how shall we say—"re-evaluation," following the failure of yet another bad relationship. This had taken the form of getting pissed and abusive in most of the high class joints in town then tapping off with the maitre d'".

"It's men in dinner jackets," she told me once. "I can't help it. They can be millionaires at Covent Garden or head waiters in Chez Gerard but if they're wearing dj's, that's it."

"Do they need to keep the dj on when you get down to the nitty gritty?"

"The nitty gritty? How coy. You mean shagging. Naturally, that depends on whether or not they're wearing a cummerbund."

It was about 8:30 by the time I'd packed my tent. I looked down at the ivy-clad walls of the pub, called The Full Moon, a trickle of smoke curling lazily from its chimney. I knew it did bed and breakfast—I'd been tempted to cheat and sleep there last night. I walked down, breathing in the fresh air.

I could see half a dozen police vehicles pulled up on the verge outside the churchyard. A group of men in uniform and plainclothes were huddled near to where I had found the body.

Bright yellow tape had been stretched in long lengths around the churchyard, hiving off the crime scene. Inquisitive locals hovered by the church itself. I saw Savage in his cloak talking to an elderly man in a dog collar.

The pub was open. I went into a cozily gloomy room, furnished with long tables set before long settles. A man was sitting at the bar nursing a pint. At this time of day, that's what I call dedication to drink. The jukebox was on. I recognized Nina Simone's version of "I Put A Spell On You."

The barmaid was an attractive woman somewhere in her forties. Streaked blonde hair, slender.

"What are you drinking?" she said pleasantly.

"I make it a rule never to drink before breakfast, at least in the middle of the week."

I was conscious the man at the bar was giving me a hard look. I glanced at him and gave a little smile. He looked like an ex-rugby player: a flat nosed, big shouldered man in his forties, his pint lost somewhere in a huge fist.

"It's a special day," she said. "May Day. The morris dancers come on here from Lodge Hill. Then there's the May Day fete at the church."

"You've twisted my arm."

As I took the first sip the man at the bar turned to me.

"You a journalist?" he said, scowling.

I assumed my alertness and general air of integrity had given it away.

"How did you guess?" I said, preening.

"You look shifty."

"Geoff, for God's sake," the barmaid said, with an embarrassed laugh. "Don't mind him, he's only joking. Cabbie came in last night, said he'd dropped a journalist off on top of the Downs."

"That was me. I'm the one found the body."

"The body?"

"All those police down in your churchyard? There's a dead body there."

Geoff started to speak and I knew what he was going to say so I quickly ran on: "I'm surprised you didn't know. There's quite a crowd gathering."

The barmaid colored slightly and glanced at Geoff.

"I've only just got up. Haven't stepped outside yet—I live above the pub. Who was it, do you know?"

"Bloke called Miles Lyttle."

"Shit. He was running a tab." She shook her head. "Who's going to pay his bar bill? Edith will be furious."

"Edith's the pub owner?"

"Lyttle's wife."

"Aha. Happy marriage, was it?"

"None of your business," Geoff said.

"Geoff, shouldn't you be getting off to work? You said you had that top field to sort out today."

Geoff stood—we were about the same height, though he was far wider—and downed the rest of his beer.

"Be in for lunch," he said to the barmaid before throwing me a final dirty glance and stalking out.

"Your husband seems to be one of the many millions who don't care for journalists," I said.

"Don't mind him—and he's not my husband."

She reached for my glass and expertly poured a pint of bitter into it. Which was very nice, except that I'd been drinking lager.

"He's alright. Especially for round here."

"Looks like a rugby player."

She nodded.

"County player in his younger days. His nose ended up that way from too many brawls in the scrums. Concentrates on organic farming these days, believe it or not. And no, he doesn't wear sandals or drive a 2CV."

"He doesn't look as if he does. But I don't work in stereotypes, in any case."

"Thought you said you were a journalist?" she said with a little smirk.

"Well, yes—and I'm afraid I've got a *Straw Dogs* image of country folk," I said. "All in-breeding, badger-baiting, and firing shotguns at strangers."

"And that's just the commuters. Wait until you meet the families who've been here for generations. Like mine."

"Oops. Sorry. You've always lived here yourself?"

"God forbid. I moved back three or four years ago to bring up my son."

I looked round.

"He's not here. He's visiting his father for a month. In America."

I nodded.

"Moving back—the right thing?"

"I'll get back to you on that. At first I felt like I'd landed on the moon. You forget there are people in the village who've never been to London, even though it's only ninety minutes away on the train. And if you're a single mother, the chances of meeting anyone who isn't married are pretty remote. Geoff, compared to some of the guys round here, is a knight in shining armour, believe me. He just gets a bit moody, that's all."

"So can you tell me anything about Miles Lyttle and his wife—Edith, did you say?"

"Childhood sweethearts —recipe for disaster later in life. Developed different interests. Edith was a scientist, quite a well regarded one in her time, I think. He got into magic and all that spiritualist stuff. They moved down here because he had a thing about Aleister Crowley. You know, the Great Beast? Crowley used to live in Ashcombe Manor."

I nodded.

"The Great Con Man, more like."

"You don't believe in that stuff?" she said, as "Do You Believe in Magic?" came on to the jukebox. I shook my head.

"So the Lyttles lived separate lives?" I said.

"Separate homes even. Edith insisted. They split the house in two and lived in their own halves, though Miles was forever pestering Edith about his personal problems."

"I suppose Edith will be grieving."

"Only about the bar bill. She's teetotal. Otherwise, shouldn't think so for a moment. She really couldn't stand him."

"Do you know where I can find her?"

"Today? Novington Church May Day fete, all afternoon. That's our other church, up the road a mile or so. The fete is the highlight of Novington's year. She'll be there running the tombola."

"Even when she finds out about her husband's death?"

"Certainly. How did he die?"

"They don't know for certain. He may have been murdered."

"Murdered? There you are then. She likes a good murder does Edith."

"Ah, the beautiful Kathleen," Savage boomed, breezing into the pub, his cloak sweeping behind him, his bald pate shiny enough to have been waxed. "And the officer of the law, drinking on duty I see."

"I'm not a policeman. I'm a journalist."

Savage shucked his chin clear of his collar.

"A journalist? I know your editor."

"I sincerely hope not," I said.

"You are from the local rag are you not?"

"No, I write for the nationals. My name is Nick Madrid."

"Indeed." He looked me up and down. "Madrid. That's an unusual name."

"It is," I agreed. I looked at Kathleen and she was looking at me with a strange expression on her face. "But not that unusual. What did you mean, Mr. Savage? About betraying Aleister Crowley?"

"Miles Lyttle, late of this parish," Savage intoned, brushing his hand across his shaved head, "—but then he always was late …"

He gave a throaty chuckle, which turned into a thick cough. He even managed to make phlegm sound theatrical.

"If he did betray Crowley it must have been years ago," I said. "Why has retribution taken so long?"

"Lyttle's offence is recent. He has been working on Crowley's biography. I must assume the betrayal lies therein."

"But Crowley's dead."

"He has … admirers."

"There's a cult of Crowley?"

"Of course. He was, after all, a fascinating character. Some say he was a misunderstood genius, a master magician. Others regard him as a criminal fraud, a sponger, a sexual pervert, and a bully. It is well known that in his life, as one biographer put it, he drove more men and women to drink, insanity, or death than most incarnate devils."

"So what did Miles do that was so terrible?" Kathleen said.

"I have not read his manuscript but I assume he reveals something that was better kept secret. He had access to some papers that were lodged in the attic of Ashcombe Manor and only recently discovered."

"But what would the secret be that would make it worth killing for?"

"Something magical, of course," Savage said.

"Do you believe in this magic stuff, then?"

"I favor a non-logical approach to life, certainly. I believe very strongly that there is energy we could all tap into if we only knew how. It is well attested, for example, that the philosopher Gurdjieff gave off great energy. He had sophisticated theories on the subject."

"Yeah, I know them," Kathleen said. "His theories boil down to: if you got it flaunt it."

Savage laughed throatily.

"And he did?" I said, smiling uncertainly.

"You bet," she said. "In a favorite Parisian restaurant, Gurdijieff's presence was so highly charged it provoked orgasms in the waitresses as they passed by."

"Service must have been slow," I said.

Kathleen sighed and looked round the pub.

"Yeah, but what a great place to work."

"I did not realize you shared my interest in hidden forces," Savage said.

"I don't really." She looked at me. "I used to have a boyfriend who was into all that."

"Well," Savage said. "It is said Crowley also had great presence. He could exert his will outside of himself. There is a story—attested to by witnesses —of Crowley falling into step behind a man walking down a city street. For some yards he aped the other man's way of walking then Crowley suddenly dropped to the floor. The man in front of him fell flat on his face."

"He tripped him?" I said.

"Not at all," Savage said. "The man was not aware Crowley was behind him. Was it some kind of power surge coming from Crowley? Who knows? There's a man doing experiments with auras—"

My scepticism must have shown on my face.

"But surely, Mr. Madrid, you know, for example, when someone is staring at you. You can feel it. Perhaps it is your aura responding."

"More likely it's some sixth sense I'm not aware I have."

"Pah—sixth sense, aura, call it what you will. But there is something there. I can always tell when someone is staring at me."

"If you didn't dress like such a pillock you wouldn't have a problem," I thought but didn't say.

Before I could think of a more polite reply he continued: "Look at animals. Dogs know when you're coming home. Cats, dogs, and birds all have homing instincts." He looked intently at me. "You intend to write an article about this?"

"That depends. But whatever you've told me is off the record."

"How very dull. My dear fellow, I much prefer to be *on* the record. So much more interesting."

He excused himself to go to the toilet.

I turned to Kathleen.

"Can I book a room here for a couple of nights?"

"You're not staying at The Happy House?" Kathleen said.

"Ashcombe Manor? I don't think they'd have me."

"Then sure—we're less picky," Kathleen said.

I smiled and looked at my watch.

"Can I call a cab from here? I need to get a train back to London, collect some stuff."

"I'll call it for you."

Whilst she was on the phone I mooched around the pub. There was a large painting on one wall of the interior of the pub with dozens of customers crammed in together. I assumed they were locals. Judging by the clothes it had been painted sometime in the seventies. On the wall beside it was a key with a name against each person in the painting.

I wandered over to the jukebox to checkout the playlist. Cliff Richard's "Devil Woman" was playing. There seemed to be a lot of tracks by the seventies band Black Sabbath. I sipped my beer and looked back to the bar. Kathleen was watching me.

"I can't help noticing a theme here. Your choice?"

She nodded, a mischievous grin on her face.

"Witchcraft and the occult have always been big in Sussex," she said. "For a couple of hundred years, from the 17th to the 19th century, Sussex was virtually cut off from the rest of the country because of bad roads. It was a lawless place and superstition was rampant. We call the devil 'Old Scratch' or 'Old Harry' or 'Mr. Grimm.'"

"There was a strong tradition up near where I was born, too," I said. "In the Pendle villages—Roughlee, Newchurch, Pendleton—all the pubs have some reference to the Lancashire witches. At least here you don't have plastic witches on broomsticks hanging from the ceiling."

"Where did you say you were from?"

You'd think after all these years I'd be used to saying but I still got embarrassed when I had to give the name of my hometown.

"Ramsbottom," I said.

"Tupp's Arse!" she declared, using the locals' name for what was actually a very picturesque place. No, honestly.

"You know it?" I said.

"Know it well," she said. "There's something I'd like to ask you."

"Go ahead," I said but she looked over my shoulder.

"Your taxi's here. It'll wait until you get back." She looked me frankly in the eye. She was a very sensual-looking woman. "You'll be back soon?"

"Is the P-Pope a bear?" I stuttered.

"Not that I'm aware of—but I'll take that as a yes, shall I?"

THREE

"Have you ever had one of those orgasms that just won't stop?" Bridget said.

Her voice seemed unnaturally loud, but then we were standing in a lift, surrounded by men in Pynchon suits holding murmured conversations. I smiled nervously, trying to appear a man of the world, albeit one who now had bright red ears.

"I was really late for work this morning," she continued. "After we spoke I was having what was supposed to be a quick, good morning shag with this bloke and he just got me in the right place and could I stop coming? I couldn't. God, it was incredible. Couldn't get out of bed at all."

All other conversations in the lift had stopped. Bridget waited for my response.

"Er ... good," I said, teeth bared in a remarkably unconvincing smile. After what seemed an age, the lift reached the ground floor.

"That'll give 'em something to think about on their trains home," she said, looping her arm in mine as we walked out of the building.

I'd got a train easily enough and reached Bridget's thirteenth floor office near Oxford Circus just as she was leaving for lunch. She'd grabbed my arm and immediately whirled me back to the lifts and the encounter with, presumably, her bosses.

Although Gravity's Rainbow was only a few hundred yards away, Bridget hailed a cab. I looked at her footwear and realized walking wasn't really an option. Bridget didn't buy shoes for the purposes of perambulation. She bought them because they looked good, although God alone knew why she thought some of the shoes she bought looked good.

She had dozens of pairs, some of them still in their unopened boxes. None of them fit her. She was a six and a half in reality but always insisted on buying a six, imagining they made her feet look smaller—imagining her feet were big in the first place. So her shoes always pinched and rubbed. Her heels were worn smooth from putting on and tearing off band-aids for most of her adult life.

This pair was almost modest. Six-inch heels.

"Stephane Kelians," she said as she caught me looking. "Don't even imagine how much they cost."

Her whole outfit looked pretty pricy. She was dressed, like virtually every other woman in the media, in black—in her case a jacket and short skirt.

The cab dropped us outside Gravity's Rainbow and I let Bridget lead the way in whilst I got a receipt from the driver. I hadn't been here since I'd bonded big time over a meal and a couple of bottles of wine with a PR who'd just separated from her husband and was in the mood to party. Embarrassingly, we'd had to be forcibly parted from each other across our dinner table. I blush at the memory but, hey, tomorrow is another day.

The maitre d', ditto black clothes, showed estimable discretion as she saw me enter. Bridget had already joined a coterie of younger editorial staff at the bar. I knew they worked for her because they were laughing too loudly. Bridget was lapping it up, of course. Bridget has many estimable qualities. Her vanity, however, is inestimable.

"You know Nick," she told the group, though there was no

reason why any of them should. "He's just back from a ghost-hunting jaunt. Found a dead man in a graveyard."

I tensed but they merely smiled inanely.

"He's also going to be writing a location piece about Dennis Paniro's new film."

I looked at her.

"Since when?"

"Since I found out they were filming in the Brighton Pavilion tonight and tomorrow night. Producer Zane Pynchon, director Stanley Marlowe. I can't believe you didn't tell me—you're always droning on about films."

"*The Great Beast?*" a tall, good-looking, very sixties young man, standing close to her, said. "I didn't think anybody was allowed to go on set."

"Think that's going to stop Nick? He may be young but he's an old style journalist—resourceful, inventive, duplicitous, deceitful—"

"I think you can stop whilst I'm ahead," I said. "Bridget, I'm already knackered from staying up all night—since when have you decided to make me a permanent nightworker?"

"Moan, moan," she said. She took my arm. "Come on—you too, Rufus." She led the tall young man and me across to a table in the window where we could watch fashionable Soho go by. I observed her with Rufus. They seemed very pally.

"I think there could be a good story about this bloke's murder, bringing in the film about Aleister Crowley, too," I said, when we were settled. "There's an increasing interest in the supernatural and the occult because the millennium is making everybody bonkers. Happened last time, too."

"End of the last century?" Rufus said. "All that absinthe and Proust and the decadents?"

"I mean the last millennium. In the Middle Ages. Bad times in Europe, extreme poverty—all kinds of weird religious sects sprang up among the marginalized and the desperate in preparation for the Second Coming."

"Second Coming—" Rufus said with the beginnings of a smirk.

"No cheap jokes," I said. "Same uncertainties now as then because basically we have the same small minds."

"Speak for yourself," Rufus said, before a remarkable, braying laugh burst from him. Along with most of the other people in the bar I stared at him in astonishment. Bridget, showing remarkable *sang froid*—or a thick skin as it's known in our language —remained utterly composed.

When Rufus had quietened, I said: "It's just that this time round technology has got involved. Remember the guys who killed themselves because they thought a spaceship was waiting behind the Halle-Bop comet to take them away from all this? They might have been Internet freaks but basically they had the same mind set as, say, the thousands of religious flagellants wandering through Europe in the Middle Ages thinking that if they flogged each other to death they would be saved when Jesus came back and triggered the Day of Judgment."

I couldn't help noticing that both of them were looking into their drinks. Rufus was stirring his aimlessly with a straw. Bridget was stifling a yawn.

"The point I'm making is that all the New Age stuff around— you know, there are about 100,000 so called pagans who will be celebrating the summer solstice come June 21—overlaps with a belief in the occult. New Age meets Old Religion if you like. Especially in Sussex."

"The Brighton connection?" Bridget said. "Brighton is, after all, the California of Europe when it comes to loopy trends."

"In Britain an estimated 5 million people read horoscopes every day," I persisted. "People are as credulous now as they were 2,000 years ago."

Rufus tilted his head and looked at me carefully.

"Do you believe in the supernatural, life after death and all that?" he drawled.

"I've got no doubts there is another life," I said. "But it's not in the beyond, it's sitting opposite you on the bus, reading about astral projection and how God is a spaceman."

Bridget sniffed. She really should patent her sniff.

"A bus?" she said. "You take buses?"

We were interrupted by more Bridget acolytes. When they had gone Bridget said to me: "Did I tell you circulation is already up 80,000 readers since I started? Which is a relief. Not that I should worry about those illiterates."

"That's no way to talk about your readers."

A smile flickered on her face.

"I was referring to the publishers. You know the type: they can read a spread sheet but they can't write their own names."

Rufus went off to the bar for refills. Bridget drained her glass then caught me looking at her.

"What?" she said.

"You know what."

"No, I don't."

"Yes, you do. Rufus is what. What are you playing at, a jerk like that?"

"He's got a lot of contacts."

"Yeah, I'm sure. Who's his father? Politician, famous actor, artist, writer, other journalist?"

"You think I encourage nepotism?"

"I think you've got a blindspot about posh people. Was he the man in the orgasm story?"

Bridget held my gaze. Rufus came back with our drinks. I gulped mine down and left them brainstorming celebrities to write a column. I got to Victoria Station with five minutes to spare and settled in a carriage pungent with the smell of the burgers and fries everyone around me was consuming.

I'd nipped home to my flat in Shepherd's Bush before I'd gone to meet Bridget. I ransacked my drawers looking for anything clean, ransacked the wash basket for anything that could be recycled, ransacked the attic for any books about the occult and Aleister Crowley. My dad's things were up there. An old hippy who'd been into the spiritual, he'd died when I was eighteen and left me enough alternative stuff to start a Wellness Center.

On the train I took from my holdall the books I'd found in the attic. Several were written by Crowley, including *Magick* (his preferred spelling) and *The Book of Thoth,* his study of the tarot. He'd produced a tarot set in which The Hanged Man bore little resemblance to the other tarot pack renderings.

Crowley was the son of a wealthy Midlands brewer. He was educated at Cambridge in the 1880s. A mountaineer with an international reputation, he climbed in the Alps and walked across the Sahara. But really he regarded himself as a poet. Unfortunately, nobody else did. He inherited a fortune that paid to have his many volumes of poetry published.

His interest in magic led him to The Golden Dawn, a quasi-spiritual, quasi-occult society, which had Yeats among its members. Crowley tried to take over the Golden Dawn so they threw him out.

When he developed his own magic, his watchword was Thelema—Will. He regarded magic as "the science and art of causing change in conformity with will." Hence his famous saying: Do what thou wilt shall be the whole of the law.

He claimed to have fought against black magic but his magical practices were designed to raise demons and spirits. He practiced sex magic with a succession of self-styled Scarlet Women, women who were often drug addicts or prostitutes and mentally unstable—at least by the time he'd finished with them. A

number of people who became part of his circle committed suicide or went insane.

He ran through his inheritance early in his life and seemed
to live thereafter by sponging off other people. In 1920 he started
a community in the village of Cefalu in Sicily for the purpose
of studying white magic. The press got hold of stories of sexual
depravity in pursuit of magic—he had sex with men and women
and, among other things, tried to force his then Scarlet Woman
to have sex with a goat. One paper dubbed him the 'Monster of
Wickedness,' another the 'Wickedest Man in the World.'

I read that one of his little habits was to defecate on the
living room carpets of people who had him as their guest. Not
many repeat invites there, I would have thought.

I got back to the pub just before three. Robert Johnson's keen-
ing voice was singing about "Me and the Devil." I took my stuff
up to my room and put my mobile on to charge. Kathleen gave
me directions to the fete via a bridleway that ran from Ashcombe Manor up to Novington Place, another grand house, in
whose grounds the May Day event was to take place.

Novington sounded like a real backwater in my guidebook. No pub, no shop, nothing public except an old red phone
box, the mailbox, and the church. Nearby there were traces of a
Roman villa, the line of an old Roman road, and the remains of
a medieval village.

I walked into the woods. The undergrowth was dense, cow
parsley and nettles almost choking parts of the path. There was
some bird song, the cooing of wood pigeons and, somewhere,
the hollow ratatat of a woodpecker high up in the trees.

I learned about birds from my dad. He was on my mind
because of all this magic stuff. He followed the Carlos Castaneda,
Aldous Huxley approach to drugs as a way of opening up the

mind to experience. Gave the drugs and the alcohol some kind of spiritual meaning. Later, it was just an excuse to get shit-faced.

Although it was a bright day, I still felt ill-at-ease in the wood. I stopped once, convinced by the rustling noises and snapping of twigs that I was being followed. I looked back down the track, peered into the trees.

As I moved further into the wood, a silence descended for which the word *eerie* had been invented, although why someone should invent a word that looks like the back end of a bigger word I have no idea. The only sounds now were my footfalls on the uneven track.

I saw a sign, roughly nailed to a tree. "Danger. Shooting in this wood. Keep to the footpath." The floor of the wood was misty blue—carpeted with bluebells as far as the eye could see. The bluebells were beautiful but they did nothing to lift my spirits. The sun went behind a bank of clouds and I was startled by the sudden cawing of rooks in the very tops of the trees.

Something moved in the trees some hundred yards away. I stopped and watched. A tall person in a long black robe was hurrying through the trees. A tall person with the head of a large dog.

My immediate instinct was to follow the figure. Okay, my second instinct. My immediate instinct, which I followed, was to duck off the footpath and hide behind the broad trunk of an ancient oak.

I held my breath, my heart beating quickly as I started to trail the figure. Although I knew the head wasn't real, there was something unnerving about the way the figure moved so purposefully, picking its way quickly between the trees. And I was more than unnerved when, as I hurried across a clearing, the figure stopped and turned to gaze in my direction.

We both stood motionless for a few moments, looking at each other. At least the dog-head seemed to be looking at me. It was a very well made head, with pointed ears, a long snout and a thick neck, which disappeared into the high collar of the black robe.

As we stared at each other we both became aware of the noise of someone else moving through the trees. The dog's head started to turn but I fell back startled as I felt a rush of hot air past my face, heard the dull crack of what I instinctively recognized as a rifle shot, and simultaneously saw something loom up in front of me.

I dived to the soft earth and lay there, unmoving, for several minutes. I'd like to think I was being cautious but actually I was paralysed with fear. Eventually I found the willpower to make my way back to the footpath. When I reached it I got to my feet—well, wouldn't you have crawled?—and looked round for any sign of either the dog-headed figure or whoever had fired the rifle. I was alone.

I wondered if the shot had been deliberately aimed at me. The thing that had loomed up in front of me, I realized now, had been a pheasant. I recalled the warning notice nailed to the tree. Perhaps I'd just blundered into a huntsman's line of fire. But I didn't really think so. The shooting season was long since over.

I doubled my pace and hurried on through the wood. Within five minutes I was in a field of brilliant yellow rape. The field beyond, where sheep and lambs were grazing, sloped gently up towards another cluster of trees. Among the trees I could see a squat, church tower, with a weather vane on the very top of its slate-lined steeple.

I cut across the field, sheep and lambs scattering in my wake, and entered a small graveyard. The 10th century church itself lay on the other side of another bridleway. Beyond the church I could see what I assumed to be Novington Place. Both church and house had flint walls. According to my guidebook, Novington

Place was Jacobean with Victorian additions. It was more impos-
ing than Ashcombe Manor, laid out in an E shape, with two
wings projecting from it.

I saw stalls and a crowd of people on the long lawn of
Novington Place. I looked back at the way I'd come and across
to my marker—the shadowy V of trees on the side of the Downs.
Ashcombe Manor and St Michael's church, where I'd discovered the body of Miles Lyttle, were hidden by the wood I'd
come through. The Downs looked wonderfully soft and gentle.
I wanted to reach out and stroke them.

There were two clergymen at the gate. One, a tall, elderly
man, with a florid face and a marked stoop, took my entrance
fee. He looked like the man I had seen talking to the Oscar
Savage earlier in the day at the other church.

The second was a good-looking young man, no older than
twenty-five, in shirt, dog collar, and jeans. He scraped back his
long blond hair from his eyes and pressed a leaflet into my hand,
looking at me keenly.

I paused to read it. It was an advertisement for Friday nights
down in St. Michael's. The leaflet referred to a "funky-mellow
worship and dance" in a "cafe-style service." I looked at the
young vicar.

"Come and chill, man," he said softly. "It's a groove."

The fete was in full swing. Let me rephrase that. The fete was
on; swinging it wasn't. But then I guessed the death of a villager
would put a bit of a damper on it.

Looking at the people meandering listlessly between the stalls,
it didn't take me long to realize how incongruous the youth-ori-
ented service the leaflet promoted was out here. So far as I could
see, there was no one at the fete below the age of fifty.

There was something slightly askew about those who were
here: the old dears on stalls selling homemade cakes and jam; the elderly men in worn blazers and hush puppies offering second-hand

books and bric-a-brac. All of them smiled a little too solici-tously. Watched me a little too closely. Groups of three or four people murmuring to each other whilst watching my progress, then smiling or giving a little wave when I caught them looking at me.

Perhaps they were just inquisitive about a stranger. Perhaps they were keen for me to spend money at their stalls.

Perhaps they were surprised I'd made it through the wood.

I wondered if I should ask anybody if they'd seen a dog-headed man pass by.

I drifted across to the church. The young vicar was on the porch talking attentively to a tall woman in very short shorts, T shirt, and trainers. She turned as I approached and I stopped dead in my tracks.

"Hi, Nick," she said casually.

I watched her come towards me, this beautiful Asian woman, a wide smile on her face. She put her arms round me and kissed me on the lips. She had a full mouth and soft lips. Very, very soft lips. Ulp.

When I came round she was saying to the young vicar: "Jake, this is Nick. He's a journalist."

"Ah, you must be the one who found poor Miles Lyttle this morning," the vicar said. "A terrible accident."

"Accident?" I said, shaking his hand, my eyes on the woman. "I don't think they know how he died yet, do they?"

Jake didn't hear, but then my voice had come out as a croak. He smiled. "I'll leave you two together. Perhaps see you later at the service, Priya?"

Priya. Say it loud and there's music playing. Say it soft and it's almost like praying. Excuse me. This is *lurve* talking. Actu-ally, *Priya* meant 'love' in the Kannada language of Bangalore, just south of Goa. The last time I'd seen her, she'd been slipping naked into the surf in a bay in southern Crete to swim with the dolphins. It was a sign of how besotted I was with her that I would even contemplate being besotted with a woman whose idea of a good time was partying with large fish—or whatever the hell dolphins were.

Priya was the only bald-headed woman I'd ever loved, with the possible exception of Sigourney Weaver in *Alien 3*. Unfortunately, she didn't love me back. In three intense weeks she'd wreaked emotional havoc on me.

I watched the vicar walk over to the stalls then I looked back at Priya. I indicated her hair, which had grown again. It was now long, jet black, lustrous. I was feeling pretty lustrous myself.

When flummoxed, my rule of thumb is always stick to the self-evident.

"You've grown your hair," I said, my voice at a higher pitch than I would have liked.

She smiled.

"Nick, what are you doing here?"

"Just visiting. What about you?"

"Teaching yoga, what do you think? Down at Ashcombe Manor for a few more days then I go to the yoga center in Crete to help out there. I saw you at the Manor this morning when I finished my meditation."

I remembered the woman sitting in the window bay.

"Still in demand, then—the Leytonstone guru."

She switched to a cockney accent. "Course. Ow' often you seen an Asian teaching yoga in this country? Gives it a bit of cachet, know wot I mean? People think they're getting it more from 'the source.' So I don't let on I'm from Leytonstone not Mysore, I keep me *mouf* shut and I wear this spot on me forehead, though I'm buggered if I know what it means. But what you doin' ere, Nick? Ow's that Bridget? She's a case, she is."

"Priya, you can drop the Bob Oskins. I've heard you speak normally, remember."

"Yes, well, what do you know? A guy with lipstick all over his mouth."

Priya always slapped on thick wodges of bright red lipstick. Most of it was now on me. I got a tissue from my pocket and started to scrub at my face. She came close, took the tissue from me, spat delicately onto it then gently brushed my mouth and upper lip with it. She was wearing some heady perfume. I closed my eyes and breathed it in.

"If you've got nothing else to do," she said, "stay on a few days down at the Manor. It's dirt cheap and it'd be good for you. For your soul. Plus, we could *"ave a larf."*

"A laugh, Priya, a laugh. I'm going to be around for a few days but I'm staying at the pub. And I've got a lot to do. How come you know the trendy vicar?"

"I went to his Friday night service last week."

"The mellow groove? Didn't know you were religious."

She looked shy for a moment.

"I'm searching."

"Thought you'd search among your own—you know—"

"Who wants to get into religions westerners have taken over?"

"True. Have you been around here long enough to get to know people? I'm looking for Edith Lyttle."

"Yeah, I know her. She's running the bottle stall. I thought she'd be in mourning. Jake asked her if they should cancel the May Day fete out of respect, but Edith insisted Miles would want it to go on."

"Did you know Miles, too?"

She shook her head then led the way across the lawn. As a gentleman, I let her. It meant I could ogle her legs as she strode across the uneven ground. She took me to a table cluttered with bottles of all shapes and sizes, each one with a raffle ticket sello-taped to it.

"Want to try young man?" the woman behind the table said. She was small, somewhere in her mid-sixties, with thick-lensed glasses, a flowered apron, and a pair of brightly colored, top of the line trainers on her feet. They looked enormous on the end of her skinny legs.

"Choose a raffle ticket and see if your number wins you anything on here."

"Are you Edith Lyttle?" I said.

"I am," she said suspiciously.

"Edith, I'm terribly sorry about your husband."

She scowled.

"You knew him?"

"No—"

"Then what are you sorry for?"

"Well—"

"I'm not. Hated the old bugger, everybody knows that. Good riddance, I say."

"Still, it must be a shock and all—"

"Are you going to buy a ticket or what? I have other customers to serve you know."

I looked round guiltily. There was nobody else near us.

"Sure, sorry," I said, handing over some coins.

"You seem to be sorry an awful lot, young fella."

"Yes. Sorry. I found him you see."

"The shock is that it didn't happen sooner," she said as she rummaged in a cash box for change. "He's been boring me to death for weeks telling me about getting death threats. Used to tell me all his problems. As if I should care. If he did get them, it's his own fault if he ignored them."

"What kind of death threats?"

"The ones that threaten you with death. Why, what kind do you know?"

Priya snorted. I flashed her a quick look. Edith looked

sullenly at the number I'd picked out. She peered over the bottles of duty free plonk, orange squash, lime cordial, home made infusions and cheap spirits with unpronounceable names from former-Eastern bloc countries. She found what she was looking for and handed me a bottle of cod liver oil.

"Your lucky day," she said.

"I meant were the threats by post, telephone, in person?"

"By e-mail, plus he was flamed on one of the Crowley websites."

"Flamed?" I said.

"His reputation gone up in flames. You're not a webhead, young man? You should wake up and smell the new millennium."

I blushed, embarrassed that my credibility as a cutting-edge journalist had been blown by a pensioner in a pair of oversized trainers. "What was it in his book that caused problems, do you know?"

She looked at me sharply.

"And what business is that of yours? Just because you found him you think you have the right to poke your nose in?"

"No. I'm a journalist investigating the story."

"You one of them check book journalists?"

Not again. Sometimes I lament the way our society has gone. Everybody thinks they can make money out of the newspapers these days. Used to be that all a freelance had to do to make a decent living was intrude on other people's grief, act as a sympathetic ear then go and sell their story to the nationals.

But nowadays it's getting increasingly difficult to capitalize on people's unhappiness. However desolate they are, before they'll talk to you honestly and openly they expect paying. Soon, there'll be no good, honest way left to use people.

"Not exactly a check book journalist, no," I said.

"Not exactly? What does that mean?"

"It means no," I said.

"Well, why should I help you then?"

"The barmaid at the Full Moon is a friend of mine. She said you would."

"Who do you mean?"

"Kathleen."

"Kathleen who?"

She cackled at my blank look.

"If you're such good friends, how come you don't know her last name?"

Her cackle distracted me. I had a sudden syllogistic thought— they happen to me some times. Witches are known to cackle. Edith Lyttle cackled. Ergo, Edith Lyttle was a witch ...

I was lost in my little syllogism for a minute whilst she fixed me with her beady stare.

"Look," I said finally, "if you let me look at your husband's manuscript, perhaps with my trained eye I can—"

"All right, all right." Edith waved her hands at me. "Stop whining. Let's go over there now. There's no hard copy mind. It's all on the computer. I'll go first and you follow in a minute or two. You never know who's watching."

Everyone was watching. As she hobbled through the lich-gate into the churchyard then into a bower of trees, I observed that every eye was on either her or on Priya and me. Priya seemed wholly oblivious, however.

There was nothing threatening about the attention. It seemed almost solicitous. Even so, it was unnerving. I made to follow Edith.

"Will you be long?" Priya said.

"Ten minutes."

"I'll wait and give you a lift back to the pub."

As I walked into the bower of trees, I looked round. Priya had gone over to Jake, the trendy vicar. About a dozen other people clustered round them. Almost in concert they waved. I half raised a hand back.

The Lyttles' house was on an extension of the bridleway that went past the church. There were two doors side by side. One was wide open. I called Edith's name then walked in. I entered a short hall that gave on to a living room. Edith wasn't there but I could see at a glance I wasn't the first visitor that day. The room had been comprehensively ransacked.

FOUR

I found Edith in the kitchen, making a pot of tea.

"Are you okay?" I said anxiously.

"Well, it's not a typical day," she said, "but on the whole I'm doing very well."

"What happened?"

Edith withered me with a look.

"I would have thought that was self-evident. The gypsies have burgled the house."

"Gypsies?"

"So called. Personally, as I have told them on more than one occasion, I don't think they have a drop of Romany blood between them. Freeloaders who move out of their council houses when they've built up enough back rent. I'd been haranguing them only yesterday. No doubt this was their revenge."

"I'm terribly sorry."

"Do stop apologizing, young man. It is very tedious."

"But you don't think this could have something to do with your husband's death?"

"Only in that he wasn't here to protect his property."

"This is his part of the house?" She nodded. "Have your rooms been trashed, too?"

"No, but then the gypsies might not have known we lived

separately. And, of course, I was in them all night and the gypsies left early this morning, so how could they do anything?"

"You think this happened in the night?" I said.

She looked at me intently for a moment.

"Is that attractive young lady your nurse or are you simply a person with learning difficulties? The gypsies did this when they were in the vicinity. The gypsies were gone first thing this morning. Therefore they must have done it in the night."

I nodded meekly. I'm good at meek. Depressingly so. I'd actually been thinking about the convoy of caravans I'd seen in the night.

Edith beckoned and hobbled into the hallway and up a flight of stairs. She walked into what was clearly a study, though one in extreme disorder. Books were scattered all over the floor, drawers left open, piles of papers tottering in corners.

"God, they really made a mess in here," I said.

"Nonsense, it always looks like this," Edith said, marching to the desk. She looked around.

"Something missing?"

"His computer hard disk and all his floppies."

"Are the gypsies likely to have done that?"

"How would I know?" Edith said. "Do stop pacing around!"

"I'm upset on your behalf."

"Are you always such a wimp? Let's go to my house and boot up."

Edith led the way into the low-ceilinged cottage next door. We entered a small but neat study and I stood by her shoulder as she sat in front of her computer.

"Miles asked if he could back-up his book on my computer, too. Almost as if he knew what might happen."

"Did he seem scared in recent days?"

"Not that I noticed. Arrogant sod, he was. I think he was more worried about someone stealing the book."

Edith spent almost two hours trying to locate her husband's biography of Crowley. It wasn't in any of her many files or folders.

I asked her about the e-mail messages.

"Were they from one person?"

"Don't know. Could have come from anywhere in the world. Do you surf the Net Mr. Madrid?"

"Er, not exactly."

"You do use the Net sometimes though, do you? You are in keeping with the times, are you not?"

"Occasionally," I said slowly. Which was true. More or less. "I have an e-mail address."

"Indeed. Give it to me."

I had to look it up in my filofax, which is where I also kept the number of my mobile phone since I could never remember that either. I wrote that down, too.

"Well, Mr. Madrid, you will know that there are countless web sites on the Internet belonging to special interest groups."

"You mean like paedophiles and the Ku Klux Klan?"

"I was thinking more stamp collectors and steam railway enthusiasts—but then I live a much more sheltered life here. Well, I think my husband may have stumbled upon a web site that those who set it up wished to keep secret. A site to do with Aleister Crowley."

"And do you know what or where this web site is?"

"I do not. I only know the ones everybody knows about. Let me show you."

Two minutes later I was looking at a screen listing 170 matches for the name Aleister Crowley. Of the first ten on display four were a different Crowley but the rest were our man.

Among them was the Aleister Crowley Memorial Text Archive and Go-Go Bar where you could enrol for a foundation course in magick. There was an advert for a "fortune casting device"—the Aleister Crowley Magick Divination Tool.

"Did any of these carry the death threats?"

"Of course not. These are quite respectable people running these sites."

Respectability and magic weren't words I was used to putting together but I let it go.

"Well, I'm sorry young man, but I can't locate my husband's book."

"Would his publisher have a copy? Or his agent?"

"Didn't have a publisher or an agent. He'd intended to auction the book in a couple of weeks time." She clenched her jaw. "Damn and blast. That means I'll have to get in touch with him."

"In touch with him? But he's—"

"Dead? Well, I know that, don't I? I mean on the Other Side. It would be ironic, would it not, if the first real conversation we ever had was when he was dead?"

"You believe in all that?" I said, surprised.

"Doesn't everybody? There's a place I go to in Brighton every so often. Very sociable. Come along with me this evening and we can ask him. Now listen young man, I need to shoo you away and I suppose I should call the police." She wrote down an address in Brighton. "I'll see you there this evening."

When I went back across the road, Priya was standing by a decrepit old car squatting on the bridleway.

"That's probably the oldest banger I've ever seen," I said, indicating the rusting hulk of what could have been a Ford Anglia but might have been yet more ancient.

Priya walked over to me. I half expected to be handed a starting handle. Instead, she passed me a towel.

"Door doesn't close properly on your side. Loop that through the handle once you're in and hold it closed."

"Has this thing got an MOT?" I said, as I slid into the passenger seat and did as I was bid.

"What's an MOT?" she shouted as she crunched the car into gear—any gear—and we set off, bucking and bouncing, down the bridleway past Edith's house.

"I only passed my test three months ago," Priya said.

"Really? You surprise me," I said as we veered off the bridleway straight on to the road below the Downs.

"Nothing coming," I said, ducking in my seat as a reflex.

She dropped me at the pub.

"D'you want a drink?" I said, trying to control my shaking hands.

She looked at her watch.

"Five o" clock. Better not. You going to come to my yoga class in the morning? Starts at nine."

She kissed me on the cheek and drove along to the Manor. I watched her go then turned to the pub.

The courtyard to the side of the pub was very busy. Morris dancers in clogs and flower beribboned hats cavorted in lines, bells at their elbows and knees, hankies in their hands. Watching from one side of the yard was a large group of cyclists, from the other a coach-load of football supporters. If I say the Morris dancers were the most sensibly dressed people there, you'll get an idea of the state the others were in.

The football supporters comprised whole families in bob caps and tight fitting polyester shirts announcing the name of their team and the insurance company that sponsored it. Gloomy, round shouldered blank-faced men and women, sagging inside the unforgiving shirts. Their dead-eyed children, thin team scarves round their necks, were bored and raucous.

The cyclists were haughty, aloof. Kings of the highways they were. I'd seen them on the Downs pedalling like fury, heads down, startling walkers, riders, and animals.

I'd always found their clothing an environmental pollutant. The brightly colored tops, those stupid, shiny plastic helmets.

And the shorts. Oh the shorts. I watched a guy with white hairy legs, his drooping bum scarcely held in place by the lycra. Another with his shorts so tight I wanted to go over to him and say "I see you've been circumcised then."

I went into the pub, making my way through the massed beards and spotted handkerchiefs of the Morris dancers' fans, treading warily over dogs on strings and small children in dungarees with painted faces. The Rolling Stones' "Sympathy for the Devil" was blaring from the jukebox.

At the bar, Kathleen raised an eyebrow.

"Happy days," she said.

I told her about the break-in at Miles Lyttle's house.

"Edith thinks it's a bunch of gypsies who left in the night. What do you think?"

She shook her head slowly.

"Seems more likely it's linked to Miles's death don't you think?" I persisted.

"Seems that way," she said, excusing herself to serve the Morris dancers, who'd just finished their stint. I sat at the bar and looked through the window as the crowd in the yard thinned out. I was puzzling over Lyttle's death and my conviction that somebody had attempted to steal his book on Crowley. What secret could Lyttle have been revealing? And more important: was it suicide or murder?

I was also thinking about the dog-headed man loping through the trees, about the bullet that had narrowly missed me, and about the strangeness of the villagers.

Most of all, though, I was thinking about Priya in Crete.

I go to a yoga center on the island to do this odd kind of yoga—astanga vinyasa yoga. Also known as workout yoga, kick-ass yoga, and power yoga. Demi Moore does it—though sadly on a different continent—and Sting and a bunch of other film stars, too. But it's no fad—it's much too difficult for that.

The popular perception of yoga is gurus, meditation, and gentle stretching exercises for people who don't like to get into a sweat. With astanga vinyasa there are no dogmas, no meditation. A lot of sweat.

I first met Priya in what was familiarly known as the Sweat Box, the small room where those who knew how to do the yoga did their practice in extreme heat. Our mats were facing each other.

"Have you sprung a leak?" she asked with a grin as, within minutes of starting my practice, sweat began to pour from me.

"Wait 'till you see the steam," I said. I wasn't joking—I usually got so hot my sodden clothes gave off heat vapor.

We talked afterwards then together walked over the headland to one of the nudist beaches in the next bay. She looked like a goddess but swore like a trooper in this strong cockney accent. When she unselfconsciously stripped off her costume I thought I was going to expire from lust there and then.

Bridget had turned up unexpectedly on that stay too, hotfoot from busting up with a married American comic she was having a scene with during his Antipodean tour.

"Who's the girl with the tits?" she said when I joined her at one of the three taverns which overlooked the idyllic bay. "They real?"

"She's a yoga teacher. I assume so."

"Well, let me know when you're further along and know for sure."

"It's not like that. She's very cultured. She's reading Proust." Bridget gave me a look. "Okay, I'll let you know."

But I never did get further along. I didn't think Priya was leading me on. She clearly liked me, but she managed to avoid my lecherous advances. Story of my life.

Kathleen disturbed my daydreaming when she came over and leaned against the other side of the bar. She poured me a pint of Vicar's Pleasure, brewed locally. I'd given up trying to get lager from her—she obviously disapproved. In London I'm a wine drinker but my rule of thumb is never to have wine in pubs, the last bastion of undrinkable plonk.

I looked at the pump with the grinning cleric on it.

"What's the story on Jake the Vicar?"

"You've met him, have you?" Kathleen said with a grin. "He's a pop star among the young round here. Sent in by the bishop to get more youngsters into church. Succeeding too. The older members of the congregation aren't quite sure what to make of it."

"Christianity has always tried to keep up with the times. I remember in the eighties they went for diversification—couple of hit shows, few name converts, the planned conversion of St. Paul's cathedral in to cathedralettes. But I thought that kind of rave thing was regarded as a bit dodgy these days? Open to abuse?"

Kathleen shrugged.

"I read in the paper that there are two new religious cults starting up every week. Christianity will go down the pan in the new millennium unless it can get young bums on seats. Jake's job is to lure them away from the New Age stuff—Buddhism, paganism, whatever."

"He won't approve of Ashcombe Manor, then."

"He's never said." She yawned. "Sorry. Long day. Keep meaning to get an exhibition at the Manor—I'm a painter. That would be apt, I've seen some things there."

"You've attended courses?"

"Naw. Haven't set foot in the place for ten years. Wouldn't be welcome there now. Moira Cassidy and I had a falling out last year. In the seventies and eighties, I mean. When Dan Wilson owned it."

"He lived there?" I said, surprised.

Dan Wilson was a megastar back in the sixties and seventies who'd wrapped his car round a tree in Barnes when stoked up on booze and drugs. His back list still sold and was featured on Classic Gold playlists. In life, in a business that was known for its excesses, he and his band had reached new heights—or plumbed new depths, depending on your point of view. He'd been famous for taking one of his girlfriends round on a lead.

"I knew him when I was an innocent young thing."

"What size of collar did you take?"

"Nothing like that in those days. He was a straightforward bloke then. Used to come in here for a few pints. He played for the darts team. After a match he'd take some of us back for a black mass."

"Very straightforward," I said. I perked up. "Did you say *black mass?*"

"Sabbats he called them. Kinky sex really. That's where 'Paradise Waits Within' came from. Yeah, he was into all that. That's why he bought the place. For the black magic room."

"I thought that was destroyed in the forties."

"Don't you believe it. I saw a lot of it. From every angle."

She poured herself a half.

"So you were into black magic?" I said.

"Not at all. It was just a giggle. There wasn't even anything very kinky. But Danny had this thing about Aleister Crowley, you know."

"Yeah, I know." I was remembering the Thelemic Album my dad used to play constantly.

"You a fan?"

"Not exactly. My dad was. I inherited his record collection."

"He's dead?"

"When I was eighteen. Heart attack. My mother died when I was three. Road accident."

"Sorry to hear that," Kathleen said quietly.

"Yeah, well. Tell me about the house. You're saying the black magic room was still there in the seventies?"

"For sure," she said.

"Is it still there now?"

"I wouldn't know. I can't think why it wouldn't be. The secret passage used to take you pretty near it."

"Secret passage?"

"There's a secret passage from the church to the house. The house itself is riddled with them. The black magic room was a secret chapel used by Catholics centuries ago. There's a priest's hole behind the fireplace too, big enough to get a horse and rider in. Story is a cavalier, escaping from the roundheads, rode into the Great Hall and disappeared. Then later smugglers used to have all kinds of secret hiding places for contraband brought over from France."

"You've not seen the priest's hole?"

"We tended not to explore much once we were there. Except on the astral plane."

"You had out of body experiences?"

She laughed.

"I'm just a straightforward girl. I called them orgasms."

"Would you come with me to the Manor and show me where the black magic room is?"

Kathleen blushed.

"That's not so easy," she said.

"Oh yeah, you fell out with Moira Cassidy. What was the problem?"

"Geoff …"

"He was Moira Cassidy's man?"

Kathleen nodded.

"So I'm not exactly a welcome guest there. But look," she said, as the first haunting chords of Cassandra Wilson's version of "Hellhound On My Trail" started, "sometime I'll show you where the secret passage starts in the churchyard if you like."

Kathleen lent me a bike and I cycled down to the station at Hassocks to get the train to Brighton. The séance was in a house in the Seven Dials. I came out of the station and looked down the hill to the sea sparkling in the distance. Seagulls wheeled about overhead. Although I was flagging after such a long day, the brightness of the town and the sight of the sea enlivened me.

The terraced house was five minutes' walk away up a steep hill. I stood catching my breath for a moment before I knocked at the front door. It came open of its own accord. A dark entrance hall lay beyond it.

"Is there anybody there?" I called, getting, you know, into the spirit of the thing.

A mangy dog appeared. It looked like something I used to put my pyjamas in. It was followed by a frizzy haired woman in her thirties wearing a long skirt and a purple jumper.

"Can I help?" she said, in a none too friendly tone of voice.

"Edith invited me to the séance."

"She didn't tell me," the woman said suspiciously.

"She told me," I said, smiling. "I'm Nick." I held out my hand. She ignored it.

"I don't know how this will affect numbers," she said, turning away and walking down the corridor. I assumed I was to follow her.

I entered a gloomy room lit by candles and a table lamp. The walls were hung with cheap cotton throws illustrated with suns and stars and various astrological figures. Joss sticks burned everywhere. The woman scowled and went off into the corner to fiddle with a CD player. She put on something soothing that went on a long time.

There were five other people in the room. They looked up as I came in. I smiled cheerily at each of them. They included Moira Cassidy. I was surprised to see the administrator of Ashcombe Manor there.

"Ms. Cassidy. How nice to see you here."

She smiled thinly.

"I wish I could say the same, Mr. Madrid. This is a private séance you know."

"Edith invited me."

A flicker of annoyance crossed her face.

"Will you be writing about it?"

"Writing about it?" a bald headed man said. He was in his late forties, a thin man with big, myopic eyes behind wire-rimmed specs. He was sitting very straight and nervous, his too tight jacket buttoned, his foot jiggling.

"Mr. Madrid here is a reporter."

"Journalist," I said quickly.

"What's the difference?" Cassidy said.

"The ideal number for a séance is four, six, or eight," the bald headed man said pedantically. "We shall now be nine. I find that most distressing."

"We can manage quite well with nine, dearie, don't you worry."

I looked round again.

"Shirley, our medium," Cassidy murmured to me.

I have to say she was a vulgar woman. She trailed a heavy scent into the room with her—I'm sure it was no coincidence that a fly went into a spluttering dive at the television in the corner. A large woman, Shirley had dressed up for the occasion in a purple and cream low backed number which revealed a black bra strap cutting into her plump flesh.

I looked at her feet. High-heeled sling backs, looking too fragile to carry her weight. And no help where fraud was involved. I'd been doing my research. Fraudulent mediums (media?) used to snap their toes inside their boots to produce the tapping noises heard during séances. Last century Thomas Huxley, the biologist, learned the trick and advised it worked best if you wore thin socks and roomy, hard-soled boots. A thin carpet also helped, since you got the resonance from the floor.

Curiously, Edith hadn't shown up by the time we went through to the dining room. No carpet at all, just lino. The only furniture was a rectangular table covered by a sheet with eight wooden chairs set round it. Correction, seven wooden chairs and a small three-legged stool. The woman who had met me at the door ushered me to the stool.

"I don't have enough chairs," she said. She brushed some toast crumbs off the table in front of me. "And don't lean too hard on the table, the flap is broken at your end."

Moira Cassidy was sitting beside me.

"You'll note how bare the room is," she said in her school-mistressy way. "Heavy furnishings or cushions absorb the psychic force."

She took my left hand. Held it firmly. The bald-headed man was on my other side. He took my right hand limply.

"Shirley prefers we begin the circle while still chatting," Moira explained.

"It helps establish the right atmosphere," Shirley said from across the table. She resumed her conversation with her neighbor. "Clairvoyants are always unhappy in their love lives," she said. "Because you know when your husband is cheating on you."

I heard a young blonde woman say to the bald man: "On her deathbed my mum told me she'd try to communicate with me using a phrase of significance known only to the two of us."

Shirley heard, too.

"Which phrase?" she asked, a little optimistically I thought.

The lights lowered and music floated into the room. Shirley

closed her eyes, smiling. She made a shushing noise. Then, sitting bolt upright in her chair, she began to click her tongue and sway. Moira clutched my hand more tightly. Shirley swayed more violently. I moaned.

"What is it?" Moira whispered excitedly.

"Your rings are digging into my fingers," I whispered back.

Shirley was making chug-chugging noises now and breathing heavily. Her large bosom heaved. I worried for the fate of those nearest to her should the strain prove too much for the black brassiere. Suddenly she stopped still, her head thrown right back. As if on cue, the music also stopped. You could feel the tension in the air as everyone waited expectantly.

I was hoping for some sort of multimedia event: glowing trumpets and bells, cold draughts, the actual appearance of a spirit. I wondered if Shirley would spew ectoplasm all over the table—the main reason séances were popular *after*-dinner alternatives to canasta in fashionable society in the last century.

Not that I believed these things really happened. The medium whose voice had the timbre of a spirit communicating from beyond the grave was often found to have a gramophone up her jumper. Her ectoplasm was her spare set of net curtains.

For what seemed an age nothing happened at all. Was Shirley asleep? Had she been overcome by the heady fumes of her own virile perfume? Nobody spoke. I got the fidgets. My stool wasn't very comfortable. It was a bit wobbly, too. I swayed.

"What is it?" Moira said. "What do you see?"

"I see it," the bald man said. "It's a face in the corner there."

"I see it, too," Moira said, twisting round.

"Please," a strange voice said. It was Shirley! "He wishes to communicate. Let us put our feelings together, bind our spirits, and make him welcome."

"Who is it?" I said. "Is it Miles Lyttle?"

"Or is it—someone else?" the bald headed man whispered nervously.

"Let us bind our spirits," Shirley repeated. And for the next five minutes that's what we did. I didn't know how to do it really so I gritted my teeth, thinking that might help.

The voice formerly known as Shirley spoke again.

"He wishes to speak to Neville. Is there a Neville here?"

"And if there is, will he admit that that's his name?" I murmured.

"That's me," the bald guy squeaked. "I'm Neville."

"That figures," I muttered.

Cassidy dug her elbow into my side.

"He wants to know if you have found it yet," Shirley said.

"Is it really him?"

Shirley did not respond. Neville gulped, his adam's apple bobbing at his scrawny throat.

"N-not yet," he said. "I was hoping he might help me in my search."

I leaned towards Moira.

"Who's he talking to?"

She shushed me again.

Just then I heard an odd noise. A kind of shuffling.

"Can you feel the draught?" Moira whispered.

And it was true. There had been a sudden rush of air into the room.

"There's someone with us," Neville exclaimed.

I could sense some kind of presence myself. I tensed. Then I felt something brush against my leg. I jerked my legs and my stool tottered. I bore down on the table with my elbows to keep my balance. Everything happened at once: the table flap collapsed, my stool tipped, and I began to fall over, pulling Moira and Neville down with me.

"Don't break the circle," Neville yelled.

"Don't break the table," the voice formerly known as Shirley yelled.

"Who let the bloody dog in?" I yelled, as I landed on the mangy creature, which yelped and lunged for the door.

FIVE

I was in disgrace, of course. Shirley called me a bloody fool and stomped off. Neville shook his head sadly before he went off on his bike, his briefcase strapped to the cross bar. Moira Cassidy gave me a long look and laughed contemptuously. I followed her out of the house.

"Who was Neville trying to contact?" I said, hurrying to keep up with her as she strode down the street.

"Why would I know?" she said.

"Aren't you both regulars here? I mean you're both into séances and stuff, I can see."

"Can you indeed? Do you think you could take the sarcastic tone out of your voice when you tell me about myself."

I tried to ingratiate myself.

"Hey no, I'm not being sarcastic," I said. "Everybody should have a hobby, and communicating with the dead, I know, is a remarkably popular one."

She stopped in the street but I plunged on.

"It just puzzles me because how exciting can that be? As conversationalists, dead people are, well, dead boring basically. I've been reading *Psychic News* reports of spiritualist meetings and the banality is, frankly, dispiriting. You get: 'How are you?' or 'It's nice here.' What you don't get is the thoughtful spirit who tells you to look under the mattress for the million pounds in used notes it left there."

Judging by the expression on her face, I could see I needed to work on ingratiation. I stepped back a pace, thinking she was going to hit me.

Instead, she said: "Why did you bother to attend if you feel like that?"

"Edith invited me to talk to her husband."

Cassidy gave me another long look.

"And you regard *me* as credulous?" she finally said.

"I didn't really expect him to speak," I protested. "But in an investigation like this—"

"What investigation? I thought you were here to spend the night in a haunted place."

"Well, I've done that. Now I'll be looking into Miles Lyttle's death."

Cassidy groaned.

"I've also got to do a quick piece about the film Stanley Marlowe is making about Aleister Crowley," I continued. "I'm going to see the filming at the Pavilion later on tonight." I smiled cheerily. "So I'm going to be around for some time."

Cassidy groaned again and resumed walking. I kept pace.

"Tell me," I said, "have you seen a man with a dog's head hanging around Novington?"

"No."

"Are you sure?"

"I think I would have remembered."

"And last night I saw a whole group of animal-headed people on top of the Downs."

"Perhaps you should take more water with it."

We were heading into the North Laines, a network of narrow, shop-lined streets, which had largely been taken over by hippies and New Age people. Shops called Asgard's Retreat or

Druid's Voice, full of stars and crescent moons.

"A lot of people are getting into theriomorphism," she said.

"You don't say," I said cautiously.

She glanced at me.

"Animal impersonations."

"What … in the clubs or something?" I said.

She laughed. It was almost a friendly laugh. It tinkled.

"Not exactly. In their spare time, some people like to be animals with which they feel an affinity. Some people pretend to be pets—mogs and dogs—others try domesticated animals like cows, pigs, and horses. One man has his own web site."

"Doesn't everybody," I said.

"There's an internet news group—pets can advertise for an owner, owners for a two-legged pet."

"Sounds a bit perverse. I don't think the ones I saw were pretending to be animals, particularly. They were wearing long robes."

Cassidy paused outside the door of the Aquarius Coffee Shop.

"Probably pagans then. A gang of them hang out in here." She peered through the window. "Some of them are sitting over in the corner."

"Are you coming in?" I said.

"No, I've got to meet my brother then get back to the Manor."

I went into the cafe and over towards a group of young people, dressed in what could only be described as Druid chic—lots of dark, flowing robes. However, when I introduced myself, I soon discovered how simplistic it would be to regard them all simply as Druids.

In fact there was only one—a tall, skinny guy whose robe wasn't quite long enough to cover bony ankles and a pair of grubby plimsolls. The others were a Priest of Isis, a Priestess of Aphrodite, a Wiccan, and a shamaness. Oh, and the King of the

Pagans. I looked at the shamaness slumped in the corner, her white face ravaged by acne, her lipstick and mascara smudged.

"A shamaness?" I said to her. She looked at me blankly.

"A female shaman," the King of the Pagans, a hollow-eyed young man sitting beside her, said. "It's a Siberian word. A shaman is like a medium. Using drumming and dancing, they work themselves up into an ecstatic state of divine frenzy. Then they pass into a trance and their spirits leave their bodies."

I glanced at the sad sack over in the corner. She looked as if her spirit had left her body for good. She stared back at me sullenly. Then she gave me a kind of dead leer and spoke.

"I'm what you might call a specialist in divine ecstasy," she said. "Plus I do thought-reading and clairvoyance."

Maybe she was having an off day but when I looked at her the words *divine* and *ecstasy* didn't automatically spring to mind.

I turned to the King of the Pagans.

"So, you're the King of the Pagans?" Well, what would you have said?

He nodded.

"For a year."

"What happens when your year's up?"

"You're usually killed," he said, rather proudly. "The priestesses cut your throat with a sickle then bash your head in with a big stone. That'll happen to me unless the women of the tribe decided I can stay for a second year."

"Looks like you've got your work cut out."

He seemed to guess what I was thinking.

"You can't fornicate with the women of the tribe when you're king," he said indignantly. "Shame," I said. "You don't go in for wearing a stag's head and antlers, do you?"

He swelled his chest a little and nodded.

"Were you up on the Downs last night with a bunch of, er, other animals?"

He nodded again.

"Did you see us?" he said.

"See you? You scared me to death."

"We go up there for all the pagan festivals. We'll be back for the midsummer solstice. There's ancient woodland there. The only known example of native large-leaved limes in the whole country. Very spiritual."

"You didn't by any chance see anything going on in the churchyard, did you? A bloke hanged himself there—or was murdered."

The King of the Pagans shook his head.

"I saw you," a low voice said. I looked at a big, blond curly-haired bloke who hadn't said anything at all. He met my gaze calmly. He looked the most normal of them all.

"He's into UFOs," the King said. "Spent last night up on the Downs waiting to be picked up by an alien space ship."

So much for normal.

"You were over Ashcombe way?" I said.

"In the V of trees," the curly-haired bloke said. "There's an unusual conjunction of ley lines there. Must be for visitors from other galaxies to navigate by. No other explanation. It was a toss-up between being there or at the Long Man of Wilmington. The Long Man's phallus is a celestial runway."

The thought of the neolithic image's erect penis being used as a runway left me momentarily speechless. Sure he was long, but he wasn't *that* long.

"Sounds reasonable," I said, hearing myself with disbelief. "Did you see anything in the churchyard?"

"Nothing. Saw some caravans early in the morning though. A Jag leading the way. Big four track bringing up the rear."

"You're sure it was a Jag?" I said

"Sure I'm sure. An old E-type."

"Great," I said. "Thanks." I smiled at him. "So did anyone

come down—from another galaxy, I mean?"

He shook his head sadly.

"Next time, eh?" I said in my special cheering-up voice.

"You a game show host?" the King of the Pagans said. I made a mental note to tone down my special cheering-up voice.

I sensed I was probably outstaying my welcome. Still, I might as well finish what I'd started.

"So are any of you into Aleister Crowley and/or satanism?"

The priest of the fellowship of Isis stopped picking at a spot on his neck and spoke up.

"Paganism is a brotherhood of white magic," he said. "We believe in the light not the dark. We believe in the spirits of the trees and the streams. There's no reason to confuse paganism with satanism." He curled his lip. "Only journalists would do that. We don't worship Satan, we worship pre-Christian gods. I read satanists are supposed to be 10 percent of the British population. But that's crap. There are probably about a hundred admitted satanists in the country."

"Any around here?" I said.

"There's supposed to be a coven over Lewes way. It was in the papers a couple of years ago. Some guy jumped off the cliffs there, leaving a note saying a black magician had it in for him."

"That sounded a bit cranky," I said. "What about the real thing?"

There was silence. Sly glances passed between them.

Eventually, the King of the Pagans sniffed and said: "There's a village near here almost entirely owned by the local lord. Some guy came to him and said the village was possessed by the devil. The Lord said 'What can I do about it?' Guy said, 'I'll get rid of the devil if you give me £750,000.' Lord apparently handed over the money."

"And did the devil go?"

"Last I heard he was lounging on some Caribbean beach with the guy who got the money," the King said, laughing.

I made my way down towards the Royal Pavilion. The walk was uneventful except that as I passed a group of people drinking outside a pub a large dog lunged for my leg. I stepped out into the road.

"Sorry, mate," a big man with a red beard said, yanking the dog back on a thick lead. "Scruffy's a bit frisky tonight."

I smiled and walked on. I didn't dare look back, although I wanted to. The dog, bigger than any dog I'd ever seen, had moved in a very unwieldy, undoglike way. I had the crazy idea it was somebody wearing a dog suit.

Although it was well after eleven by now, the town was still buzzing, the streets crowded. A pleasant breeze came in from the sea.

I wasn't sure how I was going to do this. Stanley Marlowe was notoriously secretive and kept his film sets closed, but security on night filming is always a bit lax. I was hoping I could hang out at the catering van then sneak in at some dead hour in the morning.

There were trailers and power trucks and lorries dotted around the grounds of the Pavilion. As I wandered past the trailers I almost immediately bumped into a make-up artist I knew. She was with a tall, very pretty woman wearing a baseball hat with her long ponytail sticking out of the back.

"Oh no, here comes trouble," the make-up artist said, before giving me a big hug. I'd had a little scene with a friend of hers called Sally once on the set of some TV mini-series they were shooting in Cornwall. I knew the make-up artist was Australian, from Sydney, but what was her name?

"Nick," she said, "this is Trudi, Zane Pynchon's assistant. No, it's okay, she isn't the enemy. She's on our side. Trudi this is Nick. He's a journalist but he's almost human."

"Nice of you to say."

"Come on into the make-up truck and have a cup of tea." As she led the way she turned: "So what are you doin' here, Nick? Sally lives with somebody now you know." She laughed loudly. "But I'm available."

I remembered her name—Stacey—as I was perched on a stool in the make-up van, smiling inanely at them both. Trudi was striking, but then she was working for Zane Pynchon.

"You still doing your yoga?" Stacey said. She turned to Trudi. "Nick here does the yoga that Woody Harrelson does. Good for inner peace and that."

"It's probably what I need to do then," Trudi said, in a refined east coast voice.

"Well, it doesn't always bring inner peace," I said. "As often as not you just get torn ligaments." I smiled at Trudi. "So what's it like being the assistant to the famous Zane Pynchon?"

"Oh it's just *wonderful*," she said, sarcastically but not with hostility.

"What—fed up of making coffee and picking up the kids from school?"

"Yesterday I picked up not the kid but the kid's stool sample."

"Yuk," I said.

"See this," she said, pulling out of her handbag a plastic sachet full of some kind of green slime. I jerked back.

"You carry it round with you?"

"This isn't the stool sample, you idiot. This is spinach juice. Zane is forever wanting to diet—he'd be in the Brando, Orson Welles weight category if he wasn't careful. But which diet? He gets me to test them. I've done 'em all. Fasting? Liquid only? High protein, low protein, no protein. This is the latest. Try some?"

"No thanks," I said, still suspicious of the green slime. Trudi looked efficient but anyone could make a mistake. "Why do you put up with it?"

She toyed with her ponytail.

"Because I want to be in movies. I want to produce movies. I know I'd be good at it. And working with Zane, if you can get through all the crap, is a priceless learning experience. It's just that it can get you down sometimes."

"It doesn't help that he's involved with the star of the movie," Stacey said.

"Zane Pynchon's dating Dennis Paniro?" I said, startled. "Is it one of those mid-life things?"

"Alice Denver," Trudi said. "The fact he's going with her makes it ten times worse. She's so cranky."

"And what about Dennis?" I said.

"Well, of course, we've had this whole thing about the length of his trailer compared to Alice's ."

"No, I mean his hair—you giving him a bald wig or is he shaving?"

Stacey grinned.

"Neither. He wants long flowing locks."

I looked puzzled. Every photo I'd ever seen of Aleister Crowley in his prime, he had a totally shaved head or he was wearing an obvious wig.

"You know Dennis isn't very bright," Trudi said. "Remember when he wanted to do *The Merchant of Venice* set in Nazi Germany and he wanted the German director who'd done *Doctor Faustus*? But he mixed him up with the one who'd done that pro-war version of *All Quiet On The Western Front* and all those disaster flicks? Got some great action scenes—and Shylock and his pound of flesh made *Seven* seem like a Disney cartoon—but the rest didn't really flow."

"So?" I said, laughing.

"He thinks Aleister Crowley is Oscar Wilde."

I pondered this for a moment.

"But he must have discovered his mistake about Crowley when he read the script."

"You're presuming he read the script," Trudi said.

"But I thought he liked to do heavy research for his roles?"

"That's a different thing but in any case that was in the old days. All these older method actors have twigged that whether you're wearing Mussolini's underpants or an extra hundred kilos you're still essentially playing you."

"But he still must read the script?"

"Don't be naive," Trudi said sharply.

"You sound bitter," I said.

"I just did it wrong. I went to Harvard, did an MBA. I should have hung around Venice Beach flashing my tits for the Baywatch casting team. Most movie stars are college dropouts and to drop out of U. S. colleges, you must be really stupid. But, hey, they get the multimillion dollar deals and I get the stool samples."

"Alice is bright isn't she? Didn't she go to an Ivy League college?"

"Excuse me whilst I vomit," Trudi said fiercely. "The woman is so self absorbed I have no way of knowing if she's intelligent since she never says anything that doesn't relate to her."

"I bet Melinda has read all her Virginia Woolf," Stacey said brightly.

"Melinda Taylor is in it?"

Stacey nodded.

"Playing Virginia Woolf."

"The Charleston set," Trudi said, by way of explanation. "They were around when Crowley was."

I wondered if Crowley had ever visited them and crapped on their carpet.

"Melinda doesn't need to have read Woolf," Trudi went on. "All she's concerned about is whether angst is written into her contract."

There was a knock on the door.

"You're needed on set," a man's voice called from outside.

"I suppose you want to come and watch," Stacey said. "Well, you can leave your bags here. But if you're caught I don't know you, I never met you, and I certainly never said in a moment of weakness that I wanted to bear your child."

The Royal Pavilion, the Prince Regent's gorgeous pleasure palace, is one part chinoiserie to three parts Walt Disney. My favorite story about it is that it was selected as a hospital for wounded Indian soldiers during the First World War, on the grounds it would make them feel at home. You can imagine them looking up at this pantomime Indo-Chinese confection and thinking: "*What* the fuck?"

The production was shooting at night so that the Pavilion could remain open for business as usual from nine each morning. Stacey took me through a group of crew and extras who were huddled outside the side entrance having a quick fag. Inside the ornamented corridors dozens of other crewmembers were swarming in a remarkably orderly fashion.

Stacey stopped at the entrance to the banqueting room. We both looked up at the enormous chandelier hanging from a dragon's claws in the very center of the room.

"It's a crazy place," Stacey said. "People who don't know it will think the art department is on some very bad drugs." Without looking at me she said: "Okay, I'm leaving you here. See those people in sweatshirts? Pavilion staff keeping an eye on us. Don't lean against the walls—hand painted wallpaper—or touch the furniture. And since the music room was badly damaged by fire some years ago, smoking is a definite no-no. Enjoy—and don't leave the set without coming by the make-up van."

I watched Stacey walk off, racking my brains for any occasion when she could have offered to have my child. I gave up and eased into the banqueting room. It was very quiet and I was conscious of how much the waxed floorboards squeaked and creaked as I walked over to a cluster of lights and large metal storage boxes. I squeezed in behind them, figuring it would be safe to loiter there.

Most of the cast were gathered by the banqueting table, beneath the grand chandelier. I could see the diminutive Dennis Paniro deep in exaggerated thought, his chin resting in the palm of his hand. He was having a bad hair night, his long hair going every which way.

Alice Denver wasn't around. Melinda Taylor stood slightly apart, tapping a foot, her fierce face raised to the ceiling. She exuded tension.

The camera was on a dolly on fifteen feet of track to my left. Stand-ins for Dennis and Melinda were walking slowly past the long banqueting table whilst the camera flanking them was drawn back on the tracks.

I looked for Stanley Marlowe. A man was hunched in a chair marked *Director* across the back. He was wearing long, baggy shorts and a baseball cap reversed on his head. As he turned to look at a video monitor I saw an unlit cigar in his mouth. I also saw that it wasn't Stanley Marlowe.

"Let's go for a take," the man called to his assistant director.

"Quiet on the set," the AD bellowed. "Anybody not in this scene please shut up or—better still—fuck off."

The sound diminished but nobody made an effort to move. The AD went over to Melinda and spoke to her. She nodded and walked over to Dennis. She wasn't tall, but she was a good five inches taller than he. They ignored each other.

Eventually the director went for a take. Melinda and Dennis came down the room side by side. Melinda walked elegantly, stepping daintily. Dennis hadn't quite got it yet. He was bouncing along on his toes, swinging his shoulders like a contender from the waterfront.

"My dear Crowley, I understand sex, I assure you," Melinda said crisply. "I know a little of magic. I seek clarification, however, about sexual magic."

Dennis grabbed her arm and pulled her to a halt. He pushed his face close to hers and, spraying spit, said intensely: "I doubt you do understand sex. I know you cannot understand *magick*. Sexual magic I can only demonstrate."

"What—here?" Melinda said with a low laugh.

Dennis was groping for a response.

"Fucking A here!"

"Cut!" the director called.

Melinda cast a cold look down at Dennis, turned on her heel, and walked away a few yards, wiping her face with her handkerchief. The director went over to Dennis, put his arm over his shoulders, walked him—shit—towards me. I moved behind the lights and tried to become invisible.

"Dennis, I think you're there with the emotion in this scene but I think the language—could you just follow the script?"

"What's wrong with the words? They're what Oscar—"

"Aleister—"

"Whoever—they're what he's feeling."

"That may very well be so, sport. I'm sure it is. But the language he would use would be—your words were a little—anachronistic."

"Anachronistic, that's right."

"That's wrong."

"Why—I thought you wanted it fucking historical?"

"Anachronistic doesn't mean fucking historical."

"It don't?"

"It don—doesn't. And you know, there's something else. Your accent."

"Jeez, you limeys take such pains. I told Zane I wasn't going to do no Dick Van Dyke accent and I sure wasn't going to play him as queer. All that 'A *handbag*' shit. I think this guy had balls."

"Dennis, I think it's time—over time in fact—that you came to terms with the fact that this film is not about Oscar Wilde, the Irish dramatist—who was, I have to say, definitely queer. It is in fact about Aleister Crowley, a black magician."

Dennis looked dull for a moment.

"Well, sure, I know that. But I see him as kind of *Wildean*."

"No."

"No? But he was friends with the poet Yeats."

"Even so. No."

"Okay, so gimme a handle on this Crowley character."

"It's all in the script."

"Well, sure, I know that but I like to be kind of spontaneous when I'm acting. Matter of fact I mentioned to Zane about boards."

"Boards?"

"Yeah, you know, with my lines on."

"Boards. Okay, we'll sort that out later. Well, what if I say Crowley was a hell of a swordsman? Great sexual athlete. Went at it for hours."

"Sexual athlete, huh?" He pushed out his chest. "Okay, I could maybe work with that."

"Now about the accent. I thought you'd agreed that with Zane."

"Oh sure. You want a tip-top British accent, old chap."

"Yes," the director said patiently. "But not that one. Terry Thomas won't do."

"But why do I need a limey accent at all? Redford didn't in *Out of Africa*."

"I know."

"Costner didn't in *Robin Hood*."

"He tried."

"Could I do it Irish?"

"I'd rather you didn't."

"Okay, okay." Dennis wandered off muttering.

The director raised his eyes to the chandelier hanging above him. Was he saying a prayer or a curse? Then he looked down and straight at me. Pointing a long finger he bellowed: "And who let that fucking insect on to my film set?"

SIX

I was sitting on the catering bus looking at a plate of salad when the director loomed over me with another guy.

"Nick Madrid meet Don, our line producer."

I started to stand but the director pushed me gently back into my seat.

"You've got some nerve, Madrid, sneaking on to *my* closed set. Lucky for you we go way back. And lucky for you Zane Pynchon wasn't around."

"I don't understand why it is your set. You're not now, nor have you ever been—to the best of my knowledge—Stanley Marlowe."

His name was Julian Parkinson. He was a tall, energetic man with a mass of black curly hair and saturnine good looks that made women swoon. Bastard. I'd known him for about three years. He was another yoga fiend. We'd met at the yoga center in Crete and seen each other from time to time since. Not really friends but good acquaintances. As a matter of fact, he'd turned up in Crete a couple of months ago, the weekend Bridget and I were leaving. It was a stroke of luck finding him here.

"Stanley walked three days ago," he said. "Ye olde creative differences. Mucho hush-hush. Alice suggested me—she's the only person in the world who thinks that James Hogg lump of shite I did with her was any good. *Confessions of A Justified Sinner* from the point of view of the seduced barmaid? She thought that she'd finally been able to do some real acting. Dennis went along with using me because he loved *The English Patient*."

I frowned.

"But you didn't direct *The English Patient*."

"True, but I directed *The Patient Man*. They sound the same to him and I wasn't going to disabuse him. This is the film I was born to make. But don't distract me from my central beef here—how did you get on to my set?" He glowered for a moment then shrugged. "Oh, who cares. It's lucky it was my set and not Marlowe's. If he'd found you out you'd be feeding the fishes off the soon-to-be-restored West Pier now."

He sat back.

"So how's the yoga? On the second series yet?" He turned to Don, who was tucking into a plate piled high with cold beef and ham from the catering van. "Nick does the same yoga as me. How's your friend Bridget?"

I suspected Bridget and he had done more than practice yoga together—Bridget was having anything that moved at the time.

"She's fine. She's the one sent me down here. So how's it going?"

"You've seen how it's going. And if you print one word of what you've seen or what I'm about to say my foot soldiers will do disgusting things to you *and* your pet gerbil, friends or no friends. I've got a lead who thinks he's Oscar Wilde—and further that Oscar Wilde was straight. This without benefit of drugs, mind. And every time he's in a scene with Alice he tries to French kiss her. For that matter, he French kisses any woman he comes across."

"You got him cheap though, right?"

"For scale, he and Alice both. Plus expenses. Wanna tell him about the expenses, Don?"

Don frowned. Julian squeezed his arm.

"The kid's kosher, Don, it's okay. He's done location pieces about my last two films."

Don spread his hands.

"The deal for expenses is first class airline ticket and equal lodging for family, friends, personal assistant, nannies, and own dresser. They gotta have twenty-four-hour transport—so that's a limo available around the clock with driver *plus* a self-drive rental car *plus* a noncommercial jet—a Gulf stream in this case—available at all times during the shoot. Any idea how much that costs?"

"Yeah, but at least Zane's made his own Gulf stream available," Julian said. "It's over at Shoreham. But it's the other costs that add up, too. Like hair and make up. We've got Stacey here—you know her, don't you? Wait a minute. I get it. That's how you got on set. That disloyal broad—" He grimaced.

"Anyway, we got Stacey and she's one of the best but Alice will only use her own make up and hair person. Dennis has his own hairdresser. Both of them insist on bottled water only for washing their hair. So that's another $1,000 a day per person—that's around $40,000 by the end of the shoot."

"If we can persuade Dennis to go bald we got a $20,000 saving right there," Don said.

"You know how he loves his hair," Julian said. "You'd think he was Samson, the way he goes on."

"Do you think you got the right man for the part?" I said.

"What do you do? You don't get a name, you don't get funding. Simple as that. Dennis's okay. He just thinks if he says motherfucker a few times he's giving his character depth. And improvise? Jesus. It's a depressing thing that those who want to improvise most have the least to improvise with. Inarticulacy breeds inarticulacy. 'Fuck you. No, fuck you. No fuck you, asshole.' Et cetera, et cetera."

"Yeah, well, we should be grateful he hasn't gotten seriously into the part yet," Don said.

"How come?"

"You know he likes to stay in character throughout the shoot. Could make him kind of tricky to deal with. Plus, he'll want to do stuff for real."

Julian looked at him.

"Oh, you mean the sex magic. What—the whole thing?"

Don chuckled.

"Give or take the chicken."

Julian frowned.

"Hmm. And we're going to get Mr. Method down here tomorrow for a cameo. Danny Seaford is playing Eric Gill."

"Eric Gill. There's synchronicity—Bridget and I were talking about his typeface earlier today."

"You mean somebody's actually heard of him?" Don said. "I think he should be axed from the script."

"One of this country's greatest sculptors and typographers," I said. "He did my favorite typeface."

"He did everything that moved as far as I can tell," Julian said. "I read his biography. Had sex with his apprentices, his daughters, even his pet dog. He has a couple of scenes with Melinda. Hope Danny doesn't feel the need to live the part for a cameo. At least whilst Alice's dachshund is around."

"It's not a dachshund it's a pug," Don said. "Very hip accessory in Hollywood these days."

"How'd you get it through quarantine?" I asked innocently.

Don gave me a bored look then turned to Julian.

"A famous typographer who was into bestiality," he said. "That'll get the hearts of the teenage girls down at the multiplex beating a little faster."

"Did Gill know Crowley then?" I asked.

Don raised an eyebrow at Julian.

"He may have," Julian said, a little defensively. "Gill lived in Ditchling, just down the road from Ashcombe Manor. Besides, Zane wanted him in. It's his money, so ..."

"Zane Pynchon is putting his own money into this?" I said, surprised again.

"Let's not get into that now," Julian said. "It makes commercial sense to put the cameos in. As soon as Stanley put the Bloomsbury gang in we got name Brit actors queuing up to play cameos."

"Plus we've cast a bunch of guys with initials," Don said.

"T. S. Eliot, T. E. Lawrence, and W. B. Yeats."

"T. E. Lawrence?"

"Only a walk-on part. You know the kind of thing: 'Virginia, this is Lawrence of Arabia, he's just finishing *The Seven Pillars of Wisdom*. T. E. say hello to the author of *To The Lighthouse*.'"

Julian took out a cigar, stuffed it in his mouth. I'd never actually seen him smoke one. I think he just liked talking round it.

"Okay, Nick," he said. "You can stay but these are the ground rules. Absolutely no talking to the talent—and that includes me—on set. I'll get the PR to arrange sessions in the trailers. On set, Alice doesn't want anyone looking at her—"

"But she's an actress!"

"Even so. You must never meet her eyes or be anywhere in her sightline when she's shooting a scene because it distracts her. Dennis now, we're gonna have to put boards up everywhere for him to read his lines from. So keep out of the way of those, too."

"I see a problem coming up with Melinda and Alice," Don said. "You know Melinda's only interested if there are screams or tears—well she's gonna see that Alice's got the best rage scene and she's not gonna like it."

"Can Alice do rage?" I said.

"Well," Julian said with a shrug, "we'll spray her so stuff comes down her nose and tears out of her eyes, then she can heave her shoulders. It'll look like the real thing. And for that deeper emotion I'll tell her we've been washing her hair with tap water. That'll really get to her."

"Your sense of how to deal with these people is remarkably acute," I said.

A pretty redhead came in and tapped Julian on the shoulder. "We're ready to go again, Julian."

"Thanks sweetheart. Nick, I'm just doing pick-up scenes the rest of the night. You can come back tomorrow night if you want. And let's get together daytime when it's less fraught."

He named a time, then they left the bus. I looked at my watch and yawned. It was already three in the morning. I wandered back over to Stacey's van.

"Nick," she said, closing the door behind me. "Glad you're here. I've got an hour with nothing to do. You going to keep me company?"

"Sure," I said, as I heard her bolt the door. "I wanted to ask you about you wanting to have my baby."

"Really," she said, standing very close to me. "Maybe we need to rehearse first before we go for a take." She reached down and yanked firmly on the zip of my trousers. "What do you think?"

Kathleen the barmaid had a big grin on her face when I finally came down the stairs of the pub, yawning.

"You got the mascara off, then?" she said.

"If you knew, why didn't you say?"

"Suited you."

When I woke I thought I'd been struck blind. My eyelids were gummed together. I stumbled to the mirror over the washbasin and groaned at what I could dimly see. My red eyes were surrounded by thick swadges of mascara, mascara that had now run. I looked like Theda Bara on a very bad day.

The taxi driver who'd brought me back to Ashcombe at about six in the morning hadn't batted an eye—but then he was from Brighton. That Stacey, what a case. I'd wondered why she had that sly smile on her face when I woke up after a brief post-coital nap.

Our get-together hadn't really worked out very well. She'd been very *limber*, I'll give her that. And what she could do with her mouth was nobody's business—and certainly not yours. But she used rather colorful language, which I found distracting.

"C'mon, blue," she said, after ten minutes tussling, as I lay on top of her on the cramped floor of the caravan. "When you gonna give me your big dog?"

"That is my big dog," I gasped.

"Really?"

She rummaged for a few moments.

"Okay," she said cheerfully. "We'll just have to work round it then. Size isn't everything. Matter of fact, smaller guys can usually hit the—ooo, nice—spot better. Not that you feel small. No, no, no. Yes that's good, that's good, keep it there, c'mon, c'mon, baby—fuck me 'til I fart …"

This last was not an expression I'd heard before. I suppose I must have slowed to ponder it.

"Have you just slimed, blue?" she said.

Slimed?

"Have you, darlin'?"

Slimed??

"Sorry, no," I said in a small voice. "I haven't yet."

Nor, I thought, am I likely to now.

Kathleen interrupted my gloomy reverie.

"Our community policeman came in last night," Kathleen said. "Told me they're assuming Miles Lyttle's death was suicide."

"Trussed up as he was? What about his house being ransacked?"

"They're blaming the gypsies. Don't you think that's possible?"

"Anything's possible. But I thought it was Edith the gypsies disliked." I had a sudden realization. It didn't hurt or anything. "Though, come to think of it, gypsies have strong links with superstition and the supernatural. In fact, I think the Tarot pack comes from the gypsies."

I looked at Kathleen.

"Did he say when Lyttle died?"

"Some time between eleven and one."

"I saw the gypsies leaving at around two, I think."

She went off to serve a group of youngsters from the agricultural college. I wandered over to the food area. A board above it announced the opening of a new vegetarian bar with every dish at the same £2 price all that week.

There were a dozen or so people milling round the bar, dressed variously in tracksuits, brightly colored leggings, a turban, and pairs of oversized Doc Martens. I recognized the type. They must be Priya's yoga class. I'd caught up on some well-needed sleep this morning rather than attend it.

I overheard an American bloke with a General Custer moustache and beard combination say: "I tried a Bon spiritual healer."

"Bon?" a dumpy girl, in *dungarees* yet, said in an English accent.

"Bon is the Tibetan shamanistic religion that preceded the arrival of Buddhism," the yank explained. "Anyway, my healer prescribed me a deer's heart."

"That wouldn't do for me," the woman said. "I'm vegetarian." She looked at the food counter. "I was hoping there would be wheatgrass to drink."

"I can't take wheat," General Custer said.

"I think there's glutin in that," the woman said, pointing at a salad dish. "I can't take glutin."

"You know, in Britain the big companies are taking alternative philosophies seriously now," a woman in a turban said. "I read that M & S, Orange & Virgin are all making use of feng shui for the positive focus of life forces."

"Oh sure," Custer said. "In the States lotta companies now make key investment decisions using mathematical psychology based on astronomy."

"What's that?" the turban said.

"Posh name for astrology," the dungarees said.

"Is that millet?" the turban said to the manager, who was hovering behind the bar. The manager nodded tentatively. "Millet's good. It's full of magnesium. That makes you supple."

The manager smiled as he thrust a spoon into the dish of millet. The turban lifted the lid on a steaming soup tureen. "And if I have the soup the salt in it will replace the minerals I sweated out."

"Yes," the yank said. "But the salt cancels out the magnesium. It will stiffen you up again."

The manager released the spoon. He decided to be proactive.

"The cheese is very nice," he said. "Organic, you know."

It was as if he had admitted mass murder. They looked at him in horror.

"Dairy products?" the turban said. "Dairy products are terrible for your sinuses."

I went back to the bar. Kathleen smiled.

"*Picky* aren't they?"

I nodded, then frowned when a tall man with a long ponytail came out of the toilets and crossed to join the others. I knew him. He'd been in Crete the last time I was there. Bloke called Chris. He was a psychotherapist, who at first I'd felt sorry for. I could tell he only wanted to get laid but when women found out what he did all they wanted was to tell him their problems.

In my experience that should have helped him—I was very young when I first discovered that a problem shared is almost guaranteed sex—but he was too moral to switch from confidant to lecher.

I think. I'd lost my sympathy for him when he became my rival for Priya's affections. They used to go over to another bay most days to practice free diving, an optional course the yoga center had introduced that year. Now I wondered why he was here. Were he and Priya an item? If so, what about Jake the vicar? Where did he fit in?

"You still with us or are you in another dimension?" Kathleen said, nudging my arm.

"Somebody I know," I said, turning back to her. "The night before last, did you notice anything unusual in the pub?"

"What kind of unusual? Geoff staying sober you mean? Nothing like that."

"I heard a car leave the car park pretty sharply at around 11:15. Made quite a racket."

"You still here asking your questions, Mr. Madrid?"

I turned and came face to face with Kathleen's friend Geoff.

"Just passing the time of day," I said.

"Well, it's the time of day for my lunch so Kathleen, love, I'll have my usual."

It wasn't exactly a get-out-of-town confrontation but I saw no point in hanging around, inflaming Geoff's aggressive tendencies. In principle, I don't have any problem with two grown men beating the brains out of each other. Just so long as, in practice, neither of them is me.

I decided to walk through the wood to Novington to visit Edith. I'd tried phoning and got no reply. Through the trees as I walked

I could see several farms doing their bit for a beautiful Britain. Rusting farm machinery abandoned in fields, higgledy-piggledy piles of other rusted equipment alongside tumbledown corrugated iron outbuildings. And tires. Mountains of old tires everywhere I looked, serving who knows what purpose?

As I came across the field to Novington church and the old house I was aware that a mist was descending rapidly on the hamlet.

I emerged on to the road from beneath the canopy of trees. Here the fog was quite thick. At the sound of an engine I looked towards the crest of the road and saw the headlights of a car coming up the other side of the hill. The twin beams bathed the fog in a bright, yellow light.

In this light I suddenly saw the silhouette of an immense figure, some twenty feet high, looming out of the impenetrable mist. It was a figure in priestly robes, arms outstretched in some arcane hieratic gesture. A priestly figure with the head of a large dog.

Although the image was projected against the fog only for a second before it dropped from sight, it shook me badly. I stepped behind the old red telephone box as the car came over the crest of the hill and drove by me.

Bizarrely, the sun still shone brightly over the Downs to the south of me. Yet the whole of Novington was shrouded in this thickening fog. There was a definite chill in the air under the canopy of trees.

I wondered whether to go and investigate the dog-headed figure. I didn't for one moment imagine it was really twenty feet tall. I knew that to be a trick of physics to do with the projection of light. I wondered if it was the same dog-headed man I'd seen the day before, then smiled to myself for thinking there might be two of them wandering these country lanes.

I hurried to Edith's house with a sense of foreboding. Her door was wide open. I called her name but there was no answer. I entered cautiously. I was half-expecting to find another ransacked house but as I went from room to room everything seemed to be in good order. I stood at the bottom of the stairs and called her name again. Only silence. Her study seemed undisturbed. Her computer was turned off but intact.

I eventually found her in the garden. Face down in an ornamental pond. I looked at her lying there, half submerged, tangled in a length of filtration pipe. *Dead* was the first word that came to mind.

Inspector Bradley looked at me sternly.

"Mr. Madrid, you seem to be bringing bad luck to this little community."

We were standing on Edith's terrace. I had my back deliberately turned to her body, laid out beside the pond. I'd been paralized when I'd first seen her in the water. She wasn't moving so I assumed she was dead, but I dragged her out anyway then called the police on my mobile. I felt terrible, partly because I'd trodden on something as I was struggling to get her on to dry land. When I looked down I was standing on her dentures.

I'd given Bradley my statement, mentioning the dog-headed figure I'd seen in the fog.

"I gather you're concluding that Miles Lyttle's death was suicide," I said. "Don't you think the burglary at his house makes that conclusion suspect?"

"Coincidence. I stick with facts, Mr. Madrid, and the fact is I've never heard of anyone being killed in a row over a dead black magician."

"Maybe you should get out more," I muttered.

"What was that?"

"I was wondering whether you didn't find Edith's death a bit *too* coincidental."

"I don't have a problem with coincidence, Mr. Madrid. I have a problem with journalists making up fanciful stories about dog-headed men wandering round my patch knocking people off three months before I'm due to retire to my villa on the Costa del Sol."

"In other words—don't make waves," I said quietly. Then: "How do you think she died?"

"I'm not stupid enough to make wild guesses in front of a journalist before the coroner has been along." He stuck a finger in his ear and began poking about in the fur. "Though death by heart attack or accidental drowning are my two favorites."

"Have you located the gypsies who left the night of her husband's death yet?"

"We're pursuing our inquiries," he said loftily. "But since Miles Lyttle committed suicide, the whereabouts of the gypsies is of little concern to us."

I left just as the coroner was arriving with the community policeman. I didn't fancy walking through the wood, especially if the dogman was lurking in there somewhere. I walked down the road instead. At quite a pace.

"Well, you're having an exciting stay," Kathleen said when I entered the pub. "Am I going to drop dead, too?"

"News travels bloody fast round here," I said, taking a swig of the beer she'd pushed in front of me, swaying slightly to Ella's version of "Bewitched, Bothered, and Bewildered."

"Our community policeman was in here when Bradley phoned through. He's worse than Miles Lyttle at keeping a secret. You okay?"

I looked round the pub. A dozen people scattered around in small groups.

"Tired. Frightened."

"Frightened?"

"Have you ever seen a man with a dog's head wandering around here?"

"There are a few who claim to be hung like horses but no one with a dog's head that I can think of. Why?"

"I've just seen him. It. For the second time. I know it's only somebody dressed up but it still spooks me."

"Must be Anubis, the Egyptian jackal god. He was something to do with the underworld and mummification."

"You do know about this stuff, don't you?"

"Yeah, well." She stuck her hands in the back pockets of her jeans. "How'd Edith die? The police know yet?"

"I think they're assuming heart attack, although it's possible she drowned—tripped over something and fell into the pool, you know. She was tangled in a hose pipe. I think she was murdered."

"She always did ignore the bans. Said it was the water authority's fault there wasn't enough water, because they didn't fix their leaks, so why should her garden suffer?"

"So the water fat cats killed her? No, I don't buy that."

"A heart attack presupposes she had a heart, of course."

"I thought you liked her?"

"I ... admired her. But she was very chilly. You must have found that."

"Having a heart attack now does sound too coincidental. It must be connected to her husband's death."

I handed my glass over and she pulled me another pint.

"Is a drowned woman wrapped in garden hose one of the other tarot cards then?"

"Ha ha. What do you know about those gypsies? Could they be involved?"

"Not a chance," Kathleen said firmly. "They're just ordinary people. They aren't into black magic or even any of the cliché gypsy stuff. And they certainly wouldn't kill anyone."

"Their departure that night looks suspicious."

"It's no more than coincidence. I'm sure of that. Forget the gypsies. They're just poor people trying to get by but they get demonized by certain people around here."

"They can't have been that poor to be driving an E-type."

"What do you mean, an E-type?" she said sharply.

"A young guy waiting to be abducted by alien space craft spotted it preceding the caravan convoy." I grinned. "I know—sounds like a reliable witness."

She frowned. "The gypsies don't have anything like an E-type. They have beaten up old Vauxhalls."

"Do you know anyone in the area who has an E-type, then?"

"Several people," she said abruptly. "There's a classics car garage on the outskirts of Ditchling and Novington Lane is a bit like millionaires row—a lot of very wealthy people around—except when it comes to repairs to the church roof. What color was this car?"

"Hard to tell at night. Dark—black or blue, maybe. What do people do around here? Oscar Savage, for example."

"Lives off his investments, like everybody else. Runs the local Am-Dram. He's keen on local archaeology."

Kathleen had an odd expression on her face.

"Are you okay?" I said. "Has something upset you?"

"Aside from hearing that somebody else in the village is dead, you mean?"

"Yeah, well. If it was murder I'm going to find out who did it."

"Look, Nick, there's something you have to recognize right from the off. Nobody around here cared for Edith—or Miles for that matter, although he was tolerated because he got his name in the posh papers. And some people really hated Edith.

"Passions can run deep in the country, you know. From time

to time, we all say 'I could kill so-and-so'—without necessarily meaning it. Around here, where Edith was concerned, some people did mean it. It isn't a matter of who could have done such a dreadful thing, it's more a case of where the queue starts forming."

"You're joking."

Kathleen shook her head.

"I know of at least half a dozen people who wished Edith ill. There's probably a pecking order based on the length of time wrongs have festered."

She looked across at the pool table where a trio of students from the local agricultural college were blowing loud raspberries at a fourth, presumably for making a lousy shot.

"I get all my gossip from my mum—she's a church warden. And reading between the lines, I think Edith has been almost blackmailing a number of people in the village."

"A blackmailer, eh? Agatha Christie, thou shouldst live to see this day."

At that moment the pub door opened and Jake walked in with two other men. He came over to the bar.

"Good day, Kathleen. Mr. Madrid, are you staying in the area long?" Jake said.

"I don't know yet. Why?"

"Well, you must meet some of our local luminaries whilst you are among us." He indicated the ginger-haired, ruddy-faced fellow standing beside him in a tweed suit too heavy for the time of year. "Patrick Ferguson here, for example. He owns Novington Place and quite a bit of land."

Ferguson proffered a knobbly red hand. Jake turned to the man to Ferguson's left. He was dressed almost identically to Ferguson and bore a marked resemblance to him.

"How do you do?" I said, offering my hand. "You must be Mr. Ferguson's son."

"No, no," Jake said with a laugh. "That's William Macrell." Macrell, blushing, gave my hand a quick shake and nodded at me.

"I suppose you've heard the news?" I said. "About Mrs. Lyttle?"

"That … quisling!" Ferguson said fiercely.

Jake ignored the curious outburst.

"What news?"

"She's dead. I found her body a couple of hours ago. I'm surprised you didn't know."

"Patrick and I have been out shooting rabbits," William Macrell said.

I recalled the near-miss I'd experienced on my first trip through Novington wood.

"In the wood between here and Novington?" I said.

Macrell nodded.

"Were you shooting in there the day of the fete by any chance?"

"Probably," Macrell said. "Why?"

I shook my head.

"Just curious."

"How did Edith die?" Jake asked.

I told them most of what had happened that morning and they expressed conventional but hardly effusive regret.

"You all knew Miles Lyttle?" I said.

"He kept pretty much to himself," Macrell said. "Writer, you know."

"I gather. Did he talk to any of you about his book on Aleister Crowley?"

"Certainly not to me, but then he'd hardly be likely to," Jake said with a small laugh.

"He was part of a small group which meets in the village every so often to discuss esoteric matters," Patrick Ferguson said.

"No other member of the group shared his interest in Crowley, however."

"Don't suppose the group met the night of his death," I said.

Ferguson and Macrell exchanged a look.

"As a matter of fact it did," Ferguson said.

"With Lyttle in attendance?" I said, trying not to sound too eager.

"Indeed," Ferguson said. "Oscar Savage gave a paper on the cabbala and its influence on the Renaissance. Most interesting."

"Where?"

"At my house," Ferguson said. "Novington Place."

"And did Lyttle seem like a man who was about to commit suicide?"

"I don't think any of us has any knowledge of suicides, so how would we know that?" Macrell said.

"Were you there, too?"

"I was. In fact, Lyttle and I left together. He seemed in good spirits." The others smiled knowingly. "Miles enjoyed a drink, Mr. Madrid."

"What time did you leave?"

"Around ten thirty. I live with my mother in the north of the lane. The Coachhouse. Lyttle lives—lived—in the opposite direction. We parted by the telephone box."

I had a host more questions but none that I felt I could ask at that moment. I excused myself and walked over to Ashcombe Manor, musing on what I'd learned.

Miles Lyttle had been in Novington until ten thirty. He'd been in good spirits. He'd died somewhere between eleven and one. Ample time for him to do the fifteen minute walk down to St. Michael's church.

I'd heard a car set off quickly from the pub car park sometime between eleven and twelve. The Moon Goddesses were out around then but I had no reason to think they had anything to do with his death. Then at around two I'd seen the gypsy convoy leaving.

Had the light been in the churchyard then? Or had he been brought down there in the middle of the night when he was already dead.

Could it be the gypsies? Edith had said they weren't really gypsies but I knew that some country folk had a down on any sort of traveller. I couldn't imagine a gypsy being interested in Crowley. Crowley's approach was nearer to satanism. That presupposed a belief in God and the Christian system. Gypsies, I imagined, believed in something older, more esoteric.

Then there was the odd behavior of the locals at the fete, the identity of the dog-headed man, and now the curious coincidence of Edith's death. All this and I was still no nearer knowing why Miles Lyttle was dead. Some investigative journalist I was turning out to be.

SEVEN

I'd decided to spend more time at the New Age conference center since I felt sure there was a link between the center and Miles Lyttle's death. I walked into the Manor grounds. Parked by the gate was a black E-type Jaguar.

Moira Cassidy, the administrator, was sitting behind her desk in her office, gazing into space. There were deep rings under her eyes, as if she had slept badly.

"Mr. Madrid. I suppose it was a vain hope that I had seen the last of you."

Despite her tiredness, she looked very fetching in a kind of Indian chemise. I was going to tell her how beautiful she looked but I had the distinct impression she was the kind of beautiful woman who would rather not be told about it, thanks.

She seemed very tense. I sighed and sat on the edge of her desk.

"Don't you want to know how I got on with the pagans you pointed out to me?"

"Well, you're still around to pester me so I assumed they skipped the human sacrifice part of their ritual—that's a joke, Mr. Madrid, before you start getting ideas. Terrible news about Edith is it not?"

We chatted about Edith for a moment or two, expressing yet more conventional regrets.

"What can I do for you?" Cassidy finally said.

"Since it looks like I'm going to be here for a while I'd like to sign up for Priya's yoga class."

"We're full, I'm afraid."

"I don't want to stay here. Can't I be a day-student?"

"I need to put you down for a minimum of two courses. Give me one more."

I flicked open the brochure lying on her desk. I read that Ashcombe Manor offered the experience of taking a range of courses in a community of like-minded people. The courses offered included Priya's yoga, theater, visioning, dreamwork, meditation, self awareness, the art of loving, music from within, encountering self and others, hands on healing, and personal magnetism.

"Nice E-type you have outside," I said casually. "Handles well on these country roads, I imagine."

"I wouldn't know. It's not mine."

"Really? Who does it belong to?"

"It belongs to Mr. Stassinopolos, if that's any of your business."

"I thought he was indifferent to material things?"

Cassidy almost smiled.

"Indifference is easy for a wealthy man."

"I saw a diver in your lake the other morning. What's that about?"

"One of our students is having a go at underwater archaeology. Are you going to choose a second course? I am extremely busy."

I saw Stassinopolos's name in the brochure.

"I'll do the personal magnetism course," I said. "Something draws me to it."

"It starts in ten minutes," she said. "Goodbye, Mr. Madrid."

On the way out I noticed the computer in the corner. I thought of the e-mail messages Miles Lyttle had received.

"You on the Internet?"

"Of course," she said, without looking up.

"Do you surf it?"

"Henry is our computer man. I expect he does."

Henry, the surly man who had opened the door to me on that first day.

The personal magnetism course was held in a basement room that looked like a chapel. True it had my great auntie Vi's wallpaper but it also had a lectern, banners, and exhortations on the walls, plus what looked like an altar draped in red velvet.

When I reached the bottom of the stairs I realized I had stepped into a Dennis Wheatley novel. Wheatley's usual cast of peculiar characters were all there. An Indian with an elongated orange turban, a slender oriental with slicked back hair and a spiv's moustache, a number of women who could only be described as spinsters. And there was the exotically beautiful foreign lady. Priya.

I sat down beside her. "Where's the guy with the bad breath," I said to her. She put her hand on my wrist and looked at me.

"The guy with the bad breath?"

"Yeah. You're sitting in a Dennis Wheatley novel. And in Dennis Wheatley novels the villain always has bad breath—as the exotic beauty discovers just before she falls asleep from the effects of the mickey finn he's slipped her so that he can ravish her. So, I repeat, where's the guy with the bad breath?"

Stassinopolos bounded down the stairs, shooting quick glances at us from eyes that had jet-black, pinpoint pupils.

"There he is," I said, relaxing.

I had assumed the E-type belonged to the gypsies until Kathleen had corrected me. But why shouldn't they have been working in concert with someone else who owned a Jag? Someone with an interest in the esoteric.

"When I was younger I longed for the magnetism that would have girls fluttering around me like moths around a flame," I whispered to Priya. "I tried everything to be noticed."

"Yeah but you can't hang around in parks without your trousers on in this climate all your life," Priya said.

I looked down my nose at her.

"You clearly spent too much time with Bridget in Crete," I said.

Stassinopolos had a sheaf of photographs in his hand. He held one up. It was similar to the ones I had seen on the wall in the office. He pointed at it.

"This Kirlian photograph shows an ordinary person's finger."

I looked politely at the multicolored image. It was certainly shaped like a finger. I was willing to believe him. He showed us the next photograph. Another finger—or possibly the same one, I don't claim to be an expert on digits—but this time with a flare of color around it.

"This," he explained, "is a faith healer's finger after he has done certain preparatory exercises for his work. See the energy it gives off."

We all nodded. He indicated the next photograph.

"What do you suppose this is?" He looked round the room. Spotted me. "Mr. Madrid?"

It looked like a cauliflower but I wasn't stupid enough to say that.

"A brain?" I said.

"I can see you don't eat enough vegetables," Stassinopolos said with a smirk. "It's a cauliflower."

Hmm. He shuffled the photographs and displayed another one. It looked like a cauliflower again, this time with a golden glow around it.

"And this, Mr. Madrid?" he said.

I had my doubts but I wasn't going to look foolish twice.

"A faith healing cauliflower?"

He tossed his head.

"It's the cauliflower after it has been chewed. The chewing releases its energy."

I nodded politely, wondering if keeping him here was depriving a village back home of its idiot.

I was hoping Stassinopolos would reveal himself in some way during the session, but by its end I knew no more about him. Priya and I went for a walk in the grounds.

As we drifted across the well tended lawn beside the lake, she said: "That was so stimulating. And wasn't it beautiful when he said he could see my aura?"

"Surely you don't believe this junk?" I said indignantly. When she looked at me I could see I'd made another mistake.

"Well, yes, I do believe in it. I believe in all kinds of things. I know there are angels because I know two of them. And I believe in other dimensions. I believe in magic. I believe in the moon goddess. Nick, you're so—so—*earthbound*."

I pondered this. It was true, I was earthbound. I didn't believe in any superstition, whether it was Christianity or fairies. Bridget had once asked me, apropos of someone running their life by astrology, what nonsense I would put up with just to get a woman into bed. "I'm a man," I'd replied. "Almost anything, frankly."

"The moon goddess?" I said mildly, hoping to disarm Priya with my interest. "Were you out celebrating the other night?"

"I was."

"Have the police questioned you?"

"They have."

"What did you tell them?"

"Nothing to tell. I wasn't aware of anything unusual happening."

"Apart from a bunch of women jumping over fires—" she looked at me sharply. "Sorry. Did you see Stassinopolos anywhere?"

"No. We didn't see anybody, though we heard a few vehicles on the road down from Novington to the main road, which I must admit puzzled me."

"Because …"

"Because Novington Lane doesn't go anywhere. It stops in Novington. So it must have been some cars from the village. Seemed strange at that time of night."

I told Priya about Edith's death. She took the news equably enough. I was telling her about the gypsies leaving when we reached one of the mounds of earth I'd noticed earlier, when the diver had emerged from the lake. Henry, the stringy bearded man I'd met when I first arrived at the Manor, was down on his hands and knees in the hole beside the mound. He was looking around him as if he had lost something.

"Hello," I said cheerily. "Can we do anything to help?"

"Yes, you can bugger off," he said, without looking up. He located a trowel. "The site is out of bounds while this work is in progress."

"Sorry," I said stiffly.

"So you should be," he said, still without looking up at me.

We left him there and began to walk back to the house.

"Is that guy always so rude?"

"Mostly," Priya said. "The Manor has got money from the Lottery Board to recreate the original Elizabethan garden as a teaching project with the students. That's what Henry's doing."

We arrived back at the house. I'd arranged to meet Julian at teatime in Brighton to interview him about the film. That was the last thing on my mind at the moment, but it was also going to be very lucrative and Bridget had already advanced me a healthy wad of money for expenses.

"I'll give you a lift to the station," Priya said.

"I can go by bike," I said hurriedly. I loved her company but I'd already experienced her driving.

"I insist," she said.

The drive turned out to be only mildly nerve-shattering. When we got there, she surprised me by getting out of the car with me.

"Where are you going?"

"We're going to see some friends of mine," Jake, the vicar said, walking up beside me, two tickets in his hand. He was wearing jeans again, his dog collar showing through a V-neck pullover. Priya pecked him on the cheek. Somehow her lipstick didn't come off on him.

I tried to conceal my jealousy.

"Stomach upset?" Jake said solicitously.

The train pulled in and I stood back to let them get on board first.

"What did Patrick Ferguson mean calling Edith a quisling in the pub?" I said to Jake when we were settled.

"What's a quisling?" Priya said.

"Strictly speaking it's someone who betrays Norway to the Nazis," I said. "Consequently it's not a word you should get much chance to use in day to day conversation."

"Not even if you betray Sweden?"

I shook my head.

"Other Scandinavian countries shouldn't count. However, it's another Decline of Our Language thing—it has evolved to mean any traitor who aids an occupying force."

"He meant stool pigeon probably," Jake said. "He's always getting his words mixed up. But I don't know why he would say that."

"I used to have a boyfriend who got his words muddled," Priya said. "He used to talk about my *erroneous* zones."

"Lucky bastard," I muttered.

"What?"

"You know," I said to Jake. "All this about the church going in for raves, isn't that a bit like letting the devil in through the disco door?"

"What—the devil has all the best tunes, you mean?" Jake said, smiling. Priya was sitting beside him. He sat back and casually spread his arm along the length of the seat behind her, his eyes never leaving mine. "I don't think so. We're just looking for relevance—"

"But the church isn't relevant. I know a lot of people who've left the church to go back to God."

"They wouldn't leave the kind of church I want," Jake said. "My kind of service goes back to the very roots of Christianity. The Christian church is founded on ecstasy you know—no, not that sort. The apostles after Christ's death spoke in tongues, lost themselves in the spirit. In a new millennium, such worship is even more relevant. Nick—okay if I call you that?—you a believer?"

"Atheist," I said.

"What—neither God nor Devil in your life?"

"No—but plenty of demons."

Jake smiled thinly. Priya gazed at me. I started to drown in her liquid brown eyes.

"Enlightenment is essential to us all," Jake said. "It doesn't necessarily have to be Christian enlightenment. People must find their own truth."

"Are you always so ecumenical with the truth?" I said, watching him jealously as his hand brushed Priya's shoulder. "My problem with enlightenment is that it destroys small talk. You spend a lot of time examining propositions like Blake's 'seeing a world in a grain of sand.' Which makes social situations difficult. What can you talk about to someone whose hobby is sand?"

Jake leaned forward. He had very blue eyes.

"Nick—"

"But it's where people look for enlightenment that's so

depressing," I blundered on. "When I was a kid a lot of people of my dad's generation were studying holy texts. Works about hobbits and rabbits and seagulls. Personally I draw the line at seagulls. As far as I'm concerned, seagulls make a lot of noise, have trouble with their bowels, and go to Bournemouth for their holidays. The concept of a gull with spiritual aspirations is alien to my nature."

"Oh for God's sake, Nick," Priya said, shifting in her seat and crossing her legs. Ulp.

Jake reached over to touch my arm.

"Whether you acknowledge it or not, Nick, you have spiritual needs. We all have. You might try to disguise them with drink, with drugs, with sex, with making money, or with living on the surface but they'll catch up with you in the end. I've tried it all, Nick, believe me. And the only happy people—genuinely happy people—I've met are the ones who take spirituality seriously."

"I know the kind you mean—I see them on the streets grinning to themselves. I cross the road to avoid them. Why can't they just smile inwardly like everyone else?"

The train pulled into Brighton not a moment too soon. We walked out of the station, Priya between Jake and I, but leaning towards him. I'd never had a vicar as a rival before and it threw me.

We set off down the hill, the sea glittering between the buildings some half a mile away. Priya and Jake took a left into the warren of the North Laines and I followed.

"Jake," a man said, stepping out of a doorway.

We all stopped. Jake looked from the man to us.

"You two go on," Jake said. "I'll catch you up."

I glanced again at the man in the shop doorway. Tall, unshaven, his hair in dirty yellow dreadlocks. Priya started walking and I hurried to catch up.

"All this spiritual stuff, Priya—I'm just surprised you're leaning towards Christianity."

"What, you think I should be in orange drapes, sandals, and a blue nylon anorak, chinking finger bells on Oxford Street in the middle of winter?" Priya said with a sharp laugh.

"You know what they say about the power of such beliefs," I said rapidly. "Winter or not, many are cold but few are frozen."

"Nick, it's clear we have opposing views. Can't we talk about something else?"

"Like randy vicars? You've read about these guys who run the happy-clappy services. They use their position of power to get into your knickers."

Priya stopped abruptly outside the Theatre Royal. She bared her teeth.

"And you don't want to get into my knickers, I suppose?"

I blushed. Scarlet.

"W-w-would you like me to ...?"

I saw the punch coming but not in time to jerk my head out of the way. Strong girl. I went down.

Watching her storm back down the street I called: "That's probably a no, right?"

"Now that, sport, is my kind of woman."

I looked up and Julian was standing beside me, offering a helping hand, his lustful gaze fixed on Priya as she stomped away. I watched her too, and noticed she paused long enough in her passionately headlong escape to walk round rather than under a ladder that was in her path.

"Do I know her?"

"She was leaving Crete when you were just arriving."

"Right. Recall her—but not in this reincarnation. Guess she was pissed off about you and our Antipodean friend last night, huh?"

"You heard about that?" I said, startled.

"Everybody's heard *about* it. Some people even heard *it*." He leered. "Those caravans have very thin walls you know. *Big dog.*"

I groaned.

"Don't worry, sport. You're not exactly the first. Stacey's a great kid—the original good time who was had by all."

He helped me to my feet.

"So where do you want to do this? I can give you forty minutes, tops."

It was a balmy evening so I suggested we go down to one of the bars on the beach and watch the waves wash in. Brighton council had developed the seafront to give it a European feel. Cafes, bars, clubs—even an artists' quarter in refurbished arches that were formerly used for housing fishing boats.

Once settled at a table where Julian could see all the pretty girls go jogging, walking, or rollerblading by, I set up my cassette recorder and started in.

"How's filming going?"

"Okay, really. Zane's being a pain—wanting to interfere to make sure we keep it *pure*. Seems to think that's more difficult to do now that Miles Lyttle is dead."

"Miles Lyttle?" I said, surprised. "You knew him?"

"Sure. He is—was—the technical adviser on the film. The Crowley expert."

"So who hired him?"

"Zane, I guess. It was before I came on board."

"How'd he know about Lyttle?"

"How would I know?" Julian looked impatient. "What's with all the questions about Miles Lyttle?"

"I found him. I'm investigating his death, too."

Julian kept his eyes on me as he took a long pull on his drink.

"Bridget's keeping you pretty busy," he finally said.

"You got any ideas about it?" I said.

"Lyttle's death? Nah. Killed himself, didn't he? That's all I've heard. Have to get hold of somebody else now, to keep Zane happy. Waste of money, of course."

"Lyttle's wife was found dead today, too," I said.

"You trying to make conversation?" Julian said, with a quick snigger.

"I found her."

"You got something against that family?" He squeezed my shoulder. "How'd she die?"

"Don't know yet. Drowned, maybe. Heart attack, maybe. There's some weird things going on on the other side of the Downs."

"We're heading over there day after tomorrow, sport, filming above Novington and Ditchling for two days."

"Did Miles Lyttle ever say anything to you about Crowley that might piss Crowleyites off?"

"Not that I recall," Julian said absently.

"Did he let you see his book?"

"I'm a film director, for chrissakes. I don't read books, I read treatments. But you were saying about Lyttle's wife. That's awful. The two connected?"

"What do you think?"

"Big coincidence, I have to agree. But what's it to do with you?"

"I feel involved. Responsible. I'm going to take it all the way."

"You up to that kind of investigation, sport? No offence, but I thought you were strictly a showbiz journo."

"I've had some experience of the other sort, too," I said.

"No need to get huffy," Julian said. "If you're looking for likely suspects, our film has attracted its share of weirdos."

"Aside from the cast, you mean."

"Pawky, Mr. Madrid. Definitely pawky."

"You said about a new Crowley expert. Isn't it handy to have someone—"

"We have someone," Julian said decisively.

"Who?"

"Me."

I looked at him.

"Didn't know you were a Crowley freak."

"I didn't say I was. But I wrote the initial script for this. The whole project was my idea."

"Tell me."

"You know I got lured away to Hollywood. I was offered *Confessions*—$30m budget, Alice, couple of other stars. I took the bait but they really stuck it to me. Well, you know the story. Alice wanted to play against type—mousy hair and no grin—producers wanted it to be an Alice Denver film, I'm in-between. Film was a disaster.

"So then I came back to lick my wounds. I was looking round for a project, discovered there'd never been a movie about Crowley. There's some interest—Snoo Wilson has a script called *The Beast* going around based on something he did on the telly—but I figured there could be more. Thought I'd try my hand as a hyphenate—you know, writer/director."

"What happened? How did Marlowe get involved?"

"Budgets. I envisaged a small, low budget film. You know I made my first film juggling credit cards? For this I was going to get investors in to pay £1,000 each for the privilege of playing extras in the movie. The crew would do it for expenses and deferred payments.

"Meanwhile, Zane Pynchon had turned up willing to put a lot of moolah into *The Great Beast* provided we got stars. And Marlowe had expressed an interest in the film. So, I was dropped *instantly*." He started to get up. "I need the bog."

As I waited for him to come back I noticed a man looking at me from the fisherman's pub next door. He was no fisherman, though. He looked a typical drinking man. In his late forties, open necked white shirt, sports jacket. He had a folded newspaper tucked in his jacket pocket. He stood with his head high, shoulders back, gut out. His waistband was folding over below his belly.

He held my look for a moment then casually turned away.

Julian came back, wiping his nose with a tissue. I wondered if he'd had a little pick-me-up in the toilet.

"You must have been really pissed off," I continued. "It being your project and all."

He shrugged.

"The movie business. It's what happens. I've got it back now, so that's okay."

"How's the shooting going?"

"Dennis is going to drive me mad. You know Crowley, for all his search for mastery, was actually a masochist. He liked being buggered and beaten—that's the T. E. Lawrence link right there, by the way. But Christ, can I tell Dennis that? Stars aren't on the receiving end. Stars are always in control, on top."

"If they're men," I said.

"Women too, if they're big enough stars. You know the rule of thumb in sex scenes—whoever has top billing goes on top. Do you remember the trouble they had the last time he was filming in Britain?"

"When he made Ralph Richardson rehearse opening the coffin lid for three hours?"

"I never believed that. No, when he made that film about the Civil War. He's hiding in the barn after the battle. Natalie Whatshername finds him. He's supposed to be exhausted but she's wilful and hot for him so she does him right there.

"*She* is doing *him*, right? He's supposed to lie still. Fifty four takes it took. I kid you not. I was second cameraman on that. The little bastard had St. Vitus's Fucking Dance. First he starts bucking, then he keeps trying to roll over on top of her. But she ain't gonna let him, so his little legs are scrabbling away trying to get some purchase. Looked ridiculous. Guess he didn't want to be seen as passive."

"So the information that his character likes to be penetrated anally might not go down too well?"

Julian adopted Zane Pynchon's voice. It wasn't a bad imitation: "You're asking Dennis Paniro to take it up the ass? Julian, babe, I don't *think* so."

We climbed the steps back up onto the wide promenade. I was distracted by the sight of a tall naked man, painted in black and white stripes to look like a zebra, walking down the steps from the promenade to the beach. I rubbed my eyes and turned back to Julian.

He was watching a bulky, bearded man in an expensive tracksuit, trainers, and mirror shades plough towards us down the prom from the direction of Hove.

"You're about to meet the great Zane Pynchon," Julian murmured.

"Julian," Pynchon called from ten yards away, his voice a deep rumble. "I hear from Dennis you got some strange ideas about his part."

He came to a halt in front of us, glanced at me.

"Zane Pynchon—and you are?"

"Zane, want you to meet an old friend of mine, Nick Madrid. He's the guy who found Miles Lyttle's body. He's investigating the death."

Pynchon held out a thick hand, chunky gold rings on each digit.

"That a fact?" he said, then turned back to Julian. He sucked in his cheeks. Someone had obviously once told him he had good cheekbones. I'd read that he had regular liposuction on his cheeks to keep them well defined. In consequence, when he pursed his lips he looked like a salmon. "What's this with Dennis?"

"It's your fault, Zane. You wanted it pure. And you know as well as I do that Crowley liked being a lady with men. Dennis has been having trouble getting a handle on the character so I pointed this out to him, thinking it might help."

Pynchon reached up and lowered his glasses. He had blood-shot eyes of an indeterminate color.

"Lemme get this straight. You're asking Dennis Paniro to take it up the ass? Julian, babe, I don't *think* so."

Julian flicked a glance at me but kept a straight face.

"No prob, Zane. I just thought Dennis should know."

"And you should know you gotta keep things real simple for Dennis. Helps him stay focused."

"Sure thing. So how's the power walking going?"

"Good. Try to do thirty minutes a day. You know there's quite a scene up the other end there—" he indicated back over his shoulder—"reminds me of Venice Beach. Hovey, is it?"

"Hove, actually," I said, startled by the comparison. The last time I'd been to Hove it was full of retired colonels whose afternoon naps were disturbed by little more than the squeak of the wheelchairs along the prom. Venice Beach was … different.

"Oh Julian," Zane said. "Dennis's gotta use the jet tomorrow, fly over to Paris, talk about another film he's doing for me later in the year."

"Will he be back for the opera?"

"'Fraid not."

"That mucks up the numbers."

Pynchon examined his watch for a moment, raised his hand in a languid wave, then looked at me. "Maybe your friend here can help out."

A black limo with tinted windows pulled up alongside us.

"Give you fellas a lift?" Pynchon said.

"Naw. Thanks, Zane. The Pavilion's only a couple of hundred yards away and it's nice to stretch the legs. See you later."

As the car eased away, Julian grinned at me.

"Total asshole. He tried our yoga, you know. And deep breathing. Now he's on power walking." He shook his head. "D'you see his watch?"

"Looked like a Mickey Mouse watch ..."

"Right—but a gold one—a gift from Team Disney. Not many around."

"What's this about the opera?"

"Yeah, I'm about to make your wildest wet dream come true. How'd you like to go to Glyndebourne tomorrow with Alice and Melinda?"

It's at times like this that you can judge the mettle of a man—or of a woman, though that isn't as attractively alliterative. A journalist without any morality—let's say, for the sake of argument, a *tabloid* journalist—wouldn't think twice about shelving his or her ongoing murder investigation(s) to swan off and drink champagne at the opera with a couple of movie stars.

We *broadsheet* journalists, however, are made of more ethical stuff. Was it likely I would drop everything to hobnob with Alice and Melinda? Give me some credit, *perlease*.

Then again, I didn't want to cause offence by refusing.

"I didn't think the season had started yet," I said.

"I should know about that? It's some one-off charity do, linked to Brighton Festival."

"What's on?" I said.

"What do you care what's on? I'm inviting you on a date with two film stars. Zane and I'll be there too, of course."

"You're not in my wildest wet dreams." I pondered. There was something about Zane I didn't altogether understand. "I haven't got my dj with me."

"Trudi will rent one for you. It should be fun. Alice's bringing one of her airhead retinue—her personal astrologer or something. But listen, don't for God's sake let on you're a journalist. I'll tell them you're a screenwriter. Still the lowest of the low but not quite subhuman. Plus, I'll tell them you got charisma. With a K."

It seemed peculiar to me that Pynchon should use his own money for the movie. Unless he was obsessed with Crowley. And a man with an obsession is capable of anything. Glyndebourne would provide an opportunity to quiz Pynchon that I couldn't afford to miss. The things I force myself to do for a story.

"Charisma with a K," I said. "That's me."

A couple of the crew winked at me when I went on set with Julian. Nothing much seemed to be happening. Alice was sitting in a chair looking bored, Melinda was twitching beside her. Intense? I should say. Alice was, of course, more ordinary looking than on film, though she did have a remarkably wide mouth. She looked even bonier than she did on screen.

Now, I know until Sandra Bullock came along Alice was up there with Julia Roberts, Sharon Stone, and Geena Davies as everybody's heartthrob. I'm afraid she wasn't mine. I must have been the only man in the world not to fancy her at all. Great smile, yes, but sexy, no.

Besides, she might as well have been computer-generated since nothing you saw of her body on screen was really her. For instance, her legs in the film where she played the supermodel in the microskirt and long boots—the film that made her a star—belonged to somebody else.

She'd had body doubles for most of her sex scenes in her other films, too. In the shower scene of the one where she was on the lam those weren't her breasts. That lesbian love scene in the feminist buddy buddy film? Somebody else entirely.

So I wasn't exactly sure what everybody was responding to.

She'd been going through her dull and dowdy phase, wanting to be taken seriously as an actress. She hadn't smiled once in *Confessions* and the film had bombed. Was nobody telling her that her grin added $30 million to the box office receipts?

It didn't surprise me she'd ended up—for the moment anyway—with the multimillionaire Zane Pynchon. She probably needed an older man to take care of her for a while. The tabloids had made hay with her past love life and there was a web site game, based on who she'd slept with, akin to "Kevin Bacon In Five Moves."

"What's everyone sitting around for?" Julian said. "We're ready to shoot. Wait, don't tell me. Where's Dennis?"

"He's getting focused," Melinda drawled, without looking up. "He doesn't feel he's in the character yet."

As she said this, Paniro walked on set. He was dressed in an Edwardian frock coat and carried a malacca cane. Somebody tapped me on the back. I turned.

"You're going to have to move, pal," one of the crew said. He indicated the board hanging just behind me. One of Dennis's idiot boards. Printed on it in big letters were the words "Do what thou wilt is the whole of the law."

"Sorry," I said, walking over to a space between the lights some ten yards away. I was facing Alice now. She looked at me. I smiled, she frowned.

I was trying to remember not to lean against the walls when I saw Alice speaking to Don, the line producer. A moment later he was shambling my way.

"Gonna have to move from there, fella," he said. "You're in Alice's sight-line."

"Sure," I said, almost walking into another of Dennis's boards as I set off.

Within ten minutes I had been moved six times. Once they started shooting the scene it became impossible. Dennis's boards were everywhere, Alice was staring round wild-eyed. What made it worse is that it was a pan-shot. I felt like a hunted man, ducking and weaving behind idiot boards, trying desperately to avoid eye-contact with Alice.

Finally, Julian called a halt and slouched over.

"Madrid. Got a knack for being in the wrong place at the

wrong time, I can see. Why don't I see you at the hotel tomorrow afternoon around three thirty for Glyndebourne? In the meantime—don't you have a couple of murders to solve?"

EIGHT

Iron Maiden's "666, The Number of the Beast" was playing at full blast when I walked into The Full Moon. Kathleen was standing on the other side of the bar gazing into space.

"So tell me about the unpopular Edith Lyttle," I said when I'd bought us both a drink.

"Not for me to say," she said. "But you could check out Patrick Ferguson—you met him earlier—the man who owns Novington Place."

"How come?"

"He and Edith have been at loggerheads for years. Originally, it was because whenever he tried to flog off bits of his land for building or for golf courses, Edith was always the most vociferous opponent of the scheme.

"More recently, she alone queered his pitch with the planners for his scheme to turn Novington Place into a discreet country house hotel. Nobody else in Novington minded. Rumor had it the plan was his last attempt to stave off bankruptcy: the Tories losing the elections a couple of years ago played havoc with some of his shadier investments."

"Harder to make a dishonest buck these days, I suppose. What about this quisling reference?"

"One of Ferguson's fields is the site of a Roman villa. He

took to exploring with a metal detector. Edith must have been watching him like a hawk. When he discovered a cache of gold coins in a sealed jug, the police were taking them off him as crown property before he could place his first call to Sotheby's.

"I heard the row—it was only a couple of weeks ago. I was in my mum's garden, next door to Edith's. Ferguson's parting words were, 'I'll get you for this, you see if I do.'"

I sipped my beer. Kathleen was looking better now. Gossiping clearly suited her. She grinned wickedly.

"What did you make of William Macrell?" she said.

"Seemed like a good natured non-achiever. Fancies himself as a country gentleman."

"Very true. Always dresses in clothes appropriate to whatever he's attempting. I think he must have a special 'Country Pursuits' mail order catalogue. On horseback he favors a hacking jacket, old fashioned jodhpurs, and a tight fitting bowler hat. If he could stay on a horse longer than sixty seconds he'd be just the thing.

"Mrs. MacRell's husband died as she was giving birth to their son, William. The local wags joked it was the first known case of a father dying in child birth. Malicious gossip has it he died because he was overcome by the sight of a baby which bore a remarkable resemblance to its father but, unfortunately, no resemblance at all to Mr. MacRell."

"Then who—"

"Who does he look like?"

"Patrick Ferguson is William's dad?"

"That's the assumption—though it's never openly discussed. Edith and Mrs. Macrell fell out a couple of years ago because Edith made some remarks. And that, of course, is another reason why Patrick Ferguson loathes her."

I laughed and swung round on my stool.

"Great gossip, but I wonder if that's enough reason for anyone to get murderous now."

"What are you thinking about Miles Lyttle's death?"

"I'm convinced Miles Lyttle was murdered because of the book he had written about Aleister Crowley. Did you know Lyttle was the Crowley expert used by the production company making *The Great Beast* in Brighton?"

Kathleen shook her head.

"He kept that very quiet. Which wasn't like him. When he'd had a few—i.e. almost any day—he was very indiscreet. Perhaps that's how people found out about what was in his book—the bits that are upsetting them, I mean."

Kathleen poured herself a bottle of imported beer.

"Although now I come to think of it Miles was in here a few weeks ago with a couple of trendy looking blokes who could have been film people."

"What did they look like?"

"One was drop dead gorgeous—wicked eyes. The other was a fat guy with a beard."

Julian and Zane Pynchon.

"What do you know about this esoteric group Miles was meeting with the night he died?"

"They're linked to local archaeology and history. I think they're writing a history of Novington. You know: From Domesday to the New Millennium kind of thing. Can't imagine them finishing off their meeting with their usual glass of port then ritually killing Lyttle, though. Didn't he go back home after?"

"Macrell says he walked with him as far as the telephone box at the church. Edith told me she hadn't heard him return home. Mind you, she was fast asleep and they do live in separate parts of the house."

"And what are you thinking about Edith's death if you don't take Patrick Ferguson as a suspect seriously?" Kathleen said.

"I'm not dismissing him—or anyone—out of hand. But I'm wondering if she found her husband's book."

"You're thinking she was murdered by some Crowley fanatic who then stole the book?"

"Maybe. I did see Anubis in the road just before I found her body."

I took a swig of my drink.

"I'd like to check out the black magic room in the Manor, too. There's something funny going on at that place, I'm sure."

"Aside from the courses they run, you mean?"

"I saw someone scuba diving in the lake the other day."

"What are those big mounds of earth in the grounds of the Manor?" Kathleen said. "What are they looking for?"

"They're recreating the original Elizabethan Garden. Looking for old walls and stuff I suppose."

"I wonder ..." Kathleen said. "You know, John Dee, the Elizabethan magician who lived in the Manor for a while, used scrying in a crystal to locate buried treasure. Perhaps Crowley did the same. Perhaps Henry is looking for buried treasure. And that might explain the scuba diver ..."

"There you go again, showing off your knowledge."

She flushed.

"I told you, I used to have a boyfriend who was into it all. Nick, there's something—"

We were interrupted by a customer coming to the bar for a refill. A lot of fuzzy guitar heralded the arrival of Hendrix's "Voodoo Chile" on the jukebox. I chuckled at the thought of the Manor getting lottery funding to search for buried treasure.

Kathleen came back to me and looked at her watch. "If you like, once I've shut up shop, I can show you where the tunnel in the churchyard starts."

"At this time of night? That's the kind of stupid thing people do in horror films. They always live just long enough to regret it."

"So what do you say?"

"I'm too tired tonight. But tomorrow—why not?"

In the morning I went to Priya's yoga class. I hadn't done my practice for a week plus I was keen to make it up with her. When I arrived at the Manor, Stassinopolos's E-type was still parked outside.

The others in the class were already assembled on their mats when I arrived in the yoga room. It was on the first floor of the manor, with a high-ceiling and long windows. The floor was waxed pitch pine.

From the windows I could see a ground mist in the woods beyond the lake. To dispel the early morning chill Priya had plugged in a couple of fan heaters.

She smiled tersely when she saw me. Some of the class welcomed me. One or two looked wary, as if I brought back luck. Maybe I did. I saw Chris, the therapist with the ponytail, watching me from the other side of the room. He gave me a nod and a quick wave of his hand.

I stripped down to my Calvin Kleins and unrolled my mat. The session was a taught practice, but for experienced yogis. That meant Priya issued instructions only to ensure we were all keeping to the correct rhythm of breath and movement.

I did half a dozen salutes to the sun—simple stretching and bending exercises—listening to her musical voice. It is important to stay focussed whilst doing this demanding sort of yoga. But bending my body into an inverted V, feeling the first beads of sweat trickling down my face, I let my mind drift back to Crete and the yoga center where Priya and I had met.

Once she had my heart, I hadn't seen Priya very much. She was studying free diving in the next bay with a young Frenchman who was apparently a world expert. Free diving is the kind made famous in Besson's *The Big Blue*, where divers go to incredible depths without oxygen tanks simply by breath control. They come up the same way, without getting the bends.

The breath fitted in well with the yoga, which is based on the power of breathing. In yoga, the theory is that when you breathe, you take in *prana,* the life force. Not in Shepherd's Bush you don't.

I wasn't doing the diving, as the Frenchman and I had had a falling out the first night he was there over something and nothing—bantam cock stuff. Priya, an athletic girl, was keen. So was Chris, the therapist. I'd see the two of them hike over the sandy headland together every afternoon. Later Priya would wax lyrical about it whilst I chewed my tongue off with jealousy.

I spent my afternoons with Bridget in one or other of the taverns. It wasn't very yogic. I wasn't drinking with her. I always made it a rule not to drink whilst in Crete, however tempted I might be—and believe me, with Bridget, I was very tempted. I sometimes wondered if I could only cope with her when I was drunk.

But it wasn't yogic because Bridget whined all the time. She hated it there. I told her that was the basic problem.

"There is no basic problem," she snapped, digging her knife and fork into the red mullet on her plate in a vain attempt to find some edible flesh. Red mullet was all that seemed to be fished by the local fishermen. "I just don't happen to like staring up strange people's bums so early in the morning. And most of these people are *very* strange."

There was indeed the usual smattering of narcissists and neurotics among the relatively normal people at the yoga center. This time there was an anorexic nutritionist who was, perhaps understandably, rather intense; a barrister who spoke—ceaselessly—in a nasal whine; and a blonde German woman, the healthy outdoors type, who insisted on eating a slice of the raw, steaming flesh when the locals slaughtered a pig. The vegetarians—and they were in the majority at the center—shunned her thereafter.

"You always get one or two nutters at places like this where people come to think about things or to search for something," I said.

"One or two nutters?" she said. "They're all nutters. Did someone get a cheap deal on *The Celestine Prophecies, Nine Insights from the Ancient Mayans*? Every bugger here is reading it."

"It's supposed to be very enlightening. And historically accurate."

"Historically accurate? The Mayans never wrote anything down, you half-wit, so where has all this wisdom been stored all these centuries? Forget *Men Are From Mars, Women Are From Venus*—I haven't a fucking clue where half of these people—men or women—come from. Nick, how can you fall for this stuff?"

"I don't necessarily."

"So why have you got that pile of Deepak Chopra books with you?"

She reached over into my bag.

"*Ageless Body, Timeless Mind.* This one—*Creating Affluence*—I can understand you wanting. But the *Seven Spiritual Laws of Success*? I hate this New Age shit."

"Priya recommended them to me."

"That Asian piece? She seems to be spending a lot of time with the Nietzschean Superman."

"Nietzschean Superman?"

"Yeah, big boy, I can use ten-dollar words when I want to. That psychobabbler, Chris. He's into 'will to power,' achieving one's potential by mind over body. All that 'anything is possible' crapola."

The next day, the free divers switched bays after an unexploded Second World War bomb washed up on the beach.

A crumbling pile of rocks on a headland a couple of bays along had once been a Templar castle. The Germans had occupied it during the war. Locals were now worried that they'd dumped all their explosives in the bay when they withdrew.

"I may go down there and check it out," Chris said that night at dinner. He and Priya had been on a table alone but I'd foisted myself upon them.

"Bit foolhardy, isn't it?" I said.

"Chris is a very experienced diver," Priya said, an admiring look in her eyes.

"Bully for him," I muttered underneath my breath.

"I have my scuba gear with me," he drawled.

"Tim-ber!" Priya yelled.

Suddenly I was back in the yoga room in Ashcombe and heading helplessly for a painful collision with the floor. I'd been doing *utthita hasta padangusthasana*—series C, if you want to get really technical. I was standing on one leg, my other leg pulled up—straight knee—against my chest, my shin against my nose, my hands round my ankle, when I remembered about Chris and his scuba gear.

The thought that he might be the diver in the lake here at Ashcombe was like a physical jolt, which broke my concentration and caused my loss of balance.

I managed to break my fall without too much difficulty but with no dignity whatsoever. On all fours I glanced round the class. Everybody was ignoring me, but all had superior little smirks on their faces.

"Focus, Nick," Priya called sternly.

I looked across at Chris, my mind whirring.

Maybe the diver—Chris—was looking for treasure. But how did Chris know about Crowley's treasure? Did Lyttle tell him? Which linked Chris to Lyttle's death.

As I moved into *ardha baddha padmottanasana*—don't ask, you're really better off not knowing—another thought struck me. If Crowley did have such a valuable treasure, how come he ended his life in poverty in a Hastings boarding house?

Priya left quickly at the end of the class and Chris too slipped away before I could ask him about the diving. Drenched in sweat, I made my stiff way back towards the pub. As I passed through the churchyard I saw that the door to the church was ajar. I had the jealous thought that Priya was in there with Jake, the young vicar.

In fact, the only person in the church was the elderly vicar.

"Who is there?" he called in a flustered voice, looking wild-eyed about him.

"Sorry to startle you, vicar. My name's Nick Madrid."

He fumbled in his pockets and pushed a pair of spectacles on to his nose.

"So sorry," he said. "I'm blind as a bat, I'm afraid, without my glasses. I thought for a moment you were a thief. I couldn't remember if I'd locked the church door. I'm forever having to come and check."

"Did you happen to come and check the night Miles Lyttle died?" I said.

The vicar turned and squinted at me.

"You are the journalist, are you not, who discovered poor Miles Lyttle's body? And now poor Edith, God rest her soul. As a matter of fact, I did come down that evening. But I'm sorry to say that I saw nothing. I left my spectacles in the vicarage on that occasion."

"What do you think about the idea that there is black magic being practiced hereabouts?"

"Absurd. I would know of it. I think at the college they indulge in heathen practices but I don't think devil worship is involved."

"What about Aleister Crowley?"

"That Godless man? I met him once, you know, at his Hastings boarding house. He didn't die until 1947. I was only a child at the time, of course. My father, who was vicar here before me, took me when he went to visit a friend who also lived there.

"The friend pointed Crowley out to me. A portly old man sitting in a deckchair in the garden. I'd heard of him—everybody had because of John Bull, who christened him the wickedest man in the world.

"But he seemed a shell of what I gather he had once been. I think his use of heroin had become addictive many years before. He wore the most ridiculous wig, I remember. It looked like it had been made from a mop-head. It had an enormous seam down the side …"

He seemed to be lost in his memories.

"Did Miles Lyttle discuss his book with you?" I said.

"He joked about it. You must understand, Mr. Madrid, that many religious people like to test the limits of their faith. There can be no belief in Satan without a belief in God."

I smiled.

"How long was your father vicar here?"

"Rector for over forty years," the vicar said, walking over to me.

I did a quick calculation.

"Then he must have known Crowley when Crowley was here in the twenties," I said.

"Oh indeed. And when Crowley came back for a brief period in the thirties."

"He lived here for two periods?" I said. "I didn't know that."

"Not many people did. It was in my father's papers. In his diary, I think."

"Was there much about Crowley in the diary?"

"I have no idea. I loved my father dearly but I'm afraid he was a very boring writer. My courage always flagged at the thought of wading through diaries devoted to the minutiae of his ministry."

"Has nobody read them through?"

"Oh, I think so. When my eyesight went I donated my father's papers to the local history collection in the Ashcombe Library in Lewes. It's a private library founded by the Ashcombe family last century. I think the working party is using the diary as a source for it's history."

"Working party?"

"Novington's aesthetics group has been working on a definitive history of this area. It has Lottery funding, you know. One of them mentioned the reference to two stays to me. Is it significant in some way?"

"I don't know. Very little is known about Crowley's movements in the thirties, that's all. Do you remember who mentioned it to you?"

The vicar thought for a moment.

"I'm afraid I don't. It may have been Patrick Ferguson. Or even poor Miles."

"Did whoever it was do the work on the your father's diaries at home?"

"Dear me, no. The local history collection is not a *lending* library."

"But anyone can see the collection?"

"During opening hours, if you are a member of the library or have purchased a day pass, certainly."

I thanked him and made my way back to the pub. I went to my room for a long soak in the bath. It was almost one before I was dressed and ready for the day.

I had to be in Brighton by three thirty to collect my dj from Trudi and meet Julian and the opera-goers. I thought I would go via the Ashcombe Library in Lewes.

I'd mislaid my phone somewhere yesterday so I used the call box in the pub to order a taxi. Kathleen smiled and waved from behind the bar.

The Ashcombe Library was in a Georgian building hidden down a narrow alley off Lewes High Street. It's rooms were on the first floor, down a narrow, wood-panelled corridor. It was perfect. Sagging old shelves packed with large books. Creaking floorboards pitched at all kinds of odd angles. Soft light coming through small, square-paned Georgian windows, augmented by lamps on the long, heavily varnished desks. And the smell, that musty, leathery smell old libraries have. I loved it immediately.

A kindly old lady in a big cardigan and tweed skirt had me sign in, then pointed me in the direction of the vicar of Novington's papers. It was a disappointment but little real surprise to find the diary was missing. The librarian was extremely distressed and went off searching cupboards in the other room.

Of course, she didn't find the diary. Before I left, I glanced back over the entries in the admissions book. Three names stood out from the dozens entered in the book in the past couple of months. Miles Lyttle. Patrick Ferguson. And Henry Thomas, the rude man from Ashcombe Manor.

I mooched around Lewes after leaving the library and the still distressed librarian. A pretty little town, full of tumbledown, red-tiled houses.

In a pub on the High Street, where Thomas Paine had given various inflammatory speeches a couple of hundred years before, I settled down with a pint. I thought about Priya and I thought about my list of suspects, all the while gazing blankly at a poster advertising a concert by a band called the Hofners.

My dad used to have a Hofner guitar. There was a time when he played guitar pretty well, when he handled his drink and his drugs pretty well. I'd been thinking about him, too. How little I knew about his life. How much less about my mother. I'd wondered before now whether it was the mystery of my parents that made me so persistent in unravelling mysteries I came across in my life now. Perhaps my persistence was a deflection because I was too scared to look at the mystery closest to me.

I reached the Grand Hotel in Brighton at three. The wind was fresh on the seafront, white spume frothing on the Pynchon waters, fleecy white clouds scudding across the sky.

"Hi, Nick," Trudi said as I waltzed into the makeshift office in the sitting room of Zane Pynchon's suite.

I kissed her on the cheek. She smelled fresh and clean.

"You're going to have my company too this afternoon," she said. "Alice's "astrologer had to drop out."

"Why?" I said.

She flashed white teeth.

"Unforeseen circumstances," we said together.

She pointed past me.

"Your tux is over there. You can change in the bathroom."

"Pynchon not here?"

"On his way back from London."

I started for the bathroom.

"Oh and Nick," Trudi said. I looked back over my shoulder. "Stacey sends her best," she said, deadpan.

When I came out of the bathroom, my street clothes neatly packed in a small bag I'd brought with me, I glanced round the room. Stacked on a table under the window were a couple of computers, a fax, and what looked like a satellite telephone. There was state of the art video equipment and a giant video screen over against the far wall.

Trudi came in, still in her jeans and T-shirt.

"Am I your date?" I said.

She shook her head.

"I think you're going to be with Melinda." She must have seen the panic on my face. "She's okay, really. I'll be going with Zane."

"Won't he be with Alice?"

"They're not an item any more. Mutual agreement, so it'll be okay tonight."

"So will Zane—has he …"

"Hit on me? No, he knows the score."

"Which is?"

"I have a partner."

There was something about the way she said it, or maybe it was the challenging look in her eye.

"Ah," I said.

"Ah, indeed," she said with a low chuckle.

Zane and Trudi were following on, so I went down to the bar alone and waited for the others to join me. Just the thought of Melinda terrified me. She was legendary for being an icy interviewee, unwilling to reveal anything, cuttingly intelligent, prone to rage, venom, and vituperation.

She was two breakdowns in and if there was no screaming or tears in a role, she wasn't interested. The joke about Melinda was that she always insisted a gratuitous madness scene be written into her contract.

Critics had called her a great actress on the strength of perhaps her best known distress scene, in a film about incest. Grieving for her dead father, she broke down in tears whilst clearing out his wardrobe and the camera stayed on her whilst *real snot* came down her nose and dripped off her face on to his sports jacket. Greatness, indeed.

"Nick, glad you could make it," Julian said, bowling into the bar and pumping my hand. "Alice, Melinda, this is my friend Nick Madrid."

Alice and Melinda each extended indolent hands. Melinda smiled winningly at me. She was wearing a black cocktail dress that emphasized her large breasts.

God knows what Alice thought she looked like. She was clearly wearing something left over from some long forgotten Oscar ceremony. At the time somebody must have offered her a great deal on tulle in Bo Peep Blue. In fact, with her hair in ringlets and a wide straw hat in her hand, she was a ringer for Little Bo Beep, *sans* sheep and, thank God, the crook.

I didn't know whether she was doped. She did have a lovely face, a very clear complexion, and, when she smiled, as she did now, a great set of gnashers. But she looked, frankly, vacuous.

My conversation with her in the bar went like this: "You're tall," Alice said.

"Yes, I am," I said.

"I'm tall, too," she said.

The trip in the limo passed with little more in the way of talk. Julian was on the phone to the studio in Hollywood most of the time so we all kept quiet. I looked out of the window, occasionally sneaking glances at the two women. Once or twice I caught Melinda staring at me. She looked me in the eye and smiled knowingly.

"How's the filming going?" I said to her.

"It's going to be a disaster, darling. An absolute disaster. Have you *heard* Paniro's accent? It's pure Bronx."

"But I thought he could do great accents? What about his Polish accent in *The Bridges Over Troubled Water*?"

"Dubbed by Anthony Hopkins. Tony would be perfect for this. He's never given a bad performance. Although he wasn't quite convincing as Picasso. He can't play earthy."

"Can't play earthy?" I protested. "What about as Hannibal Lector? He ate a guy's kidneys with fava beans—how earthy do you want him to be?"

"Mmm yes, Hannibal the Cannibal," Melinda said. "He and Cruella de Vil are my two screen heroes."

"Really" I said, smiling weakly and willing the journey to end.

NINE

I'd only ever been to Glyndebourne once before, to research a color piece about the first morning that tickets for the Festival Opera go on public sale. The box office opened at ten, customers were advised to begin queuing at eight. I arrived at seven thirty to find some four hundred people milling in the lobby. People with cut-glass accents, sleeping bags, fold-up chairs, and picnic hampers.

It wasn't quite like that today. Today, the men were for the most part soberly dressed in dinner jackets, the women were— well, mostly the women looked like dogs' dinners. When it comes to female fashion, the rich are different. They don't have any taste. What a tragedy places like Glyndebourne are for them.

Everywhere I looked women were wearing things that had to be seen to be disbelieved. I've always thought women with more money than sense should be obliged to wear a standard dinner suit, as men do, to avoid making spectacles of themselves and to save the rest of us from embarrassment.

For here they all were, the wives of captains of industry, of the country's business elite, and of members of Parliament, done up like Christmas trees in uniformly awful outfits. Ball gowns, swathes of taffeta, giant polka dots, oversized bows, saucer-sized buttons, the inevitable court shoes or heels so high that walking across the grass with any dignity was impossible.

I overheard snatches of conversation.

"I bought it in Dotty P's actually, mummy. Is what a statement?"

"Did I tell you I bumped into Johnny in Covent Garden? We met his sister in The Ivy. He's the one who used to have in his passport under occupation: socialite. No, social*ite*, daddy, he'd hardly be one of those would he?"

The chauffeur set up our table and chairs underneath an ancient tree near to the house. He placed a couple of large wicker hampers in the shade beneath the table. I added my little bag of clothes.

Julian passed round the glasses of champagne. Melinda was staring at me intently again. I smiled and looked away. When I glanced back she was still staring. It unnerved me.

Alice piped up.

"I wonder when people first started clapping as a means of appreciation?"

The remark proved to be a bit of a dead-end, conversation-wise. I shrugged and sipped my wine. I could tell it was going to be a long evening.

I looked around. There were already a couple of hundred people scattered around the grounds on rugs, blankets, and fold-up chairs. The form was that you had drinks before the opera then during the interval had your picnic either in the gardens or in one of the marquees.

One or two people drifting by looked across at Melinda, recognizing her from the telly or the theater. No one seemed to recognize Alice, perhaps because she was doing her best to hide her face behind the long brim of her hat.

"The house looks kind of spooky," she said, tilting her head to look at the ivy-clad old mansion. "But it gives off good vibes."

"There is a ghost here," I said. "The owners keep quiet about it. In one of the bedrooms. You get a sort of smothering feeling. Opera director I know told me about it."

"My therapist told me the supernatural is just your own guilt," Alice said. "Some kind of displacement thing. You into therapy, Melinda?"

"I'm on my fifth therapist," Melinda said matter-of-factly.

"You must be mad," Julian said.

She levelled a look at him.

"I beg your pardon," she said.

Julian grinned.

"I mean they're all charlatans."

"Rather a sweeping statement, don't you think?" she said slowly.

"If you can harness the power of your own mind, you can heal yourself of any mental or physical scar," Julian said with a shrug.

Just then Zane Pynchon and Trudi arrived. He was your velvet cummerbund, red satin bow tie, and brightly colored waistcoat kind of guy. She looked stunning in a very simple long black dress and gold pumps.

"Madrid, good to see you again," Pynchon said when they were settled. "Do what thou wilt is the whole of the law—only keep your hands off Alice, eh?"

He laughed loudly, the rest of us less so.

"We were just talking about therapy, Zane," Alice said. "You know, I've been staying at a wellness center in Colorado? I went because I was suffering from spiritual abuse."

"Spiritual abuse?" I said.

She nodded.

"I used to go to a medium for spiritual advice. She only did A list people."

"Fancy," I said.

"At the center they poured oil on to my third eye."

"The bastards," Julian said.

"No, it's good for you. You should read Deepak Chopra's books. Do you know them, Trudi?"

"Essential reading," Trudi said.

"He's quite remarkable," Alice continued. "He believes in perfect health through mind control, you know. He has terminal patients at the center. Some had spontaneous remissions whilst I was there."

"Isn't he the one who says that age is self inflicted?" Melinda said.

"Yes, yes, he does."

"If only," Melinda said, touching her face.

"And death is a mistake of the intellect."

"Miles Lyttle screwed up big time then," I said.

"What?" Alice said.

Pynchon gave me a thoughtful look.

"But how do you balance your belief in these, er, things with your Ivy League education, Alice ?" Trudi said, smiling sweetly.

Alice shrugged.

"I don't see that the two are exclusive."

"Weren't you also once called a genius trapped in the body of a goddess?" Melinda said silkily.

Alice sighed and nodded, apparently unembarrassed. Melinda pursed her lips.

"I've never been into spiritual things," she drawled. "I suppose I should have been. I was brought up in India—place is full of superstitions. Daddy was in the army, commanded a troop of Ghurkas. When I was back here at public school he'd send me a couple for my birthday. I used to keep them in the dorm. The other girls and I loved to play with them."

Alice looked at Melinda blankly. Melinda sipped her champagne with a smile and a little shudder of her shoulders.

Alice turned to Julian. "Are you a Scientologist, Julian?"

"Me?" Julian grinned, reached for the champagne and started to replenish our glasses. "Nah. Flirted with it. You know the guy who founded Scientology—old L. Ron Hubbard—broke up an Aleister Crowley cult in California in the thirties."

"I didn't know that."

"Guy called Wilfred Smith met Crowley in 1915, went on and founded an Ordo Templis Orientis Lodge in Pasadena—the Agape Lodge, part of the Church of Thelema. Rocket engineer called Parsons took it over. He wasn't some weirdo. Or not *just* some weirdo. He's the guy who founded Cal Tech.

"Anyway, Hubbard was sent in by Naval intelligence to get to know Parsons and break up this evil black magic group. Succeeded too, though a Pasadena sect was still paying Crowley's rent in the forties, when he was in Hastings."

I'd been watching Pynchon whilst Julian was talking. The producer was listening intently.

"Thing about Crowley," he said now, easing his belly under his cummerbund. "He knew about the mind, man. And the mind, that's where it's at. I've been interested in that for as long as I can remember. I used to play these games with myself. Locked myself in the bathroom and said my own name over and over into the mirror. Like a mantra. And I became *absolutely nothing*. I remember being locked in the bathroom, sitting on the edge of the bathtub, having repeated my own name until it became gibberish."

He paused for a long moment, staring fixedly at the ground.

"And I had this absolute lack of sense of self. I would have to sit down and literally regroup my point of view and orientation. I would have to travel back to wherever I thought I was when I started."

He shook his head and balled a hand into a fist, half-raised it.

"I remember almost not making it back on two occasions. I remember saying, I better stop this shit, because I felt I was in touch with my personal power and I could destroy myself."

I looked at Trudi. She gave me a quick wink then got to her feet.

"I need the little girls' room."

"Me, too," Alice said. They linked arms and sashayed across the grass.

"Zane, love," Melinda said. "Let me show you the gardens."

Julian and I watched them head towards the lily pond.

"Now listen, sport," Julian said. "Just so you know: I'm intending to be in Alice's bed tonight. Which leaves Melinda for you."

"What about Zane?"

"You wanna sleep with him, you might have your work cut out."

"I mean he and Melinda."

"She's not his thing. He likes 'em young and innocent."

"Alice innocent?"

"Okay then, straightforward. Alice has a healthy appetite. Zane's appetite is distinctly unhealthy. He's not real interested in straight sex, you know. He likes to corrupt them. Calls it 'turning them out.' That's why he and Alice split. She didn't like what he was offering."

I was thinking about Pynchon's obsession with power and his interest in perverted sex and putting it together with his investment in the Crowley film.

"Is *The Great Beast* a very personal project for him?" I said casually.

"I guess."

"This 'turning out'—I assume it's S & M. Does he get into ritual sex, too—you know, Crowley's sex magick?"

"I should know the details of his sex life? Ask him yourself, you're so interested."

I sipped my champagne.

"What about you and Alice—aren't you taking a bit of a risk since she's just turned him down?"

"He's cool. Besides, it'll be for old times' sake. We were an item years ago when she was just starting out. Plus a bit of a mercy fuck. She's feeling insecure about her acting. As well she might."

Melinda and Pynchon reappeared some twenty yards away, deep in conversation.

"So make your play with Melinda," Julian said. "You'll be okay."

"What's she going to want with me?"

"Sex. Sport, she ain't exactly picky. Let it be known on the first day of shooting that she needs sex every day. Doesn't seem too fussed who with."

"That makes me feel wanted," I said.

We both took a swig from our glasses.

Pynchon and Melinda plonked themselves down. A moment or two later, Alice and Trudi rejoined us, too. One look into Alice's eyes and it was pretty clear she had been powdering her nose. Julian excused himself, presumably to do the same.

"So, opera," Alice said. "It's what—like a musical?"

"Sort of," I said. "I'm afraid I don't know what we're seeing today."

"Some guy called Peter Grimes," Alice said. "What's it about?"

"It's about ninety minutes between champagne and dinner," Zane Pynchon said. "It's air conditioned, we're in a box, we can doze off. Who cares what it's about?"

Alice seemed to accept that. "You know, I met one of those three tenors once at the Hollywood Bowl."

"Pavarotti?" I said.

She looked puzzled.

"Not just now, thanks. I wish I could remember his name. One of them anyway. We had a real interesting conversation, except, of course, he spoke Italian and I don't speak it."

"Er …"

"Oh that's nothing. I once had a relationship with an Argentinian dancer that lasted a year—he didn't speak a word of English, I didn't speak a word of Spanish. Worked out fine."

Julian rejoined us and soon after we made our way over to the auditorium. We took our seats in our box and I scanned the crowds.

I did a double take when I saw Bridget sitting on the other side of the auditorium. In a room full of men in dinner jackets she looked like she was in hog heaven. Her head was swivelling from side to side—she didn't know who to ogle first. I grinned but my smile dimmed when I saw who she was with. Rufus, the sixties looking young man from her office, was sitting, very upright, beside her.

I can cope with Peter Grimes because I like the sets but I can see for a girl raised on *Fame* and *Flashdance*—even one who was also Ivy League—it would be a bit of a culture shock. Alice was basically a Valley Girl. First she got impatient, then she got sleepy, then she got … horny.

I didn't take it personally. I understood boredom and dope when I saw it. To be honest, I don't think at first she realized it was me she was playing footsie with. I think she thought it was Julian. Or maybe even Melinda. But I have big feet, which kind of dominate any small space. When she realized, she looked at me blearily.

Things got heavy at the interval. She glugged down a lot more champagne, by which time she was willing to grope anything. Thankfully, she focused on Julian. He good-naturedly fended her off whilst the rest of us pretended not to notice. Conversation was a little slack.

At the end of the interval nobody seemed too bothered about going back in. Zane said he'd prefer to get back to the hotel. Trudi said she'd go with him.

"Let's stay out here in the grounds and have some more

booze," Alice said. Pynchon and Trudi said their goodbyes as Julian popped another bottle of champagne. Alice lunged at him.

Melinda got up and walked towards the lily pond. Julian, holding Alice off, looked at Melinda's retreating back, then at me.

She didn't look up when I fell into step with her. But she spoke.

"Dennis Paniro has just learned about the serpent's kiss and is insisting he has his teeth filed down," she said, apropos of nothing.

"The serpent's kiss?"

"Crowley's customary greeting to women. His two incisors were filed to sharp points so that he could draw blood."

"From their necks?"

"Their wrists, usually. Miles Lyttle told me."

"You knew Miles Lyttle?"

"Met him, can't say I knew him. Have you ever sucked a lover's blood?"

I stole a glance at her whilst considering this question.

"I'm just a grammar school boy," I finally said.

"It's the ultimate orgasm," she said, glancing across at me. "It's very popular in the States. There are vampire communities in New York and Los Angeles, you know. There are around 15,000 people on the circuit, although most of them are Goth types who wear black lipstick, drink red wine, and pose. Probably only about 1,000 actually drink blood."

She caught me trying to look at her teeth and gave me a deliberately wolfish grin.

"Some people do have their teeth filed to a point. Or you can get fake fangs for $1,000. But most people use a razor blade to open a vein." She saw me wince. "Others use a syringe and put the blood into a wine glass."

"You're well informed," I said nervously.

"I know a dominatrix who runs a commercial dungeon in New York," she said. "She tells me vampire dominatrixes are all the rage."

"Is this part of a general interest you have in black magic?" I said politely.

"No." She stopped and faced me. "It's part of a general interest in sado-masochistic role-playing."

I flashed a quick look around us. We were walking beside the lily pond. A number of other people were doing the same, en route for the second part of the opera. I'm not saying we could be overheard, I'm just saying that Melinda, as a sometime stage actress, knew how to *project*.

"How interesting," I said, smiling cheesily. Out of my depth again. "I'm just an ordinary Joe, you know. I'm not into rubber or leather or whips and spikes."

A smile played on her lips as she led me into the trees at the far end of the pond. When we came to a clearing, she turned to face me.

"Pity. I was hoping you'd take me back to the hotel for some fun and games."

She raked me with her eyes, pushed me back against a tree, then closed in on me. Five minutes later Bridget and Rufus walked into the clearing.

In the limo back to Brighton, Melinda ignored everybody, Alice pawed Julian and he raised an eyebrow at me. I was impressed by the blasé way he was handling the importunings of one of the world's most desired women.

I smiled to myself recalling Rufus's look of utter astonishment as he recognized who was with me in the clearing. Bridget, grinning from ear to ear, raised her hands and silently applauded. Melinda had noticed nothing, although it was only a few moments before she pulled away and straightened her frock.

"You're sure you don't want to come back to the hotel," she said huskily.

"Since you insist," I gulped.

It was still only about half past eight when we piled into the Grand.

"'Night," Alice said, dragging Julian out of the lift when it reached her floor. He looked back over his shoulder, a mans-gotta-do-what-a-man's-gotta-do expression on his face.

Melinda and I ascended to her floor in silence. I have to admit I was nervous. I certainly wasn't into S & M and I wasn't sure what would be expected of me.

"Let's take a bath," she said as she let me into her suite and walked straight through to the bedroom. "I'll start running it."

I undressed, folding my clothes neatly, as I've been taught to do, then walked through to the bathroom. I would have liked to shower before getting into the bath, but Melinda beckoned.

I got the tap end. Gold taps mind. We worked out a mutually satisfactory arrangement of limbs so that no private parts were trespassed upon straight away. By accident, as we shifted about, my foot made contact with her bum.

"Bet you think that's my toe," I said racily.

"Your little toe," she replied without a pause. I hugged my knees.

The bath was all right. Nothing to write home about. That's what she said, anyway. I went ahead into the bedroom and slipped between the sheets, feeling remarkably like a sacrificial victim.

Melinda came back in from the bathroom wearing a tight basque, her plump breasts perilously close to falling out of the top, her thighs very white above her stocking tops.

"These rooms are supposed to be haunted, you know," she

said, glancing at my neat pile of clothes then back at me. "The ghost of some suicide."

She went over to the closet and dragged out a suitcase. She put it on the bottom of the bed and, leering, flipped it open.

I swear I heard the ghost gasp.

The suitcase was full to bursting with sex aids of every description. Plastic and leather, metal and rubber, each one with strange extrusions and knobs. I was unfamiliar with the use of most of these devices—where I come from the only sex aids we had were walls.

"Pandora's box," she breathed. She climbed up on to the bed and, on all fours, leaned over me, her full breasts only a few inches from my face. She licked my face. I made a little squeaking noise. Well, it tickled.

"Be my little incubus, Mick," she growled.

"Not so much of the little, if you don't mind," I said weakly. "And it's Nick actually."

"Old Nick. Have you got the devil in you, Nick?" As she said this she reached her hand down underneath me. I'd noticed the length of her pointed scarlet nails.

"No and I don't want him in me, thanks very much."

She grabbed hold of my hair and pushed her face close to mine.

"Are you rough trade? Are you, Nick? I think you are—"

"It's just my accent. I'm from Rams—"

I yelped as she scraped her nails across my buttocks.

"I bet you like to be rough with girls, don't you, Nick? And I bet you like to tell them filthy things. You like to abuse them. You do. I can tell. I can see it in your eyes. Well, do it. I want you to hurt me. Really hurt me. Tell me terrible things. Tell me the worst you can think of …"

I cleared my throat and gave it my best shot.

"You're a really lousy actress."

"You bastard!" she yelled, bursting into tears and rushing to the bathroom.

I lay on the bed, staring up at the ceiling, for a couple of minutes. Listening. Then I walked over to the bathroom door and tapped on it. I could hear her sobbing.

"Sorry," I said through the door. "Did I get that wrong?"

There was to be a big firework display to celebrate the opening of this year's Brighton Festival at nine thirty that evening. I'd changed and left my dinner suit with reception—Melinda had tactfully ignored how tightly I had clutched my little bag of day clothes in the lift up to her suite—and I now had ten minutes to reach the Palace Pier before the fireworks started.

I made it in five—embarrassment lending wings, etc. The sky was darkening but there was also, I noticed for the first time, a fog coming in fast from the sea. People were streaming on to Madeira Drive, to the east of the pier, where the fireworks would be set off. I walked onto the pier, bright as daylight beneath its strings of white lights. It was crowded with people.

I stood at the railing for a moment, looking across at the Pynchon hulk of the West Pier. Famously used in the filming of *Oh What A Lovely War*, it had been derelict for years, although now it was connected to the mainland by a thin thread of metal as work began on its multi-million pound refurbishment. It looked ghostly as the mist from the sea swirled around it.

"You're thinking *Oh What A Lovely War* but Barbra Streisand filmed on that pier, too. The Minnelli film, *On A Clear Day You Can See For Ever*? The one where Jack Nicholson sings?"

I turned.

"Priya. You've been going to pub quiz nights again haven't you?"

She grinned. I tried to catch my breath.

"What are you doing here?" I said.

"There's nothing quite like a firework display to set the blood racing."

"I can think of other things I prefer in the blood racing department," I said roguishly.

"Ah, bless him," she said, squeezing my hand. She winked. "The night is young."

"Try it with the other eye," I said.

She laughed as she found herself scrunching up the entire side of her face.

"It's been my observation that very few women can actually wink effectively with either eye," I said in my best man-of-the-world voice.

"You're quite an intellectual under that game show host exterior, aren't you?"

"Game show host?" I said, indignantly. "You're the second person to tell me that this week."

"Maybe you should listen to people more."

"I'm just observant. For instance, I've also noticed that men will tend to push a swing door, women will tend to pull it."

"That's because women read the sign that says 'pull,'" Priya said, shooting me a sharp glance. "The foibles of women, eh, Nick. Who can fathom us?"

I got the distinct impression I'd started out on the wrong foot. Again.

"Are you with Jake? Or Chris?"

"That asshole," she said, scowling.

"You've had a falling out? So I was right about the happy-clappy vicar wanting to get into your pants."

Priya flashed me another look.

"I was referring to Chris. He followed me here, you know. I thought I'd got shut of him in Crete."

"I thought you liked him."

"I did like him. I could talk to him and he would listen. He listened to all my troubles."

"You have troubles?"

"Bloody right. You should try being an Asian woman in Britain."

I looked across at her.

"I'm not talking about racism, I'm talking about being brought up in one culture and having to live in another."

"You mean sex."

"Not just sex." She gave me a kind of lopsided grin. "Though my dad would bloody kill me if he knew half of what I got up to."

"Not with me, though," I muttered.

"What?"

"How come you've avoided an arranged marriage so far?"

"Deviousness. But my mum is very keen on that for me. It's only a matter of time."

"So what about Chris?"

She pouted. I bit my lip. "It turned out we weren't on the same wavelength. I thought he realized that too, but now he turns up here."

I thought of Chris and his scuba gear and wondered if Priya was the sole reason he'd turned up.

She took my arm.

"Let's walk to the other end."

As we started off Moira Cassidy hurried past.

"Moira," Priya called after her. Cassidy stopped and turned.

"Priya—and Mr. Madrid."

"Walk with us?" I said.

"In a bit of a hurry," she said. "Got to find my brother on the end of the pier."

I looked around at the crush of people.

"You'll be lucky to find anyone in this scrum."

She gave me a curious smile.

"Oh, I don't think I'll have any problems. See you later."

Priya and I continued along the pier, her hip against my thigh, her head against my shoulder. I didn't know what was going on but, hey, if the girl had finally come to her senses, who was I to argue? You can't fight *kismet*, right?

"What about Jake?" I said into her hair.

"What about him?"

She yawned.

"Is he still chasing you?"

"He never was."

"Tell me another one."

"Tell you another one?" she said, lifting her head off my shoulder to glance up at me.

"Yeah. There's something suspicious about him. Secretive."

"Nick, Jake is gay. He likes it squalid. If you were a vicar, you'd be secretive about something like that."

"That guy who called him over that night in Brighton?"

"One of his friends. He's glad to be gay, but he has to be careful."

"He's glad to be gay, I'm glad he's gay," I murmured. I was starting to feel better.

We walked along in silence. I watched the choppy water far below through the gaps in the boards. Within fifty yards the fog had closed in around us.

"We'll see bugger all if the fret keeps on," Priya said.

"Fret?" I said.

"Sea frets—that's what they call these mists down here."

We passed the candy floss stall and the computerized 'Analyse Your Handwriting' booth. There was a rock shop and a gypsy caravan where a gypsy read your tarot cards. There was another gypsy caravan next to the first where another gypsy (or possibly the same one doubling up) read your palm.

Priya insisted on buying me a large stick of red rock from the shop. We were surrounded by exuberant people: rowdy locals, yappy foreign students, teenyboppers hanging around asking for trouble.

A mix of sweet and fatty smells wafted over us as we passed fish and chip, popcorn, toffee apple, hot dog, and candy floss stands. And there were the sounds. Snatches of music blaring from individual stalls, raucous shouts, girls screaming and laughing.

When the first fireworks went off, the fog smothered them. We could hear the dull crumps but could see little more than dim flashes of color in the blank sky.

Priya steered me into an amusement arcade in the center of the pier. The noise was deafening: blaring music, sound effects from motor racing games, video games of bone crunching human combat, and intergalactic nuclear wars and SAS jungle missions.

A big man with a newspaper stuck in his jacket pocket, his trouser waistband rolled over under his belly, was standing by a football game. He looked familiar but he turned away as we passed and I quickly forgot about him in the din.

There was so much barracking noise it seemed to dull all the senses. I assume that's why I didn't notice the two men until they began to jostle us. And it was only when they had wedged us against a bank of video games I realized we had a problem. Even then, I thought maybe they were a couple of chancers, up for a quick mugging whilst everybody was focused on video screens and nobody could hear what was going on.

But when I looked more closely I saw they looked too serious for muggers. Big, burly guys, each over six foot tall. Ex-paras judging by the tattoos on their thick forearms and bulging biceps.

Priya looked from one to the other and didn't hesitate. She pushed forward and waved the stick of rock at the man nearest to her.

"See this?" she said. "You'll need to have it surgically removed if you don't piss off right now."

The two thugs grinned and looked at each other. Their mistake.

Priya twisted and swerved round the guy she'd threatened. She raised the stick of rock in her right fist and drove the end of it with all her strength against the back of his skull.

I watched, dumbfounded, as, pole-axed, the guy went down. The other guy was slow to react. Too slow. Priya jabbed her left palm towards his face. He reached for her wrist but she was too quick. In a blur I saw her stiffen her bent fingers, jab her nails towards his eyes, and rake down his face. At the same time she twisted slightly and trod down hard with the sharp heel of her high-heeled shoe on the guy's instep.

He cried out and Priya jabbed him with stiff fingers in the throat. As he too went down, gagging, Priya grabbed my arm and pulled me past his prostrate form. I looked at her slack-mouthed.

"If the wind changes you'll stay like that," she said, swerving between banks of one armed bandits and more bragging video games. We came out on to the funfair at the end of the pier. As she tugged me along, I was trying to catch her eye.

"That was amazing," I said. "Amazing. Where ... how ..."

"The clawing was Leytonstone Womens Action Group Self Defence class. Clawing's better than poking. You might hit the forehead or the cheek with a poke but with a claw you're going to cause a lot of pain even if you miss the eyes."

She looked back at the exit from the arcade.

"The rest was kalaripayit—a southern Indian martial art. Girls aren't supposed to do it but Indian classical dance has a lot of the same postures. So I learned them, then got my brothers to show me what to do with them. They taught me the secret art of striking vital points—like the one at the back of the cranium—with a short stick."

She looked at the shattered stick of rock in her hand.

"I had to improvise a bit with that one."

"Think we've seen the last of them?"

"Doubt it, and if they're armed—"

The paunchy man I'd noticed earlier appeared at the exit. I remembered where I'd seen him before. Last night, when I'd been chatting to Julian down on the seafront. I was congratulating myself on my memory when I noticed he was holding a gun down at his side.

I nudged Priya and indicated the gun. She tugged me away towards the dodgems and waltzers. Here too the usually garish lights were muted and ghostly in the fog. Sound was refracted, making the amplified voices of the fairground barkers sound even more distorted than usual.

Although it was noisy here, I comforted myself with the thought that a gunshot would not go unnoticed. Very small comfort, I admit.

We reached the railing at the far end of the pier. There was nowhere else to go but back.

"We should be able to sneak past him," Priya said, "if we just follow the railing round. He won't be able to see us in the fog."

"What about the other two?"

"They won't be capable of following for some time," she said grimly.

I led the way along the railing. The fog made it seem as if we were entirely alone. No sooner had the thought crossed my mind than a shape loomed out of the fog. The paunchy one, gun in his hand.

"You can go, he stays," he said to Priya.

"Stick it in your ear," she said scornfully.

"Look, love, you're a game girl, but you won't catch me out with a stick of rock."

"No, I'll only need a stick of celery for you."

He looked at her with something like love in his eyes. I recognized it, because I had the same look in mine.

"What do you want with us?" I said, dragging my attention back to him.

"Nosy journalists need to be taught a lesson."

"Shooting me is a bit of an extreme lesson isn't it?" I said, my smile a rictus.

"Ain't gonna shoot you, pal," he said, his eyes flicking to keep a watch on Priya. "Just gonna pistol-whip you."

"Oh—that's okay, then," I said, moving back a pace as he raised his gun.

Priya was tensed to do something martial, I was tensed for the first smack of the pistol, and the thug was tensed to whack me when the zebra walked out of the fog.

It appeared on the thug's left. The man glanced towards it and his eyes widened. Then the zebra kicked him in the head. The thug fell against the railing and, almost lazily, toppled backwards over it. A second later I heard the splash as he hit the water.

"Whoops," the zebra said.

TEN

"Gordon used to be a kick-boxer, you see," Moira Cassidy said.

We were sitting in the Aquarius Cafe with a bottle of red wine. Well, Cassidy, Priya, and I were sitting. The zebra—Gordon, Moira's theriomorphic brother—was standing. He was covered from head to toe in stripes of black and white paint. Disconcertingly, his posing pouch—the only thing between him and an indecency charge—was at head height. My head height.

"I have to stand because I don't want to smudge the paint any more than I did on the pier," Gordon said. "It's water-based. Takes ages to put on."

When the thug had gone over the railing, Priya had rushed across to see if she could see him in the water. Gordon reached round to pull his tail to one side, sank to the planks of the pier and let his tail drop into his lap.

"The fret's too thick to see anything," Priya said when she came back. She looked down at Gordon. "Is that a tail in your lap or are you just pleased to see me?"

"Do you think he swam to shore?" Cassidy said now.

"No idea," I said. "He could easily have drowned."

"Good," Priya said shortly.

None of us at the time had felt inclined to go into the water after the thug. But now we had a dilemma. We felt we should report it to the police but we didn't want Gordon to get into trouble. We were sure we could prove self-defence but there would still be a lot of hassle.

"I don't know how I feel about killing someone," Gordon had said when I first broached the subject of the police. "We zebras are very peace-loving, you know. But I can't bear the thought of being caged, like an animal in a zoo, even for a day."

He looked at me with pleading eyes. I held no brief for going to the cops. My main concern was whether or not our attacker was dead. If he wasn't it meant that out there somewhere there was still a gunman—albeit a very soggy one—on our tail. Or more specifically my tail. Not to mention his two henchmen.

I looked at Gordon.

"I don't want to appear intrusive, but why do you want to be a zebra? Is it some superhero thing? You've taken on the attributes of a zebra to do good, as you did tonight?"

"I got the idea from a piece I saw in a Sunday paper about another man in Brighton who likes to become a zebra. He said a zebra had certain qualities—shy but arrogant—that he identified with. And I identified with that so strongly."

"I see," I said, though I had never been blinder. "So what do you do? Just hang around Brighton being, erm, zebra-like?"

"That's right, in the evenings and on my days off—I'm a local government officer, you know. I love being out and about. I'm trying to get a herd together to go up on the Downs. I was up there on my own the night before May Day."

"Wasn't everybody?" I said.

He looked at me and tossed his head. I half expected him to whinny.

"Roaming the veldt," he said. "That's what I like to do most. The moonlight on my body." He shimmied his hand down his chest and belly.

"Steady on, old chap," I said, worried where his hand was heading next. "The Downs is hardly the veldt."

"It's the nearest you can get to it round here."

"Where exactly were you?"

He looked down his nose, flared his nostrils and bared his teeth.

"Why?"

"Just curious. Wondered if you saw a convoy of three caravans led by an E-type, with some kind of four-track bringing up the rear."

He took a long pull on his beer.

"Saw it? That E-type nearly ran me down. Going far too fast on a bridleway. Spoiled my night in fact. Covered me in dust, which I couldn't get off without smearing my paint. I gave the driver what for, I can tell you."

"What did he say?"

"Told me to fuck off back to the game reserve. Threatened to shoot me and put my head on his dining room wall. Made a crack about a zebra crossing the road should be more careful to look both ways. Brute."

"Did he have a gun with him?"

"Certainly did. He stuck it out of the window and aimed it at me."

"What did he look like?" I said.

"Sorry. All humans look the same to me. Besides, I was looking at the gun not him."

"Accent?"

"I'm from Totteridge originally but I've moved around a lot."

"*His* accent."

"Local, I think."

"Where was this? Where were they going?"

"They'd come up Novington Hill, off the main road. I presumed they were heading for the A27. You cut out quite a bit of road going that way. You need to be local to know about it. Why are you so interested?"

"I saw them, too. You sure you don't you remember anything about him?"

"Broad shoulders, gap in his teeth, flat nose as if he'd been a boxer."

"Or a rugby player," Cassidy said quietly.

Priya had told me I'd left my phone in her car yesterday afternoon. She went over to use the phone on the bar to call a cab. Gordon wanted to be off so I thanked him again for his intervention.

When he'd gone, I drew Cassidy to one side.

"What did you mean by rugby player? Do you know who was driving that E-type?"

"It just reminded me of an old boyfriend, that's all."

"One that Kathleen in the pub also got involved with, by any chance?" I said, recalling the big hulk who had been hostile to me when I'd gone into the pub on May Day morning.

"Geoff," we both said together.

"He has an E-type," Cassidy said. "Didn't you know?"

I shook my head.

"But are the caravans connected with what happened to you tonight?"

"I haven't the faintest idea," I said, with depressing honesty.

Cassidy drove us all back to Ashcombe Manor, then tactfully left Priya and me alone at the heavy door.

"D'you want to come in?" Priya said.

I looked at my watch. Midnight.

"Well …"

"I've got your mobile phone in my room. Do you want to come and get it."

"Your room?"

Never has a man opened a heavy door more quickly.

Priya's room was on the second floor, facing the Downs. Once inside the door, she turned and kissed me very quickly all over my face. Then burst out laughing. I caught sight of myself in the mirror on the wall. My face was covered in bright red pouting lips.

I put my arm round her waist and pulled her gently towards me. "Ha-bloody-ha," I said, dipping my head down towards her face.

"All this occult stuff," Priya murmured, before we kissed. "I've got second sight, you know."

"Oh yeah?" I murmured. "Can you tell what I'm thinking now?"

She pressed herself against me for a moment.

"Definitely."

She insisted on wearing pyjamas in bed, with a complicated knot at the trouser waist. I went into my slow seduction technique. It differs from my rapid pounce technique in that it's, er, slower. That's the only difference really.

After sighs and passionate kisses and stroking through cotton for twenty minutes—a marathon for me, frankly—I started to fiddle with the knot one-handed.

"All fingers and thumbs," I murmured as I slid down the bed to nuzzle her belly button so that I could use both hands to untie the Gordian knot.

"Nick," she whispered, stroking my hair.

"Hnngh," I replied, as I tried to hook my chin into the waistband to slide the pyjama pants down. Trust me—it could have worked.

"Nick," she repeated, tugging at my ears.

"What?" I said, wondering if I should nip next door to borrow a pair of scissors.

"There's something I have to tell you."

I moved up beside her and began kissing her ear.

"Say whatever you want."

"I don't know how to say it."

"The words?" I put my mouth right against her ear. "Use whatever words you want. I won't be shocked. Anything is permissible in bed."

She said nothing.

"Whisper it," I encouraged her.

She put her lips next to my ear and breathed something into it. Her breath tickled.

"What?" I whispered back. "I didn't hear."

"I'm a virgin."

I didn't move a muscle. For a moment, I didn't say a word. This may or may not sound weird, but I'd only ever met one virgin before. As a girlfriend I mean. I knew they must exist. Obviously. But over the age of sixteen? Not in my lifetime. Mind you, I'd never met a boy over the age of fourteen who admitted to being one—because, of course, men lie. "Me?" they say. "Lost it when I was twelve. The French mistress at school." In your dreams pal.

I thought I should ask, just on the off chance.

"Er, do you want to stay a virgin?"

"You're supposed to, in my culture, incha?" she said, switching to mock-cockney out of embarrassment. "For the arranged marriage and that. So me, I'm all talk. Always 'ave been."

"Frustrating for you."

"You learn to make do."

I know the feeling. When I was a teenager my dad caught me masturbating. He wasn't cross or anything but he said I should try for the real thing instead. I thought masturbation was the real thing.

A lot of men have a thing about virgins. Not me. The only virgin I've ever slept with, I did so in ignorance. I was sad that

I hadn't known because I would have done it with all the frills. Two minutes for your first time is hardly memorable, especially with me.

Actually, I've yet to find a woman whose first time was either memorable for the right reasons or with the right man. Almost every woman I've ever met has told me how disappointing her first time was. That's a big responsibility for a sensitive man. I prefer being a disappointment later in their love lives.

"Let's just lie here and talk," I said to Priya.

"You're sure it's not frustrating for you?"

"No, no," I said, cramming my fist in my mouth and biting down hard. "Not at all."

We talked through most of the night. Well, she talked, I listened. Until, as it was getting light, she said: "But here am I wittering on about me. I really want to know about you. You must have had a fascinating life."

"I have actually. When I was younger ... Priya?"

She was fast asleep.

I dressed quietly and slipped from the room. Once outside, I inhaled the sharp morning scents then strolled across to the churchyard. I'd picked up my phone from Priya's room and now I dialled the answering service to see if I'd had any messages in the time it had been out of my hands.

There was one. A voice from the dead.

It was Edith. The computerized message service for my mobile kept messages for forty-eight hours before deleting them. She must have phoned me not long before her death.

Her message was to the point. She'd finally found the back-up files of her husband's book on her computer. She'd posted a copy on disk to me at The Full Moon and also sent it to my e-mail address.

Kathleen was coming down the stairs when I let myself into the pub. She stopped and put her hands on her hips, a stern expression on her face.

"And what time do you call this? Must have been a bloody good opera. Use this place like a hotel …"

"It is a hotel and you don't know the half of it. Did anything arrive for me in the post yesterday?"

"The post?"

"Yeah. You know, there's this thing called the postal service? Delivers to lots of houses?"

She came down the remainder of the steps.

"Fuck off. I just wasn't aware we'd become your *post restante* address."

"Edith sent me a copy of her husband's book on disk."

"Nothing came for you yesterday. Maybe it'll be here this morning. Post usually arrives around eight."

I looked at her for a moment. She looked troubled and I thought I knew why. She knew about Geoff and the gypsy convoy. And she knew I knew. However, now wasn't the time to get into that.

I gave her a quick hug and started up the stairs.

"Oh, someone phoned for you last night," she called after me.

"Who?"

"Somebody who wanted to talk to Shagger."

Bridget, who else?

"What did she say?"

"Intended to come over for lunch."

There was no disc in the post, but then there was no post. The pub phone rang as I came back down the stairs. Kathleen came away from it looking pale.

"That was Mrs. Deacon at the sub-post office. Our postman was mugged this morning and his postbag stolen."

"Interesting timing," I said. "In that case I'm going to go back to my flat for a few hours to retrieve the e-mail Edith sent. If my friend Bridget arrives before I get back, give her a bottle of vodka to keep her occupied."

"And if there's a later post?"

"If there's anything for me, just put it to one side. And don't, you know, defend it with your life or anything. If someone wants it, give it to them. I don't want you to risk getting hurt."

"Sounds like I'm going to have a fun day."

"I'm only offering you the worst case scenario."

"Well, not quite the worst case scenario. That would be that I end up dead."

I was in London by nine-thirty. The concourse on Victoria Station was packed. Even so, as I threaded my way through the crowd, I was aware of someone else's footsteps dogging mine.

A moment later I fell flat on my face. I'd like to think my superb, yoga trained body allowed me to break my fall with ease but, in fact, I fell really heavily.

I lay there for a moment, shaken. Ignored, of course, by all the people bustling past me. I hadn't slipped, I hadn't tripped, but somehow I was on the floor. I started to get to my feet, in that embarrassed way we have when we do something stupid and try to pretend nothing happened and hope nobody noticed. As I did so I was aware of someone close behind me. I started to turn but suddenly found myself back on the floor again. Looking round all I could see was a sea of legs. And a glimpse of Stassinopolos's retreating back.

I took the tube to Oxford Circus and walked down to the Central Line, looking back over my shoulder every few moments to see if I was being followed. I had no idea how I had come to fall in the first place, but I was pretty sure someone—and Stassinopolos seemed as likely a candidate as any—had pushed me back down the second time.

When I reached the door of my house I checked along the street. It seemed deserted. The house is a three-storey Victorian, my flat third floor rear. I grabbed my mail from behind the main door and hurried up the three flights of stairs.

I wasn't scared of Stassinopolos but I couldn't help remembering the two thugs on the pier. I double locked my door, bolted the three bolts, put the burglar chain on. My door has so many locks because of the area I live in. It is a peculiar mix of working class, yuppies, homeboys, and jackboys. The jackboys, always on the prowl for valuables to sell to feed their serious drug habits, aren't averse to bashing a door in to get at your goodies, whether you are in or not.

However, my locks would have little practical effect when it came to keeping anyone out. My flat is part of a cheap conversion. A very cheap conversion. It has papier-mâché walls.

If anyone seriously wanted to get in they could simply punch a hole in the wall and walk through. And, since I was tangling with the supernatural, my new enemies probably wouldn't even need the hole to come through the wall.

I made myself a herb tea—a carrot and coriander zinger, actually—and looked round. My flat is undoubtedly the smallest in London. There is this room and there is ... the other one. The bathroom.

I'd been swindled when I'd bought the place a couple of years ago. The vendor was an out and out crook. The day I moved in, the matter of a small outstanding debt he'd run out on had been brought up on my doorstep by a large outstanding debt collector. I'd had to produce my passport as proof of identity before he'd take the handcuffs off.

The only thing the crook left me of the fittings he was supposed to leave was blue corduroy wallpaper on every wall.

There's a place for corduroy in the world but it isn't on my walls, thanks. Either it had to go or I took to wearing cravats with loud striped shirts.

Of course, I didn't realize at the time that the corduroy was there to keep out at least a fraction of the chill that came through the aforementioned *papier mache* walls. In winter, the place was an icebox. Sure we've all known cold flats. I guess I just overreacted when I saw those seals lounging in the kitchen.

I left the tea bag in the mug so the herb tea would be good and strong—nothing wimpy about me. I turned on the computer and tried to remember how to work the e-mail software. It took me twenty minutes or so but eventually I clicked on the Check Mail box and sat back to wait.

Half an hour later, Edith's e-mail was still downloading. I prowled the flat impatiently, making sure I steered clear of my one house plant. It's a Busy Lizzie. A Very Busy Lizzie. It's rampant and I swear every time I go by it lunges for me. Paranoid, you say? So was it only coincidence my neighbor's cat had disappeared?

I sat back at my desk and shuffled then reshuffled my list of suspects. The convoy of gypsies, led by Kathleen's boyfriend, Geoff, in his E-type, I was pretty sure was out of another story. And I'd only linked Stassinopolos to the case because of his E-type so he was probably in the clear. But then again, I didn't know what to make of my semi-encounter with him on Victoria Station.

Then there was Patrick Ferguson, who hated Edith and was involved with that weird Novington discussion group. He'd been to Ashcombe Library and read the vicar's diaries. As had Henry Thomas, who was digging holes in the grounds of Ashcombe Manor as if he knew what he was looking for. Then there was Chris, the psychotherapist, busy exploring the lake.

Who was walking around pretending to be Anubis? Who

had sicked the thugs on the pier on me? I wondered again about Zane Pynchon. There was something about him that made me suspicious. Maybe the fact that he was as crazy as a sackful of cats.

After an hour, and two more carrot and coriander zingers, downloading was complete. It took me another ten minutes to find out which file my computer had hidden the e-mail in. Then, then, I nervously opened Lyttle's book.

I found all I needed in the introduction. It was obvious why Miles Lyttle had been killed and why someone had wanted to suppress his book.

Miles Lyttle had stumbled on a closely guarded secret, which his book was set to reveal. How long the secret had been closely guarded depended on your sense of history. Fifty plus years if you dated it from Crowley's death. Well over 2,000 years if you took the long view.

His crime was twofold. One, his introduction revealed the existence of a disparate and hitherto unknown band of hardcore Crowleyites, whose communications he had by chance inter-cepted on the Net. Second, he revealed what they were looking for: viz. an ancient book of magic, known as *The Key of Solomon,* some 2,000 years old, which had been in Crowley's possession in the thirties. *The Key of Solomon,* according to legend, contained all the secrets of the universe.

I know, I know. But some people believe this kind of stuff.

I was copying the text onto disk when I heard the floor-boards creak outside my door. I stopped and listened. Tiptoed over to the door. My T'ai Chi training means I know how to move elegantly and silently. Sadly, advancing age means my knees and ankles crack like rifle shots.

I stood behind the door, holding my breath. The only thing creaking now was me, but I thought I could hear faint breathing on the other side of the wood.

Breathing slowly myself, I waited for something to happen. And waited. Now I couldn't hear anything on the other side of the door. Had I imagined the breathing? I thought about opening the door suddenly to take whoever was on the other side—if anyone was on the other side—by surprise. Except that by the time I'd fiddled with all the locks and bolts, there wouldn't be much surprise left.

I stood for ten minutes then walked quietly back to the computer and continued the disk copying.

What had happened on the station had made me uneasy. Could I be confronted by people who had supernatural powers? I was too sceptical to believe it, but I couldn't help recalling the story Savage had told about Crowley making someone fall over.

According to tradition, I'd be safe from the forces of evil in a church—but given the vandalism round here, finding one unlocked within a radius of ten miles would be a miracle. I thought of going up into the attic for my dad's old Dennis Wheatley books. Wheatley's Duc de Richleau and his chums knew what to do when up against a bunch of dastardly satanists.

Like some occult Blue Peter presenter, the Duc would demonstrate how to keep out the hordes of hell using only a piece of chalk, some holy water, and a liberal supply of crucifixes. It usually involved drawing a pentacle on the floor, however, and I wasn't sure you could do that on coir matting.

I spilt my tea when the phone rang. Carrot stains are a real bugger to get out, too. After two rings the ansaphone cut in. I turned up the volume to hear who was calling. I heard my message then the beep then … silence. Yet not silence. Was it breathing I could hear on the other end of the line?

I'd seen the movies. I knew how this went. My nerves at breaking point, I should pick up the phone and shriek: "Speak, damn it, why don't you speak?"

I carried on copying Lyttle's book instead. Then I hid three of the disks around the flat, put one in an envelope addressed to Bridget, and the other two in my pocket.

It was almost one. I got ready to leave. I drew the bolts and turned the locks. Then, keeping the chain on, I opened the door and peeped through. The landing directly outside was empty. If someone was lurking round the corner down the next flight of stairs I would at least have the advantage of coming at them from above.

With infinite patience, I unhooked the chain and opened the door wider. I stepped out into the corridor, closing the door again silently with the help of the key.

Now I had two choices. To get down the stairs I could either tiptoe or run like hell. I'm a run like hell kind of guy, I guess. I added a banshee cry for good measure, clattering down the steps and yelling at the top of my voice. It was quite cathartic actually. I just hoped all my neighbors were at work.

I rushed at the front door, yanked it open, and dashed into the street.

I ran all the way to Shepherd's Bush Green, dropping Bridget's envelope in a mail box as I cut through the shopping center. I flagged down a black cab that was motoring fast in the outside lane. It cut across three lanes of traffic and jerked to a halt some ten yards beyond me. I climbed in and slammed the door.

"Leave it on its hinges, will you, mate?" the cabbie said peevishly.

"The British Museum, James," I said, "and don't spare the horses."

"Very original," he said sourly, pulling back out into traffic with the near-loss of only one cyclist's life.

The cab fare used up almost all my cash but at least I arrived at the British Museum unscathed. Other cyclists had not been so lucky.

Our journey had been punctuated by the metallic clang and crash of several racing bikes as my driver chose lanes at random. Or maybe he was really aiming at them.

I knew a woman in the prints department of the museum, name of Claire. I'd met her a couple of years before when I'd been researching a magazine piece about Richard Dadd, the insane Victorian artist who cut his father's throat and, understandably enough, ended up in Bedlam.

Some of his spooky, neurotically detailed paintings now hung in the Tate but I'd visited The British Museum to see its collection of his earlier watercolors and drawings. Claire had been very helpful and we'd become friends.

A pretty young woman at the information desk phoned through to her. Claire came straight out and gave me a kiss and a hug. She was tall and very striking, although she hid her face behind large owl-glasses.

"Nick. What favor are you after?"

She knew me so well.

"I need some info from someone in your manuscripts department about old occult manuscripts."

She put her hand to her cheek.

"That's part of the new British Library now. They've all moved up there. What is it you want to know?"

"Just a general chat."

"Now?"

"If possible."

"You're in luck. Two of them are down here for a couple of days working on transferring the database on to a new net-worked system."

Claire led me into a room where an exhibition was being mounted. I remembered this as the manuscripts display room. I used to enjoy browsing here whenever I visited the museum. It was the mix of things I liked. In one cabinet you could see beautiful illuminated manuscripts, like the Matthew Paris one, on which some bored copyist had doodled in the margins; in another, early handwritten drafts of novels and poems by various august writers. *The Magna Carta,* in all its splendor, was only a few yards away from a cabinet containing the first drafts of Beatles songs written on odd bits of paper torn out of exercise books.

Claire took me through to an office where a young man with a long pony tail was sitting in front of a computer screen.

"Ben, is Nev around?"

"Meeting. Can I help?"

"My friend, Nick, here wants to discuss the occult."

"Specifically *The Key of Solomon,*" I said.

He looked too young to know about such stuff but as soon as he opened his mouth I knew I was hearing an expert speak.

"*The Key of Solomon?* Okay. It's probably the most celebrated and feared work in the whole of ceremonial magic. Only the legendary *Emerald Tablets of Hermes Trismegistus* are more awesome. It has existed, in one form or another, since remote antiquity. Clerics who wrote condemning witchcraft called it *The Book of The Devil* but Western occultists insist anything diabolical was added later, that the true work is the purest spirit of High Magic."

"Hermes who?"

"Trismegistus. The Egyptian founder of magic—though it's doubtful he ever really existed. Or his tablets."

"Is this book generally known then? Are there any extant copies?"

"Dozen or so. But all corrupt later versions. Nothing much earlier than the eighteenth century. But we can trace the *Clavicle*—that's the other name for *The Key*—down through the centuries from Josephus in the first century AD."

Ben swivelled in his chair.

"But, as I say, there is no surviving Hebrew version of the *Clavicle* anywhere. All the manuscripts that exist in the great libraries of Europe are copies handwritten in French or Latin. We have one here in Latin."

"They'd had printing for ages by the eighteenth century— why so many handwritten copies?"

"Occultists say a printed text has no power. Magicians believed— believe, I guess—that it is the combination of the magician's mind with the spells that give magic its potency. So *The Key* had to be written in his own hand by the person who wished to use it—" He caught Claire's look. "Magicians or magi were always male."

"Were they all copying from a common source?"

"What we have are corrupt copies of corrupt copies of corrupt copies."

I turned back to Ben.

"So if an original were to turn up, would it be valuable?"

"You kidding? It would be priceless. Priceless. People are offering large fortunes for *printed* copies of *Magus: The Celestial Intelligence*, the book of magic by Francis Barrett, the so-called 'Last of the English Magicians.' And that only dates back to 1801. Simply as a manuscript, an original Hebrew version of *The Key of Solomon* is of incalculable value."

He laughed and spread his hands.

"And if the magic actually worked ... shit. How much would you pay for all the world?"

"What shall it profit a man if he shall gain the whole world ..." Claire said, musingly.

"Consider the lilies of the field," I countered, to show I knew my Gospels. There was silence for a moment. "I forget why," I added sheepishly. Then: "But no way is this mumbo jumbo going to work."

"There are people around who believe very sincerely that it will," Ben said.

I thought for a moment. "If an original were to turn up, where is it likely it would be found?"

Ben looked at me oddly, then at Claire, as if for confirmation that I had all my pencils in my pencil case.

"An original isn't likely to turn up," he said. "Ever."

He shrugged.

"But if you want to play pretend ..."

He tapped his teeth with the end of his pen.

"... if it's not buried in a cave in the desert like the Dead Sea Scrolls, it's probably right under our noses somewhere."

"How come?"

"Every library in the world has collections of uncatalogued or mis-catalogued manuscripts. Every great house and palace has attics full of old documents, also uncatalogued. Half the world's knowledge has been forgotten and is lying around waiting to be rediscovered."

"So which library would be your best bet for *The Key?*"

"If it isn't already in some wealthy crank's private collection, you mean? Because that is the other possibility—if it does, in fact, exist."

"Let us postulate the following ..." a voice said from the doorway.

We all turned.

"Nev," Claire said. "This is a friend of mine, Nick Madrid. Nick this is—"

"We know each other actually," I said, as Neville, the bald-headed man from the Brighton séance, walked into the room.

ELEVEN

An hour later I was back out in the street, my mind teeming. I looked at everyone I passed suspiciously—any one of them could be following me. But then, if there was anything in the occult, they wouldn't need to be. Somebody could be propped up in bed with a mug of cocoa and a crystal ball watching my every move.

I used up the last of my cash on a ticket for the tube, so when I got to Victoria I joined the queue at a cash point. It was situated beneath the overhang of the balcony of the mezzanine pub on the station. I looked up to see a young couple directly above me, glasses in hands, leaning over the balcony, squinting at the departure board.

They moved back from sight and I looked over at the board. It was twenty minutes before the next train to Hassocks. Time for a much-needed pint, once I'd got some money. I looked up and noticed the couple had finished their drinks and were coming down the escalator.

There were two people ahead of me in the queue. A guy with a big rucksack on his back was at the machine keying in his pin number. Behind him was a woman fighting a losing battle with the shoulder strap of her handbag.

She was tilting her body and hunching her shoulder to try

to stop the strap from sliding down her arm, taking her jacket with it. Her freedom of manoeuvre was limited by the polystyrene beaker of coffee she was trying desperately not to spill.

The inevitable happened just as I was reaching out a helping hand. The strap slipped down to the crook of her elbow, the weight of her bag jogged her arm, and she dropped the beaker of coffee.

I stepped back quickly as the scalding coffee erupted from the flattened beaker. At the same moment something plummeted past my shoulder. A full glass of beer shattered on the floor pretty much where I'd been standing a second before.

My shoes and ankles were immediately drenched in coffee and beer. Splinters of glass exploded everywhere. But I scarcely noticed. I was craning up to see who had dropped the glass and whether it was by accident or design.

Nobody was visible on the balcony above me.

"That could have killed someone, that could—" the woman said.

"I know," I said. "Me."

"Yes. Another foot to the left and you'd have known about it," she said, nodding sagely.

My hand was shaking so much it took me twice as long as usual to get my money from the machine. I jammed the notes in my pocket and walked quickly across to the other pub on the station, beside the Lottery booth. The barman watched me impassively as I walked up to the bar.

When I reached him he sniffed the air and peered over the counter at my sodden trouser legs.

"Seems like you've had more than enough already. Eh? Eh?"

I took my pint out to a table and looked across at the other pub. There was nobody at all on the balcony now. Had it been an accident? I decided until further notice not even to ask the question I seemed to have been asking since my first day down in Sussex. From now on, I would accept nothing as either accidental or coincidental.

I looked for my assailant among the bustle of people on the station. People eating burgers, sucking on coke, using mobiles, staring blank-faced at the information boards. A girl in short tight flares and high-heeled boots gave me a bored look. A tall geeky guy, thinking he looked cool in a straw hat, green linen suit, and T-shirt, turned away when he saw me watching him make a hash of eating a burger from a styrofoam container.

When I went for my train, I checked every compartment. I was expecting to find Stassinopolos but there was no sign of him. I walked the length of the platform until I found the buffet, one carriage from the front. I looked back down the platform to see if anybody was following me. Not that I would have known, if they were any good.

All my knowledge in this area came from films. But nobody turned to look at the nearest wall, nobody suddenly hid behind a newspaper—although an old biddy weighed down with Harrods shopping bags did look a bit suspicious.

I stayed in the buffet all the way back to Hassocks, thinking about what Neville had said: "I thought you might have come to me sooner, Mr. Madrid," he said. "I imagined Miss Cassidy would have told you about me."

"Not a word," I said. "Go on with what you were saying."

"Let us postulate that *The Key* we know was in the possession of Aaron Isaac, the court magician of the Greek Emperor Manuel Comnenus, in the eleventh century, was the original, handed down from generation to generation of High Priest."

"Greek?" I said.

"The Byzantine Empire was the eastern half of the old Roman Empire. It had its capital in Constantinople but much of its territory was in Greece."

Was this a link with Stassinopolos?

"The Fourth Crusade pillaged Constantinople and ransacked its great library. Perhaps *The Key* was destroyed in that sacking, perhaps it was carried off to Venice or to one of the other cities of Europe. Or perhaps it was already in the Empire's other great library, in the Monastery of St. Catherine."

"I don't know it," I said.

"It is in Sinai, currently part of modern Egypt. It was founded in the mountains, surrounded by desert, on the site of the Burning Bush of Moses. A Greek Orthodox brotherhood built a monastery there.

"It has the largest collection of ancient manuscripts in the world, after the Vatican. The manuscripts have never been properly catalogued. The library's most important—and valuable—possession is the oldest translation of the Gospels in the world. Called the Codex Syriacus, it dates from the fifth century, when it was first presented to the monastery.

"Yet it was only discovered among the library's manuscripts in 1892. It had lain forgotten there for fourteen centuries. If such a thing is possible, anything is possible."

Neville smiled sourly.

"I know what you are wondering, Mr. Madrid. You are wondering if Aleister Crowley ever visited Sinai."

"Is it Crowley you were attempting to summon at the séance?"

I recalled Neville asking the medium, Shirley, "Is it *him*?"

He nodded, sadness in his eyes. I looked across at Ben and Claire, who were both looking slightly bemused.

"We'll be back," I said to them. Then to Neville. "Let's take a walk."

The museum was packed with tourists but I took him through to the Assyrian rooms, a relatively quiet haven between the Elgin marbles and the wonders of Ancient Egypt. We sat on a bench in the shadow of the copies of the two giant bulls of Khorsabad—winged bulls, some fifteen feet high, with human heads.

"The Assyrians' texts seem to consist of nothing but spells to avert demons," Neville remarked.

"Did you know Miles Lyttle?" I said.

"Yes. He came here to research *The Key of Solomon.*"

"When?"

"About six months ago."

"Did he know of your interest in magic?"

"Not then, but later."

"And what did he tell you about *The Key of Solomon?*"

"He was very garrulous when drunk. When he discovered I shared an interest in magick and the work of Crowley, he insisted we go for a drink in the pub across the road from the entrance there. I'm not really a drinker but he drank enough for both of us. More than enough."

"And he told you that he had discovered that Crowley had had what might well be the original of *The Key of Solomon* in his possession."

"Yes!" Neville's face glowed with excitement. "Can you imagine how excited I was. To think that something so ancient might still exist."

"Worth a fortune, I gather."

Neville's face clouded.

"It was not its monetary value that interested me," he said. "It was the beauty of the thing itself. So venerable, such a link with the ancient world. And, of course, if—"

"Yeah, yeah. If the magic really worked …" Another nutter.

Neville looked indignant.

"But if you don't have some belief in such things why were you at the séance? Just to mock?"

"Very good question but let's get back to you and Miles Lyttle. What else did he tell you?"

"He told me that he'd stumbled upon a web site utilized by a small group of people to coordinate their search for *The Key of Solomon*. They knew about it through some reference in a letter Crowley had written to an Ordo Templi Orientis chapter in California somewhere during the war."

"Pasadena?" I said, frowning.

"I think so. The chapter was paying his rent in Hastings in the forties, I believe."

"Go on," I said, trying to stop my mind racing.

"The letter indicated he had obtained *The Key* early in the thirties but they had no idea where or how."

"In Sinai?" I said.

"Unlikely. How would he know it was there? The monastery is hardly a place you would just happen to visit and *The Key* was hardly something that you could go straight to in the library. No, he must have obtained it in some other way. And then the mystery followed of what he had then done with it."

"And Lyttle knew?"

"Not exactly. However, for some reason he did not divulge to me, he assumed that *The Key* must still be somewhere around Ashcombe Manor." Neville put his head in his hands. "Then I made a terrible error in judgement."

Whilst he composed himself I glanced across into the next room, crowded with visitors. I was startled to see a tall marble statue of Anubis, the very dog-headed figure I had seen twice as a harbinger of doom in Novington. Was it my imagination or did someone slip from sight behind the statue?

"A couple of weeks ago at the séance—I'm one of Shirley's regulars, I think she's marvellous, I really do—I did something very foolish. Lyttle had been getting nowhere trying to puzzle out where *The Key* might be. To be honest, he didn't care. The man had feet of clay. He just wanted to make a bit of a splash with his biography. So I asked the spirit to contact Aleister

Crowley and ask him if *The Key* was hidden in Ashcombe Manor."

"Was there a response?"

"None from the spirit world."

"Ms. Cassidy was there? And she got really pissed off with you?"

Neville nodded bleakly.

"She disrupted the séance, said it was nonsense to link the Manor with Aleister Crowley. There was quite a to-do."

I thought for a moment.

"Who else was at the séance? The same people as the other night?"

"Nobody else I recognized. Though I think Ms. Cassidy had come with someone from the college."

"A tall, bearded guy? Quite intense?"

"Yes, that's the one. You know him?"

"Henry Thomas. He's been searching for *The Key* in the grounds of Ashcombe Manor."

Neville put his face in his hands again. I was puzzled for a moment, then I realized what he was anguished about.

"Ah, you think you signed Lyttle's death warrant in some way by revealing Crowley's possession of *The Key*."

"It was his secret, you see," he said, clasping his hands before his chest. "And he died soon after."

I pushed on.

"So, to your knowledge, Neville, has anyone been able to locate Crowley's manuscript of *The Key?*"

"No one. I have tried everything. I confess I have even scryed with the piece of crystal John Dee used for the purpose. It is in the museum here, you know."

"If it's any comfort," I said. "I don't think you were responsible for Lyttle's death. He himself told enough people about *The Key.*"

"I don't really understand quite why he was killed."

"Don't you? A handful of people knew *The Key* had been in Crowley's possession. They were on its trail. But to succeed, they had to work in secret. If Crowley's possession of *The Key* were generally known, they'd be trampled in the rush of other people searching for it. Lyttle was killed to prevent that from happening."

As I got up to leave, Neville grasped my sleeve.

"I had one thought about where Crowley might have picked up *The Key*. Lyttle said he thought Crowley had been offered it by a Mediterranean trader who knew of his reputation for wizardry."

"In Sicily, when he was living in Cefalu?"

"He lived there in the twenties. This would be in 1931 or 1932."

"Where then?"

"In Crete."

The Full Moon had about four customers when I arrived back there. One of them was Bridget, who was propping up the bar, talking to Kathleen, an almost empty bottle of rioja and two full glasses between them. Bridget was tapping her foot to John Martyn's husky voiced version of "Call Me the Devil."

"Bless him!" I heard Kathleen say, then she saw me and nudged Bridget.

"Hi, sweetheart," Bridget said, giving me a hug.

"What have you two been talking about?" I said.

"Your love life," Bridget said. She glanced at Kathleen and they both started laughing. Their laughter built hysterically. Kathleen was so overcome she fell to her hands and knees behind the counter, sobbing.

"Bloody charming," I said. "How many bottles have you two had?"

"Who's counting?" Bridget said, gasping for breath.

"Is Doofus with you?"

"*Rufus*." She dabbed her eyes with a handkerchief. "Yes, as a matter of fact he is."

"Handbag or pocket?"

"Ha ha. With me in this vicinity, not actually here. His family has land in the county. He's back at their humble abode."

I remembered Kathleen saying that was how you distinguished wealthy people in the country: most of us have a garden; the wealthy have land.

"D'you find this place okay?"

"Rufus went to school down the road. Spent a lot of time here as a teenager."

"What, last week you mean?"

"I don't know what you've got against him. He spoke very highly of you."

"Really?" It's depressing how suddenly I perked up. "What did he say exactly?"

"Said he liked your name."

"And …"

"And nothing. That was it."

"Effusive guy," I said. I looked at Kathleen, who was back on two feet again. "So you two have been getting to know each other?"

"Getting to know you, actually," Kathleen said, holding down another snigger.

"Got to admit, I thought at first Kathleen was another one whose heart you'd broken with inadequate rogering," Bridget said. "I was telling her you should carry a printed warning: Not Worth the Heartache, Ladies."

"It's not like that."

"So she said. And so we moved on. To your shag with Melinda Taylor. I'd heard about her but I didn't necessarily believe it until I saw you in the grounds last night."

"Heard what about her?"

"That she'll shag anything."

"Thanks a lot," I said, looking anxiously round the pub. Faces were turned towards us. Bridget thought *sotto voce* meant something drunken in Italian. "Do you want to shout a bit louder? I don't think that couple over in the corner quite heard you."

"They're not interested. This is the country. They're all sheep-shaggers. You fit right in."

"Stick it in your ear," I said.

"Only place it'll fit from what I hear," she responded as she lit a cigarette. "Next week," she added, noting my disapproval. "Post-coital fag."

"How near does Rufus live, for Christ's sake?"

"Who said it had to be immediately post-coital? Kathleen, love, I need food. Something rural—swineherds soup or thatcher's platter?"

"I don't know what you've got against the country," I said.

"If you could get a decent cappuccino in the country I'd love it. Except the place names all sound like sexual practices— Fulking, Fletching ..."

Kathleen went to get food and Bridget took a swig from her glass.

"Nice woman. Okay, fill me in."

"Where do I begin?"

"Start with Melinda. Does that mean I have an exclusive or are you selling your story to the tabloids?"

No way was I going to tell Bridget—Ms. Discretion-Not— what had or hadn't happened the previous night. I brought her up to date on my investigations instead.

"So this *Key of Solomon* is worth a lot of moolah?" she said. "Enough to murder people for it?"

"Neither you nor I would hesitate." I dug one of the computer disks out of my pocket and passed it across to her. "I've posted one of these to your office but take this, too. It's a copy of

Miles Lyttle's biography of Crowley. I think he was murdered in an attempt to suppress it."

She put the disk in her handbag.

"But then there's a link with Crete, which could tie it in to a guy called Stassinopolos over at the Manor."

I told Bridget about my visit to the British Museum and my conversation with Neville.

"Crete?" I'd said in surprise when he'd told me that was where Crowley had most likely acquired the manuscript.

"It makes sense, you see," Neville said. "If you accept my postulation about the Monastery of St. Catherine. And *The Key* need not have been stolen at all. During the seventeenth century, the monastery ran a school where the greatest Greek savants were educated. In Heraklion, the capital of Crete. Perhaps the manuscript was merely transferred there, then when the school closed down some two hundred years ago, the manuscript remained on the island."

Now I rubbed my chin.

"I've had the feeling I've been followed all day," I said to Bridget.

"You seen anybody?"

"No, but there's definitely some weird stuff going on."

"Define weird."

So I told her about the beer glass and about my falling over at Victoria earlier in the day.

"You really believe some power knocked you over without physically touching you?"

"What else can I think?"

"Next you'll be saying Shirley Maclaine really is 9,000 years old."

"I'm just saying it's not as straightforward as it might be."

Bridget patted my hand.

"Nick, come home. All this country air is obviously doing

bad things to your head. Get back to the filth of Shepherds Bush and the squalor of your flat."

"Squalor?" I said indignantly.

"I've been there," she said.

Fair enough.

"So carry on with your exegesis. You looking at? I'm an editor now. Have to use big words in the Monday editorial meeting. Even know what some of them mean. Go on."

"Nothing more to say."

"So where is this book of magic?"

"My bet is that it's somewhere at Ashcombe Manor, but who knows? One guy is trying to explore the lake—though how he thinks an ancient manuscript will have survived in there, I have no idea."

"How do you know Crowley didn't destroy it?"

"I don't think even he would have dared do that. I think he hid it. I think he left clues to its whereabouts. And people at Ashcombe Manor have figured out the clues."

"Is this a Maltese Falcon job, people searching for years, tracking it over continents?"

"I think the focus on Ashcombe Manor only came to light quite recently. I think there's something in the vicar's diary that points in that direction."

"How come?"

"Because somebody's nicked it."

"What were you saying about some gypsies? What's happening with that?"

Kathleen came back in with two bowls of soup.

"Something odd, I think," I said. "But I don't believe they're involved in this."

When we'd eaten, Bridget yawned—we'd finished another bottle of wine.

"I need a nap. Where's your room?"

"Aren't they expecting you in work at all today?"

"I'm the editor. Theirs to expect, me to arrive *when*—and more essentially, *if*—I feel like it. Besides, I have Rufus to take care of things for me. He'll be going back up to London later to work his cute little butt off for me. Sexual slavery breeds a certain sort of loyalty."

"Got your celebrity writer yet?"

"Thought we'd do a gardening column instead. Everybody's going bonkers for gardening."

"You'll never guess who's here, by the way. Remember that Asian yoga teacher in Crete? Priya?"

"The one who wasn't having any of you? How could I forget your morose little face?"

"She's teaching at Ashcombe Manor."

Bridget gave me an old fashioned look.

When she'd gone I went to find Kathleen. As all the customers had left by now, she was sitting in the far corner of the bar doing the crossword in the paper.

"No more post, then?"

She shook her head.

"Fear of the number thirteen—seventeen letters."

"Very-sad-indeed? Okay, something *phobia*?"

"We always used to be told don't sleep thirteen in a bed," Kathleen said. "Supposed to be bad luck. Personally, I think it was because it would be too complicated to work out the sexual permutations. Without a rota system anyway."

"You were *always* told that? Thirteen in a bed was a popular topic of conversation was it, when you were little?"

"Well, yes. Why—what did you talk about?"

"D'you mind if I ask about Geoff? Haven't seen him around lately."

"You won't either," she said tersely. "He and I aren't together any more."

"I'm sorry," I said.

She tossed the newspaper on the bar.

"So am I. But ..."

"But you couldn't forgive what he'd done?"

She stood and came over to me.

"You've guessed then?"

"Moira Cassidy recognized the description a witness gave—a zebra actually."

"A zebra. Of course."

"Doesn't like gypsies, does he?"

"Hates them. Most people do round here. You should try having them camping outside your front door for months at a time." She sighed. "But that doesn't mean I approve of what he and his mates did."

"Gave them a good kicking then ran them off."

"The old ways are sometimes the best," she said with a grimace.

"Where'd he take them?"

"Just over to the A27 and told them to piss off out of it. If they ever came back here he'd use the shotgun. They believed him."

"I'd believe him. And everybody else in the village colluded?"

"Not everyone. But most people, yes."

I'd already decided that was why everyone had looked at me so strangely when I turned up at the church fete. Smiling and waving as if butter wouldn't melt in their mouths. Vicious sods. They'd heard I was a journalist and were worried I was going to write about what they'd done to the gypsies.

"Was William Macrell driving the four-track?"

Kathleen nodded. That figured. I wondered if he had deliberately shot close to me in the wood to scare me off, too. Though that still didn't explain old Anubis.

"And you knew?" I said.

"Certainly not. He didn't tell me because he knew what I'd say. When I found out I was so angry with him. And ashamed."

"What about when I told you about the E-type?"

"Geoff's E-type is red. You said you were looking for black or dark blue. It was only when I checked the other night I realized that red looks black at night. I wanted to tell you but I didn't know how. I did try to tell you the gypsies weren't anything to do with the death of the Lyttles."

"You could have told the police."

"What—you think the police don't know? Our upstanding community copper was one of the gang that sent them on their way."

"They chose the wrong night for it."

She shrugged.

"You going to do anything about it?"

"If the cops are part of it I don't see what I can do," I said. "I'm more concerned about the Lyttles."

"What are you doing now?" she said. "Do you want me to show you the tunnel leading to the black magic room?"

I phoned the Manor first to see if Stassinopolos was available. He wasn't expected back from London for a couple of hours.

Kathleen was locking up when I rejoined her. On the bar were two torches, a screwdriver, and a hammer. She pushed them into a small rucksack.

"You misread the sign," she said, when she saw me looking. "We do B & E here, not B & B."

I looked puzzled.

"My wit's wasted on you, I can see. B & E—breaking and entering," she said.

She led the way to St. Michael's churchyard. It was another bright afternoon: wisps of cloud, swollen sun in a blue sky.

"You know," she said, "Edith must have had a reason for being the way she was."

"Yes, she was an old bag."

"No, an unhappy life. Maybe she changed when she married Lyttle. Maybe he broke her heart."

Kathleen took my arm and walked me between the gravestones to a small mausoleum on the right of the church entrance. She looked around to see if anyone else might be lurking. We seemed to be alone.

"Follow me," she said, squeezing between the mausoleum and the church wall. The next moment she had disappeared. When I squeezed into the space too, she was standing at the bottom of a short flight of steps, fiddling with a door latch. The door came open as I joined her.

The interior of the mausoleum was surprisingly spacious. There were a dozen coffins on shelves around the chalk walls. It smelled of damp. I put my hand to a wall and the chalk crumbled under my palm.

Kathleen shone her torch on the west wall. There was a rectangle of metal, some four feet wide and six feet high. Kathleen went over to it and pulled. It was hinged and opened on to a long passage.

"This has been oiled," she said. "Recently, too."

She led the way into the tunnel. I had to bend to avoid banging my head on the roof but it was easy enough to walk down the tunnel since the floor was even and solid.

"I think at one stage the Manor must have been a center for smuggling," Kathleen said in a low voice. "Boats used to dock at Lewes and I remember reading there was a big smuggling center at Horsham, a few miles up the road."

I grunted. I was wondering about a group of men carrying, not rum or contraband, but the body of Miles Lyttle down this tunnel from the Manor and into the churchyard.

Shortly, the tunnel swung to the left. As we rounded the bend Kathleen pointed ahead to the light at the far end of the tunnel. We reached a second iron grille, with an ascending flight of worn steps on its other side. The light was spilling down the stairs.

We stopped and listened. I thought I could hear a murmur of voices. Kathleen looked at me then carefully pushed the grille open. Its hinges too were oiled

The stairs gave on to a narrow corridor. There was a doorway a few yards to the left. The murmuring grew louder. We tiptoed down the corridor and flattened ourselves against the wall.

After a moment I peeped through the doorway into a kind of chapel, its walls and floor painted with pentacles and strange astrological symbols. I guessed it was what we in the trade call a black magic room.

I poked my head further into the room. At the far end of the chapel were half a dozen people in long white robes, each wearing a conical white dunce's cap-cum-hood which concealed faces and necks completely. They were sitting in a semicircle facing an altar on a raised dais.

Kathleen was looking over my shoulder.

"The Ku Klux Klan?" she muttered. "Aren't they a bit off their patch?"

"Must be a breakaway group," I whispered.

"Very breakaway," she said.

I drew her back down the corridor.

"You should go back before they spot us," I said. "These people could be responsible for two deaths."

"What about you?" she said.

"I know I don't have much of an alibi but I don't think I'm a serious suspect."

She punched my arm.

"Come back with me."

"I'd better wait around for a while," I said.

"Why?"

"That's what you're supposed to do if you're investigating murders."

"I'm not leaving you," she said, looking round nervously.

"I'll be okay." I puffed out my chest.

"It's not you I'm worried about. I've seen the same horror films you have." She gestured at the stairs. "If you think I'm going back down there by myself, you've got another think coming. How do I know what's waiting at the other end?"

We looked back down the corridor, having done a pretty good job of scaring each other silly. Kathleen opened her knapsack, handed me the screwdriver. She hefted the hammer in her hand.

"I'm sure it should be crucifixes and silver bullets but these will have to do. Plus you're supposed to be able to wack someone with these torches without them breaking. Do you know any prayers?"

"I know some Christmas carols—they should do the trick."

"I hardly think so."

"You obviously haven't heard me sing. Less charm the birds out of the trees, more mid-air collision of panicked crows."

"Okay, let's go back in. But I warn you—if we get out of here alive, I'll kill you for this."

Which made a kind of sense.

We crept back down the corridor and ducked into the room. The groined roof was held up by half a dozen thick, squat pillars. We hid behind one at the rear of the chapel.

One of the robed figures hung an incense burner on a hook near to the altar. The incense was mixed with something heavier, more intoxicating. A painting on the wall behind the altar depicted the devil as the Goat of Mendes: cloven-hoofed, fiery eyed, breathing fire and brimstone. The kind of painting done to frighten superstitious peasants. Of course, it worked on me.

Although I didn't believe in the occult for a single moment—okay, maybe for one moment—I clutched the screwdriver tightly.

A stooped figure in a white robe, wearing the same conical hood, crossed in front of the others and stepped behind the altar. There were crude eyeholes in the hood. He looked down at the gathering.

"Welcome, O' members of the Ordo Templi Orientis Prometheus," he said in a quavery voice. "We gather for devotion to the service of The Great Work."

"D'you recognize the voice?" I whispered to Kathleen. She shook her head and put her finger to her lips.

I knew that the Ordo Templi Orientis or Order of the Eastern Temple was the magical order Crowley had fashioned, putting together tantric yoga—the sex one—with gnostic secret ceremonies. It had always sounded like X-Rated Freemasonry to me. It had split into a number of rival groups in the years since Crowley's death.

"We attend for the … er … the obtaining of the knowledge and conversation of our Holy Guardian Angel, um, Seripoth."

The chief priest didn't seem too sure of the script. I suddenly thought of Stassinopolos and his talk on the confidence and power that make you personally magnetic. For public speakers, he said, the first rule is to project confidence. The second is to know your lines.

"Once he has appeared we must call forth the three Great Princes of the Evil of the World, whose names are …"

The chief priest faltered again. Stassinopolos would have been appalled but I felt for the guy. I've been in similar situations. Well, not exactly *similar* but—you know what I mean.

The priest started patting his body.

"Shadrach, Meshach, and Abednego?" a reedy woman's voice suggested from his audience.

"No, no," the chief priest said impatiently, sliding his hand into his robe. "I'm afraid I haven't had time to memorize all the names but I have a crib here somewhere."

He drew out a crumpled piece of paper and looked at it. Held it closer to his face.

"Oh dear, my spectacles—"

"Do let's get on," a voice that I recognized boomed. "If you really intend to call forth and name the three Great Princes of the Evil of the World, the eight sub-princes, and the three hundred and sixteen servitors we need to get a move on or we'll be here all ruddy night."

"Oh shut up," the chief priest said testily, delving in his robe again to produce a pair of spectacles. "You can't stand for anyone else but you to be up here doing this. You've had your turn. Now it's mine."

"I've never seen the point in buggin's turn," Savage said, for it was his voice I'd recognized.

"It's in the rules," the woman said. "It's more democratic this way."

"What democracy has to do with raising demons I have no idea," Savage grumbled.

"Can we please continue?" a clipped male voice said.

But the man whose turn it was to be chief priest was having trouble getting his specs to stay on his nose, given that his face was covered with the white hood.

"For Vedana's sake, take the bloody hood off and get on with it!" Savage boomed.

"May I help you?" a man's voice very close to my ear said.

TWELVE

I jumped. Kathleen yelped. I yelped. Kathleen hit out.

"For Christ's sake, William," she said, whacking young William Macrell across his face with her open hand. Stocky as he was, he stumbled. "You scared me to death. Don't you ever do that again."

"Sorry, Kathleen," William said, regaining his balance and glumly rubbing his cheek. "But this is a private meeting."

"What's going on?" the quavery voiced man called. "Is that you William—I mean, Ephiras—oh, how I wish I could remember all our magical names—who is that with you?"

"Hello everybody," Kathleen called heartily. "I was just showing my friend Nick here the secret tunnels. Didn't mean to butt in."

"Outsiders? There are outsiders here?" the reedy voiced woman said in alarm.

Kathleen walked towards the group in robes. She reached for the woman's hood and lifted it off.

"Don't worry Mrs. Macrell," she said to the alarmed woman beneath it. "It's only me."

I followed. I'd already twigged that the only potentially lethal thing about this shower would be if they tripped over their robes and broke their necks.

"Hi, Mr. Savage," I said, nodding at him. "*Nice* robes. Custom made?"

"I made them," the woman Kathleen had identified as Mrs. Macrell, William's mother, said proudly, patting her hair into place.

"A job well done," I said. "Smocking, isn't it? And I noticed they have concealed pockets."

"Quite capacious ones."

"I imagine they are. But I mean it—you all look very well turned out. Neatly pressed. And your robes are so clean. Pristine, in fact."

"Thank you," she simpered.

"You do the washing, too? But they must be a *major* wash-day headache."

"You've no idea."

"I assume you can't exactly take them down the launderette, you being a secret society and all."

"Precisely," she said. "Frankly, it's a nightmare. But have I ever had one word of thanks in all the time I've been doing it? I have not."

"Shameful," I said. "And being white, I expect you only have to wear them once before they need a wash. Just get a spot of blood on—I suppose that's a kind of occupational hazard among you satanists—all those human sacrifices and such—"

"Mr. Madrid," another man said, his voice trembling, "we are not satanists."

Kathleen leaned across to him and pulled off his hood.

"Patrick Ferguson. What *do* you think you look like?"

"Good evening, Kathleen," Ferguson said, rather sheepishly. "I am dressed in the sacred robes of the OTO initiate."

"More OTT than OTO," I muttered. "What were you up to just now?"

"Conjuring up the Abra-Melin demons—Oriens, Paimon,

Ariton, Amaimon, and one hundred and eleven servitors," Savage said.

"Do not reveal our secrets," the quavery voiced man said.

"I don't think we've been introduced," I said. I looked around the group. "Don't you think it's rather rude to leave your hoods on with a lady present?"

They all sheepishly lifted off their hoods. In addition to Patrick Ferguson, William, and Mrs. Macrell there were three men I didn't recognize. All were in their sixties, all looked shame-faced.

"We are not satanists," Patrick Ferguson said. "We practice Thelemic Magick. Our interest is in the occult, which is very different."

"How different?"

"Our magical practice is natural and thus *good* magic in contrast to the evil magic of sorcery or witchcraft."

"Still sounds iffy to me," I said. "You follow Crowley and everybody knows that he practiced the Black Mass—and worse." I looked at Mrs. Macrell. "As I understand it, a validly consecrated host is used to make the mockery of the Christian Eucharist more obvious, whilst the naked back of a woman often serves as the altar—"

"There's no need to look at me like that young man," Mrs. Macrell said indignantly. "We do nothing like that here."

I pointed at the painting of the Goat of Mendes.

"Really? This room is rented out for Rotary Club meetings is it?"

Savage drew himself up.

"We are scientists, sir, engaged in serious scientific endeavor."

"Come on—magic is a pseudo science in which you incorrectly postulate a direct cause-effect relationship between the magical act and the desired event."

"It's worth a try," Mrs. Macrell said glumly.

Kathleen looked at me wide-eyed.

"I read it somewhere," I murmured. I looked at the group around me. "What are you hoping to achieve? The inside track on the winning lottery numbers? World domination?"

Savage looked from one to the other.

"We are searching for a treasure."

I sighed.

"A treasure Lyttle talks about in his book?"

Savage nodded.

"And what is it?"

Savage shifted from one foot to the other.

"We don't exactly know. That's what we want to find out."

"Lyttle didn't tell you?"

"Garrulous fool," one of the others huffed. "He told us enough to whet our appetites but not enough to enable us to find the treasure."

Hmm. They knew even less than I did.

"So you killed him," I said, without much conviction. I couldn't see these jokers committing murder.

"We haven't killed anybody!" Mrs. Macrell said, shocked.

"Not even Edith Lyttle?"

"Certainly not," Mrs. Macrell said, with at least a semblance of feeling.

"How long have you been meeting here?" Kathleen said.

"Six months or so," Ferguson said.

"And do people from the college participate?"

They all averted their eyes. Finally Ferguson cleared his throat and said: "The college doesn't know about it. We come in through the tunnel from the church."

"Moira Cassidy doesn't know you're here?"

"Certainly not. These rooms are sealed off from the rest of the Manor."

"Bit of a cheek, isn't it?"

"Certain members of the teaching staff here are going about searching for the treasure in their own way," Savage said. "Frankly, it's every man—" he caught Mrs. Macrell's eye—"forgive me, person for himself—herself—themselves."

"Does that include the clergy around here?" I said. "They turn a blind eye to this—or maybe even participate. Are there usually more of you? Don't you need thirteen for a coven?"

"We are not a coven!" Mrs. Macrell insisted.

"Do either of the vicars take part?" I persisted.

"Of course not," Ferguson said firmly. "They would not want to be involved, nor would we want them. Christianity— pah, what a farce. In its early days Christianity was an epidemic rather than a religion. It appealed to fear, hysteria, and ignorance. It has survived for so long only through alliance with the secular powers. But now they realize they've backed the wrong horse. This world was created not by the Christian God but by a stupid conceited demon. A demiurge."

"Nick has those when he's had a few drinks," Kathleen said.

I flashed her a look, wondering how she knew.

"God is above creation. He is the alien, the abyss, the non-existent. If the demiurge or archon who created the universe is a God it is the God of the Old Testament."

"Thank you very much for the explanation," I said. "As Woody Allen once said, 'We have to go now, we're due back on the Planet Earth.' Enjoy the rest of your, er, invocation. Give our best to the archon."

Kathleen and I withdrew and walked slowly back down the passage.

"Is this what the world is turning into?" I said. "A load of loony people believing in absolute garbage?"

"When was it ever different?" Kathleen said. "At least they

seem harmless. I can't believe any of them were involved in the deaths, can you?"

"Not really—although you probably never expected to see your neighbors wearing long white robes and dunce's hats either."

We emerged from the mausoleum into bright sunlight.

"There's something I want to show you back in the pub," Kathleen said. "I've been in two minds about whether it's a good idea. But you'll see a family resemblance."

I frowned.

"One of your paintings?" I said. "Your son?"

She shook her head and smiled a lopsided smile. We walked the rest of the way in silence.

Bridget had left a note at the bar saying she'd gone back up to London and would phone later. Kathleen waited whilst I read it, then beckoned me over to the big painting, the one full of all the regulars. I shuffled over and stood beside her as she flicked the switch for the light above it.

She peered at the picture for a moment.

"There's Dan Wilson, rock superstar and former owner of Ashcombe Manor," she said, pointing to a frizzy haired guy grinning over his pint of beer, standing by the bar, clutching a book to his chest. "Mr. Magic. May he rest in peace."

She moved her finger along to the far end of the bar, to a tall man with long hair and Jesus beard, wearing a black beret and leather jacket.

"Now look at this guy. It's a good likeness."

I stared at the face for a moment. It only needed a moment. It was a very good likeness.

"You have his grin," she said.

I frowned.

"And his frown."

She was right. Everybody who knew him used to say how

much I looked like my father. What was causing my bemusement was trying to figure out what his face was doing painted in to a group portrait of locals in a pub in the middle of Sussex when we had lived in Lancashire. Kathleen must have read my mind.

"He used to visit me, Nick. I knew your father well."

I remembered my dad used to go walkabout for weeks at a time late in his life. I used to assume he was on a bender. I looked at her and looked again.

"That well?"

She nodded.

"That's how you knew about Tupp's Arse?" I said.

She nodded again.

"He was quite a fella, your dad."

"Really?" I said. "You should have tried being his son."

"He gave you the greatest gift anyone could give. Freedom."

"He was too out of it to do anything else. He was a doper and an alcoholic and he did bugger all with whatever talent he had."

"You don't seem to have come out of it too badly."

"How would you know?" I snapped. I took a deep breath. "Sorry. You should ask my girlfriends how I came out of it. I'm not into therapy but I know the jargon. Can't commit, always looking for reassurance, constantly needing affirmations of love."

"What's that mean in English?"

"Means I sleep around."

"Like father like son."

"I don't want to hear that."

"Nevertheless. And for the same reason. When your mum died your dad was destroyed, he loved her that much."

"He still had me," I said, surprised at how small my voice had become. "I don't remember my mum. Did you know her?"

"Sorry. I knew your dad much later. I thought him kind, considerate, good hearted."

"—drunk, doped—"

"—innocent. I'm sure he was a lousy father but I'm also sure he meant no harm. He talked about you all the time."

"What? As in, 'Should be home looking after him but fuck it?'"

"He didn't leave you alone, did he?"

I looked at the smiling face of my long-dead dad, brought to life with a few light brush strokes.

"No. He was usually home. It's just that I had to put him to bed all the time."

"So?"

"I was seven at the time."

"Yeees. I can see that might have been a problem."

We were silent for a moment.

"When I knew him he was into all this magic stuff," Kathleen said. "Not the eye of newt and leg of toad shit. His bag was white magic, telepathy, the power of the mind, mind over body. He got into spiritualism after your mum died—to try to get in touch with her. That's how come I know so much."

I couldn't speak for a moment or two. I suddenly felt exhausted. My body had all but seized up, my brain felt like blancmange, I was bleary-eyed, and had a b-a-a-d headache.

I pretended to examine the rest of the painting with great care. I looked closely at the book Dan Wilson was holding. Looked again through the fog in my head.

I cleared my throat.

"What's that book Dan Wilson is clutching?"

Kathleen glanced back at the painting.

"That was his prize possession. Some book belonging to Aleister Crowley. Had it with him all the time. He'd found it at the Manor."

"What was in it?" I said, my imagination stirring.

"Dunno. Don't think he ever read it, he just liked to carry it around, dip into it for the odd sentence. Not much of a reader wasn't Danny." She raised an eyebrow. "Preferred actions to words."

I smiled dreamily, my eyes fixed on the book, with its cover of red leather and the design like an inverted T on its spine. The same book I'd seen in the library of Ashcombe Manor when I had first arrived there.

Despite my exhaustion, I hurried across to the Manor, trying to suppress my excitement. I didn't expect the book to be *The Key of Solomon* but it might point towards it. I was also prepared to find that the book might have nothing to do with all this. Crowley was always writing something—he'd published a hundred books in his lifetime.

I entered the library and let out my breath when I saw the book where I had remembered it, wedged among the volumes of Needham's Chinese history. I noticed nearby a set of Somerset Maugham's novels. I recalled that Maugham had written a potboiler about a magician, based on a meeting with Crowley.

I flicked through the pages of the book. The script was tight and florid. It looked indecipherable. I put it in my pocket and headed for the office. The great hall was thronged with people dressed casually in jeans and trainers, although there were a number of women *d'un certain age* with floaty dresses, a lot of tangled hair and heavy mascara, their arms and necks weighed down with ethnic jewellery.

Moira Cassidy was sitting at her desk, deep in conversation with an intense looking woman in her mid-thirties. The woman was very thin, pretty in a pallid sort of way, with a mobile face and big, panicked eyes. She looked destined to be taken advantage of.

"Mr. Madrid," Cassidy said. "How nice to see you. Meet

Doreen Hacking. She does our visioning. Mr. Madrid found the dead man in the graveyard the other day, Doreen."

"Dear me," Doreen said. She raised herself on tiptoe. "But I suppose if you are going to find a dead man, what better place than a graveyard."

She tittered nervously then looked upset when I didn't react.

"How can I help you?" Cassidy said.

"I think I need to talk privately with you."

"I was just leaving," Doreen said. "See you in the next personal magnetism session, Mr. Madrid—I noticed you there the other day."

"Well?" Cassidy said, when we were alone.

"I can't decide whether you're involved in the things that are going on here or whether you're being deceived," I finally said.

"What things are you referring to?"

"Whose idea was it to restore the Elizabethan garden?"

"Henry's. Why?"

"And the underwater archaeology?"

"As I said, one of our guests asked permission to explore the lake."

"But the lake didn't exist before Luytens created it in the twenties, did it?"

"I don't believe so."

"So your diver must be looking for comparatively recent archaeological remains. Is it Chris Ellington, the psychotherapist?"

"Yes. There's no secret about that. I repeat, why?"

"Henry and Chris are really looking for *The Key of Solomon.*"

"Don't be ridic—"

"Ms. Cassidy, what I'm telling you is true. I know you know about *The Key* because you were at a séance when Neville mentioned it."

"That fool."

"Maybe so. Henry was at that séance too. But I don't think

you know the half of what goes on here. I know you don't know what goes on right under your feet."

"What do you mean?"

I told her about the regular meetings in the black magic chapel. When I'd finished she said nothing for a moment or two.

"What you're saying about the ulterior motive of Henry and Mr. Ellington might well be true. But surely you can't want to implicate them in murder?" She shivered. "I know for certain Mr. Ellington could have had nothing to do with the first death."

"Why so certain?"

"On the occasion of Miles Lyttle's death he was with me all evening." I looked at her. She flushed. "All night, in fact."

"Fine," I said, embarrassed. "And when Edith died?"

"I don't know. But I know that Henry left that evening."

"He's gone?"

"Just for a couple of weeks."

"Where's he gone?"

"To Crete. You needn't look so astonished. It was arranged months ago. We have links with a yoga center there. Priya is going to teach on the island in a few days."

"I know the place. Is Stassinopolos going, too?"

"He is not."

"Is Mr. Stassinopolos from Crete, by any chance?"

"Athens, I believe."

She laughed her musical laugh.

"I'm afraid you're going to be disappointed again, Mr. Madrid, if you suspect Theodakis. You have just met his, er, *alibi*."

"Doreen Hacking?"

"You interrupted her telling me—in more detail than I would have wished—how wonderful Mr. Stassinopolos is in bed. They have been together every night this week. He is tireless, apparently."

"It's quality not quantity that matters," I said hurriedly.

She gave me a steady look.

"So I've heard. Is that all you want to ask me?"

I left her in her office and went in search of Stassinopolos. I couldn't decide whether I was whittling suspects down or leaving myself with no suspects at all.

Stassinopolos was in the library. When he saw the book in my hand he gave a small smile.

"Do join me."

He looked again at the book I was carrying.

"Another seeker after *The Key of Solomon,* eh, Mr. Madrid?"

"I'm seeking the truth."

"The truth? Pah! In a book of magic? Such things are rubbish. I am not interested in such superstitious nonsense. My interest is in our own potential for spiritual enlightenment, not on reliance on some outside power. I see you start to mock, but that is your blindness."

"I'm not interested in superstitious nonsense either. The truth I'm looking for is the truth about who murdered the Lyttles."

"Such a trivial truth. I am a spiritual being, I regard this world as unreal, imaginary or at best irrelevant. Most of us have felt this on some occasion. You too, surely?"

"Around closing time maybe."

Stassinopolos smiled frostily.

"People like Crowley always look for shortcuts. I fear his reputation is grossly inflated, I think because he has always been fashionable—his image appears, as I'm sure you know, on the cover of The Beatles' *Seargent Pepper* album."

I couldn't help glancing down at his Cuban heels when he mentioned The Beatles. But his view came as a surprise to me.

"Crowley, I believe, had some small power but alas the writer was correct who borrowed a description of the actress

Mrs. Campbell and applied it to Crowley: Crowley had 'an ego like a raging tooth.' And he broke his sacred oath, which he took when he participated in the Abra-Melin ritual—an oath to use his powers only for good and to submit himself to the divine will."

"That's all very well, but can you tell me what's been going on around here? Did you follow me in London earlier today?"

"No, but I saw you on the concourse at Victoria Station and I do owe you an apology. I have found your scepticism rather irritating, so when I saw you by chance I gave you a small demonstration ..."

"You tripped me?"

"No. I did not. But you fell nevertheless."

"And the beer glass?"

"The beer glass?"

The puzzled look on his face seemed genuine.

"Never mind. What do you know about the vicar's diary?"

Stassinopolos sighed.

"Lyttle had mentioned that the account the vicar gave in his diaries of his conversations with Crowley in the early thirties indirectly told what had happened to *The Key of Solomon*. He implied that it was somewhere here at Ashcombe Manor."

"And Henry and Chris Ellington had read those diaries."

"Henry only recently. I don't know what information the diver was working on at first but I believe they are now working together."

"Will you tell me what the diary said?"

Stassinopolos smiled again.

"It reported an obscure conversation. Misquoted Shakespeare's *The Tempest*. Do you know it?"

"Fairly well."

"Then you will know that in it Prospero, a great magician, also has a book of magic."

"And a magic wand," I said.

"Indeed. And you will recall what he did with them."

"So that's why they were looking in the lake and digging those holes!" I shook my head. "But how did they know exactly where to look?"

"They didn't. They were guessing."

"But you know, I think." I indicated the book in my hand. "From this? I've glanced at it. It's indecipherable."

"It would appear so. But in fact, if you look closely, you will find you can decipher enough."

"How long have you been aware of this book?"

"Since I first arrived here. I am nominally in charge of the library."

"You told Henry and Chris about the book?"

"I did not. but I gave them a clue from it."

He looked out of the window for a second.

"Henry has gone to Crete. It is such a lovely island. Do you know Prevelli?"

I nodded. Prevelli is unlike anywhere else in Crete, yet an indication of how the island must have been before centuries of bad cultivation denuded it. It is a bay which has a freshwater river running into it.

The river has lush sub-tropical vegetation growing on its banks. It looks like a South Sea paradise—and indeed it stood in for the South Seas in the eighties movie remake of *Mutiny on the Bounty*, which filmed at Prevelli for several weeks. It was one of the homes of the hippies who settled in Crete in the sixties, until they were turfed out in the mid-nineties.

"I regret that your compatriot Lawrence Durrell entitled his book on Corfu, *Prospero's Cell*. For when I think of Prospero's magical island, I think of the shady clearings in the foliage alongside the river at Prevelli."

"Do you?" I said. "You know Crete well?"

"I have relations there. My cousin owns several taverns on the south coast. I have spent many months there." He smiled. "My great aunt—a fascinating woman."

He looked out of the window again and had an odd smile on his face when he turned back to me. He held out his hand.

"Good luck, Mr. Madrid."

When I took his hand, he held mine firmly for a moment, peering intently into my eyes. I was startled to feel a great heat in his hand. It sounds crazy I know, but I felt as if a jolt of energy had surged up my arm.

Just before I entered the pub I looked down at my hand. It was tingling. And my headache had gone.

Kathleen wasn't in the pub when I got back so I retired to my room and started work on the book. It was written in Crowley's own handwriting, I presumed. Aside from the illegibility of his hand, it also seemed to be written in some strange language I didn't understand, with here and there the odd word of English.

I took a break to consider what I knew. As far as I was concerned, the gypsies, Patrick Ferguson, and Stassinopolos were out of the frame for the murders. That left Henry Thomas, Chris Ellington, and—in the form of Anubis, the dog-headed god—persons unknown. And Zane Pynchon. I'd nothing solid on him but he was rich, he was powerful, he was into Crowley, and I was sure he knew where to hire the heavies that had been causing me problems off and on.

I thought about how Henry and Chris knew where to look for *The Key*. The way I had it figured was that they knew from talking to Lyttle that in his book he talked about Crowley having the key around the time he was staying at Ashcombe Manor, for the second time, in the early thirties.

The assumption then was that it would be somewhere on

the Manor. Henry—and Chris when he arrived—started looking around. Where to look? Lyttle had given them another clue,
presumably from the vicar's diary, relating to *The Tempest*. So
they knew vaguely where to search.

I was sure the Crowley notebook I had gave the exact location of *The Key* if only I could figure it out. I looked at my
watch. Almost midnight. I phoned Bridget. I knew she'd be
awake. I didn't know if she'd be alone.

"Entirely," she said, when I asked her. "Rufus is still at the
magazine putting it to bed. That boy works hard."

"Gratified to hear it. Listen, I think I've nearly cracked the
location of *The Key.*"

"Thrill me with your acumen."

"No, I need your help. I've got this book Crowley wrote.
A notebook or diary. I'm sure the answer is in there if I could
decipher it. But it's written in gobbledegook with odd words of
English scattered through."

"Put them all together."

"What?"

"All the English words. Put them all together. I bet you get
a narrative."

"What makes you think that?"

"Went out with a cryptographer once. I'm a good listener.
Told me things about cryptography I'll never forget—no matter
how hard I try."

I spent the next two hours doing as Bridget suggested. If she'd
been there I'd have kissed her. What came out was Crowley's story
of his acquisition of The *Key* and exactly where he'd put it. By now
excitement was battling with exhaustion in me. I'd had half an ear
on the door, wanting to tell Kathleen what I'd discovered, but I
heard nothing. I assumed she was staying over at her mother's.

The last thing I did before I went to sleep was phone and
book a flight to Crete.

THIRTEEN

Late the next morning I went looking for Priya. I couldn't see her in any of the public rooms. I went to her room. She opened the door rubbing her eyes.

"What sleeping draught did you give me the other night?" she said. "I've been dozing off between classes for the past two days."

"Sleeping draught? You've been reading Proust again, haven't you?"

She drew me into the room and gave me a sleepy hug before climbing back into bed and pulling the covers up round her.

"Didn't mean to wake you," I said. I was alarmed by the saccharine tone in my voice and the fact that I had to bite back the words "my darling." Get a grip, Madrid, I cautioned myself.

She checked her watch.

"It's good you did. I'm going for a hack in half an hour. Want to come?"

"Horseriding? Er, I don't think I can. I've got things to do."

"Like what?"

I could feel the weight of the Crowley notebook in my pocket. I didn't dare let it out of my sight.

"I need to talk to Chris, your therapist friend."

"He's gone. Left this morning."

"Gone where?"

"To Crete."

Henry already there; Chris on his way. The vicar's diary must have been more explicit than I had imagined, but not as explicit as Crowley's own notebook.

"Don't look so despondent," Priya said. "I'm not interested in him. And I don't think he's interested in me. It's because of Crowley."

"How come?"

"You know he's another Aleister Crowley freak?" she said. "He's forever listening to a CD he has of Crowley propounding his philosophical nonsense. *The Beast Speaks*, it's called. He lent me Crowley's *Confessions* to read when we were in Crete but I thought it was pretty turgid. But you know what they say: '666, the Number of the Beast; 667, the Neighbor of the Beast.'"

I smiled.

"But what's the link with Crete?" I said casually.

"Chris rates himself as a magician, you know. He did a foundation course in magick with the Golden Dawn Society."

"Makes a change from media studies, I suppose."

"Every morning at dawn, when he was last there, he went over to the castle ruins to spout his mumbo jumbo."

"I still don't see the Crowley link," I said, though I did really. I wanted to know what Chris knew.

"Well, obviously, because Crowley lived there for a bit in the thirties. Chris told me yesterday that Crowley lived in the ruined Templar castle at Agios Pavlos"

She pouted.

"So you have nothing to do. And the hack will only take an hour."

"Sure," I croaked. In fact she was right. The bucket shop had got me a flight for the following morning. I'd already cleared with Bridget that I could use the film article expenses to pay for it. All I had to do before then was keep out of trouble. "I don't have any gear though."

"Don't need it. What you're wearing is fine. They'll give you a helmet."

"Okay. But I need to check Chris's room first. Where is it?"

Priya gave me directions and the key to her room, explaining that every room had the same key. I walked down the corridor to Chris's room and knocked on the door, just in case. When there was no answer I unlocked the door and went in.

I found the head of Anubis and long robes under the bed.

I waited for Priya downstairs. She appeared in tight fitting jodhpurs and a polo top. I bit my knuckles again.

The stables were on Novington Hill, on top of the Downs, about half a mile along from the V of trees. They had their own private road leading up from the public highway. The road that Geoff had used to send the gypsies on their way. It was steep and winding and I worried that Priya's banger wouldn't make it.

I'm six feet four tall. At the stables the only horse big enough for me was an enormous brown mare. Called Cynthia. I watched with admiration as Priya slid easily on to a small, dappled grey horse. Then I clambered up Cynthia's enormous flank and hoisted myself on to her back.

"Cynthia," I muttered.

"What's the matter with you?" Priya said.

"Nothing," I said. "Absolutely nothing."

"So why is your lower lip trembling?"

"It's hardly Hi-yo Silver—awaaay—is it?" I grumbled. "Having a horse called Cynthia. Hardly John Wayne."

"No, but it suits you perfectly," she said.

"Just what I wanted to hear," I said, but she was already

heading out of the gates on to the wide bridleway that ran along the top of the Downs.

We passed a few walkers and a couple of cyclists passed us, whipping by, heads down, bums in the air. For the next half an hour, however, we had the Downs more or less to ourselves.

"You know I'm going to Crete tomorrow?" she said.

"Me, too."

"What?"

I told her all that had been going on around the Lyttles and about Crowley and *The Key of Solomon*.

"An uncle of mine in India was into Crowley," Priya said. "Joined the Kaula-Nath Community."

"Kaula-Nath?"

"Mr. Madrid, I thought you'd been doing your research. In the thirties one of Crowley's disciples went to India and became a *sadhu*. He founded this community combining western occultism with magical Hinduism. So there's a big link between Crowley and yoga."

Priya reined her horse in and we surveyed the landscape laid out below us for a moment. From this height the gentle slope up to Novington and beyond looked as flat as a table. There was a heat haze in the distance but we could just make out the North Downs.

"If we come off the Downs here we can take a bridleway up to the racecourse then do a big loop back round to Novington Hill. Should take about an hour."

"I didn't know there was a racecourse here."

"Plumpton. Supposed to be Dick Francis's favorite. It's a mile or so west of Novington. They don't have races at this time of year, except for one-off charity events."

We came down the side of the Downs on a flinty, chalky track and crossed the road on to a bridleway shaded by a long line of trees. Twenty minutes later we were approaching the junction of four bridleways when I noticed a bunch of riders approaching on a track at right angles to us. Priya started laughing.

"They're at it again."

"Who?" I said.

"The old Novington Hunt. I bumped into them last year. Not that they Hunt anymore, of course. They just go through the motions."

"There aren't many of them."

"Never was. They were frightened of the hunt saboteurs— Brighton's a hotbed of animal rights activists, you know. So they never advertised and hunted in secret."

"How do you mean?"

"They'd phone each other, meet at the gates to Plumpton racecourse and try to find enough open space to have a gallop. Open space was a problem round here 'cos the council and most of the farmers wouldn't let them use their land. So they sneaked across open land, hoping nobody would notice. Any fox with a bit of nous would nip into land the hunt weren't allowed on and thumb its nose at them."

As we and the group of riders both neared the junction, Priya frowned.

"Actually, they're not the hunt, though those two at the front look familiar," she said.

They looked familiar to me too, but I couldn't place them. They reined in their horses at the junction to await our arrival. One of the men who looked familiar was having a bit of trouble with his mount, a big white stallion that, as we approached, was sniffing the air and rolling its eyes. The stallion's unease began to communicate to the other horses. They all started to snort and shake their heads.

"Afternoon," I said cheerfully as we rode into the middle of them.

"Afternoon," a man with scratches down his face said,

rather fiercely, as the big stallion sidestepped somewhere behind me.

"Oh shit," Priya said as we both recognized the man she had clawed on the pier. At the same moment the stallion, carrying, I realized, the other man from the pier, reared and lunged at Cynthia from behind.

Until then I'd regarded Cynthia as, frankly, a deeply boring horse. Despite my best efforts, she hadn't gone faster than a slow plod since we left the stables. But faced with this unprovoked assault from a frisky stallion, she showed an impressive turn of speed. Indeed, ignoring, I'm sure, all the rules of horse etiquette, she went from slow plod to Charge of the Light Brigade in a split-second. In a word, she bolted.

I was dimly aware that Priya's horse had bolted alongside me but I was too busy trying to cling on to pay her much attention. Cynthia's leap forward, pushing through the other horses impeding her progress, took me so much by surprise I almost fell off backwards. I yanked on the reins to pull myself upright, then leaned forward to cling to her neck for dear life. I was aware of shouts and whinnying horses behind me as Cynthia hurtled off down the bridleway.

My knowledge of horseriding was limited. I had no idea, for example, that riding a galloping horse could be such a juddering, jolting, downright painful experience.

I knew there was a rhythm I was supposed to get into, so that I went down when the horse went down, but Cynthia seemed to have a running rhythm all her own. In consequence, as she came up I was invariably going down, each time bringing renewed tears to my eyes. I was convinced she was going to cripple me for life.

I tried to slow her but Cynthia simply ignored my increasingly frantic tugs on the reins. In the end I simply clung on and wrapped my legs as tightly as I could round her belly.

Priya appeared to my left, her horse running flat out, head forward, ears back.

"How do I get this bloody horse to slow down?" I yelled.

"If I were you I'd concentrate on going faster," she shouted back.

"What?"

"You're being followed."

I risked a quick glance behind me. The thugs, led by the one Priya had crowned with the stick of rock, were in hot pursuit.

"Why did that horse attack me?" I gasped, as the jolting knocked the breath from me. "Can you train horses to act like rottweilers?"

"He didn't attack you. Cynthia was the popular one. And he didn't attack her," Priya said. "He tried to mount her. Cynthia's in season. You're being chased by a bunch of sex-crazed stallions."

I looked down at Cynthia and across at Priya.

"Bloody great."

"Look on the bright side," Priya called. "You're getting a good gallop."

"Whoopee."

Priya looked over her shoulder.

"They're closing. If one of those horses actually catches up with Cynthia, believe me you don't want to be on her back when he mounts her."

I looked down at Cynthia's wild eyes.

"She doesn't seem too keen on the idea either."

Up ahead the bridleway curved to the right. Directly before us was a five-barred gate. In the field beyond I could see a herd of long horned white cows. Priya saw me looking.

"Patrick Ferguson's herd of wild white cattle," she shouted. "Nobody handles them and nobody goes close to them. If they pick up human scent on one of the herd, they've been known to gore or trample it to death. Whatever you do, don't go in there."

I heard Priya loud and clear. Unfortunately, Cynthia didn't. As we barrelled up to the five-bar gate it was apparent that we were about to leave the bridleway.

"Cynthia!" I yelled in her ear. "I've never jumped … ouf."

Going up and over was scary but quite exhilarating. Coming down on the other side was something else again. Cynthia hit the ground about a second before I did. For that second I was in airborne limbo. Then I crashed back down on to the saddle and the pain shot through my body. I'd never wanted to have children anyway.

As she hit the ground, Cynthia broke wind in the most spectacular fashion. Very loud. Very long. Thereafter, at every other stride, she let rip again. Onward, onward, into what was clearly going to be the Valley of Fucking Death, Cynthia volleyed and thundered.

The herd of cattle with their wicked looking horns eyed us calmly. I glanced back again. I couldn't see Priya but I could see our pursuers thundering towards the gate. The white stallion took it first, the others close behind. I just had time to see the first rider leave his saddle and sail through the air before I turned back to concentrate on my imminent goring.

I closed my eyes as Cynthia cut a swathe through the middle of the herd. But no horns ripped into me. Instead, when I opened my eyes again, I saw that now we had an entourage of stampeding cattle running alongside us.

The Wild West comes to Sussex. Finally I could pretend to be John Wayne, if I could ignore Cynthia's flatulence. And I'd seen enough Westerns to know I didn't want to fall off my horse underneath the cattle's hoofs.

There was clearly going to be no end to Cynthia's remarkable windiness. I would rise up, she would drop down. I would drop down, she would rise up. I would hit the saddle with juddering force, she would let rip.

I was so distracted by this that at first I didn't hear the disembodied voice in the air around me. A male voice, distorted, amplified. I wondered only for a moment what it was—I had my mind on other things. Then I began to make out words.

"The final race of this afternoon's special meeting is the Plumpton handicap …"

"You want a handicap race?" I shrieked maniacally as I saw the racecourse on the other side of a rapidly approaching gate. I looked at the cattle thundering along either side of me. "Well, you're about to get one."

Cynthia jumped the gate at the far end of the field without breaking her stride. I don't know if cattle can jump. The wild whites didn't bother. I heard the clang as they ripped the metal gate off its hinges in their headlong progress.

A race official was standing in front of the entrance to the course. He looked startled at the sight—and sound—of Cynthia bearing down on him. But with commendable bravery his first instinct was to hold up his hand for us to stop.

His second instinct was to run like hell. By then he'd clocked the rampaging horde accompanying us—I couldn't help noticing that one of the bulls had the metal gate skewered on its horns without impeding its progress a jot.

With a roll of drums and a fanfare of trumpets—both courtesy of Cynthia's wildly exploding backside—we swept past astonished people eating picnics out of the open boots of their jeeps and estate cars, on to the racecourse, where the final race was about to start.

A dozen or so jockeys wheeled their horses to watch in awe as Cynthia galloped past them at the starting post, hotly pursued by the Novington Hunt and the wild white cattle. The racehorses panicked, rearing, jumping, and kicking, but thank God none of them came in pursuit of Cynthia. She was tiring now and I didn't fancy being mounted by the eight to five favorite.

It was a steeplechase course, but Cynthia swerved at the first fence and continued to run along the flat. The cattle, as was their way, ran straight through the jump. However, a quick look back confirmed what I had suspected. The cattle were losing their impetus. Our pursuers had got embroiled with the steeplechasers. I glimpsed the man with the clawed face and a minuscule jockey lashing at each other with their whips.

Cynthia was responding to me now and I steered her without too much difficulty through an exit at the bottom of the racecourse beside the railway crossing. We weren't followed.

Priya was sitting her horse a couple of hundred yards up the bridleway. Cynthia slowed to a canter and Priya wheeled in alongside.

"That was fabulous!" she said. "I didn't know Cynthia had it in her."

"I doubt she has any more," I gasped.

It took a long time to get back. Cynthia was, quite frankly, knackered. I felt I should get off and offer to let her ride me. In the end I did get off to lead her. The girl at the stables was surprised at how tired and lathered up Cynthia was when I took her in.

"Did she have a bit of a canter?" she said, throwing a blanket over Cynthia.

"A bit of one," I said, and staggered away to Priya's car, wondering if my testicles would drop again one day.

Priya drove me back to The Full Moon. I was surprised to see Julian Parkinson sitting outside with a pint of beer in front of him. He looked equally surprised to see me.

Priya gave me a long kiss.

"Come see me tonight," she said throatily. I knew I would be frustrated—even supposing I was ever able to function again—

but still I nodded. Is that a ring? Put it through my nose and lead me by it, would you, thanks very much.

"You're nobbing her, right?" Julian said, as I hobbled over to him.

"*Nobbing* her? Jesus, Julian, you're as bad as Bridget."

"But you are, right?"

"Well, it's none of your business but no, I'm not. Actually, she's a virgin."

I regretted it as soon as I'd said it. It wasn't, after all, my secret.

"Gedouttahere!" He looked incredulous. "She must be—what—twenty-five, twenty-six? You can't find virgins over the age of about thirteen these days. Especially round here—convent schools. Believe me, I've tried."

He said the last sentence with such vehemence I looked away, embarrassed.

"Well, she is," I said. "Her religion and all that arranged marriage stuff, you know."

"Of course," Julian said. "Of course." His mind seemed to wander. "The power of adult virginity, eh? Better not let any black magician know about her, sport, or she'll be on some altar before you can say black moon rising. Learned all this stuff when I did the Crowley script. Rare commodity in magic, an adult virgin. Very rare."

He looked at his glass of beer.

"Buy you a drink?"

"I'll get you one." I said.

He came inside with me. There was a young girl serving behind the bar, one of the students from the college. I ordered beers.

"I lost my virginity to a VW Golf," Julian said when we sat down.

"In a Golf?" I said.

"No, *to* one. Was with my girlfriend in the back of my mum's car. I'd been drinking, my girlfriend—future wife, in fact—had been drinking. Anyway, we get it on and I'm banging away and I have no idea what I'm doing really but it feels, you know, okay. And I finish and, still on top of her, I ask her how it was and she says, real bored, it was great. But when I start to withdraw I discover I've not been where I think I've been. I've been banging away in the gap between the two back seat cushions." He laughed. "Best I ever had, actually."

"I didn't know you'd been married." In fact, I realized, I knew very little about Julian's past. "How long were you together?"

"Stuck it out for eight years. Of course, by the end we weren't talking at all. I would sit there like a character in a Francis Bacon painting, all tightly coiled agony. She was like that painting by Munch. 'The Scream.' Unbelievably tense, nerve endings almost visibly jumping on her skin. We communicated entirely by waves of hostility."

He sipped his beer and shook his head wearily.

"Why are you here?" I said.

"I came to tell you Zane and I are leaving for a few days. Location hunting. Filming's on hold whilst Dennis convalesces."

"What happened to him?"

"Insisted on getting his teeth filed for the serpent's kiss. Bit his own lip, the dumb fuck. Contracted septicaemia. His lips are swollen up like footballs. Out of action for a week. Unexpected holiday for everyone. Melinda's already booked her flight to Jamaica. Which reminds me—how did you get on with the Voodoo Chile? I have to say she didn't look exactly ecstatic the other morning."

"They never do," I said ruefully. "We had a pleasant evening."

"You know what I'm asking."

"Julian, in my circles, gentlemen do not discuss women in a sexual way."

"Fags, are they, your *circle*? I seem to recall you asking me questions about Zane Pynchon's sex life. Or is it okay to talk about men?"

"That was because I was suspicious of him. Julian, you know the deaths of the Lyttles look very suspicious. Plus, somebody's been trying to kill me."

"Wow. Didn't realize you were *that* lousy in bed."

"Not a woman," I said impatiently.

I told him briefly about my encounter on the Palace Pier, the weird things that had happened in London, and my recent horserace. Julian leaned in closer to the table.

"Shit, Nick. Why didn't you tell me earlier all this was happening? I could have helped." He looked at me. "What, you thought I might have had something to do with it? Thanks a bunch."

"Not you. Not you at all. Never crossed my mind. It's Zane who's been worrying me."

"Zane?"

"There's been a certain theatricality about all this. The Hanged Man death position. The Hand of Glory. Even the Anubis figure. So tell me Zane couldn't have had anything to do with it."

"He couldn't have had anything to do with it. You crazy, sport? What would a multi-millionaire film producer be doing going around murdering little old dears on the South Downs."

"There's a really valuable book of magic—*The Key of Solomon*—at stake here. Did Lyttle tell you about it?"

"Not a word. I didn't hear anything I didn't already know from him. But then we only really had the one meeting. Here, actually. I think he and Zane had been getting together regularly before I came on board."

"Well, *The Key of Solomon* could be the genuine article— and even if it isn't, it's worth a ton of money."

"How much is a ton?"

I shrugged.

"Millions."

"Dollars?"

"Pounds."

Julian sighed.

"Even so. That's chump change to Zane. Do you know how many millions he's worth? Why, he's put 10 million into this film alone."

He scratched his head.

"Then again, we did have a Hand of Glory among our props."

"And a dog's head?"

"Don't believe so … . But, no—Zane? For some old book? I can't believe it."

"Yeah, but Zane is into all this Nietzschean will to power stuff. There's a popular line, for people who are bright but not bright enough, from Nietzsche to necromancy. Hitler followed it. Zane could have followed it too. And if he believes the magic really works …"

"But it can't, can it? Because if Crowley had this book and it's the real thing, how come he ended his life in poverty in some Hastings bed and breakfast joint? If this book of magic was so fucking great, sport, how come he wasn't ruling the world?"

It was my turn to shrug.

"That's what I'm going to Crete to find out."

"You don't say?" Julian said, producing a cigar from his pocket and sticking it in his mouth. "You think the answer's there, do you?"

"Pretty sure. But please don't tell Zane. I think he may be behind these attacks on me."

Julian reached over and squeezed my shoulder.

"Don't you worry, sport, I'll stay mum. And I'll keep an

eye on Zane. But until you know for certain what's been going on, old buddy, I should be cautious about who you accuse of what."

I stayed in the pub when Julian left. I heard the roar of his car as he set off down the road to Ditchling. I gazed into my beer.

"Triskaidekaphobia," Kathleen said.

I looked up.

"Huh?"

"Fear of thirteen. Crossword before? Triskaidekaphobia."

"Great word. Unpronounceable, but great word. I've missed you. You been at your mum's?"

She nodded then put her hands on my shoulders.

"Fear of arrest, seven letters?"

I twisted to look at her.

"*Scarper*," she said.

"I don't get you," I said.

"Not strictly correct but I bumped into Chadders Chadwick earlier up in Novington. Our community copper? Did you know we went to school together? Used to offer me ciggies to go behind the bike shed with him. As if! Chanel scent, now, that might have been different."

"And?"

"And I think they're going to take you in for questioning tonight."

"Me? For what?"

"Edith was murdered."

"And I'm a suspect?"

"I think that man with the woolly ears is a bit concerned that you keep falling over dead bodies."

"I can't help being clumsy."

"And they've had some kind of anonymous tip."

I tugged at her sleeve so that she would sit down in the chair Julian had vacated.

"So it wasn't a heart attack?" I said.

"Aside from the fact it had stopped beating, her heart was apparently fine."

"Did she drown?"

"There was some water in the lungs but no she didn't drown. When a person drowns, thousands of tiny blood vessels in the eyes rupture."

"And they hadn't?"

"They had. But they do the same when you're strangled. The coroner decided she had been strangled rather than drowned."

"How come?"

"The pathologist doing the post mortem took it into his head to dissect the voice box. He found that the upper horn of the thyroid cartilage in the right side was fractured. A tiny blood clot meant it had been done in life. This little bone never gets broken on its own. The pressure of a fingertip or thumb does it—when someone strangles you."

I looked at her steadily.

"You recite all this effortlessly. I'm very impressed."

"Always had a good memory. So I won't forget you when you *scarper*."

"Why should I do that, if they just want to question me?"

"Because now they're looking at Miles's death again. And the police round here don't exactly put themselves out. You were the first on the scene at both deaths. You'll do."

I'd been a bit of a suspect in a murder once before, in Montreal, but this sounded altogether more serious.

"It probably will come to nothing eventually," she said. "But in the meantime, what's going to happen to your investigations into the deaths? How are you going to find the real killers—and be the first to get your hands on this book of magic? At the minute you're odds-on favorite." She yawned. "And talking of odds, you owe me money for the last race at Plumpton this afternoon."

"You were there?" I said.

"No, but I had friends who were and who put bets on for me. Quite a sight apparently."

"They recognized me?"

"Didn't know you from Adam. Thought you were on a cattle drive from Texas and had taken a wrong turning."

"A very wrong turning," we both said together.

"But I guessed," Kathleen said. "Who else could it be?"

"Well, I'm sure it could be lots of other people but I don't have time to get into that now."

"The only question now, Nick, is—are you one of those flash buggers who always has his passport with him?"

"Guilty," I said. "It's in my room."

"There's a scheduled flight from Gatwick to Athens in two hours. Geoff has agreed to drive you to the airport."

"I don't think that's necessary—"

"He's doing penance. It's very necessary. He won't say anything to anybody. He's expecting you."

I packed my things in five minutes flat. Kathleen took me to the back door and pointed out Geoff's farmhouse a couple of fields away.

"Good luck," she said, holding me close and kissing my neck. "When I see you again I want all this to be sorted."

"You and me both," I said.

When I reached the farmhouse Geoff was standing by a compost heap. I thought he was holding a hosepipe, despite the hosepipe ban. Then I realized it was attached to him. My God. Best not tell Bridget about him. Now I knew what penis envy was. 'Size isn't everything,' I tell my girlfriends, hopefully. 'Yes it is,' they invariably reply.

Geoff saw me but carried on pissing on his compost.

"Good for it," he said. "Keeps badgers away too, if you piss around your garden border."

"Not sure my neighbors in Shepherd's Bush would approve."

"You think you're a real clever bastard, don't you?" he said as he zipped up his trousers.

"Never think I'm clever enough, actually—though thank God I'm not too clever by half."

He grimaced at me.

"Car's over here."

We scarcely exchanged two words as he drove me up the A23 then the M23 to Gatwick. I got out and he was driving away almost before I'd shut the door.

I booked on a scheduled flight to Athens with no difficulty. You can only get charter flights to Crete itself. Horrible cramped planes, which are always delayed and leave at some god-awful hour of the morning. This way I could go down to the port at Piraeus and hop on a ferry to Crete. I was too tired now to figure out what I'd do when I got there.

I got to Athens at two in the morning but the streets were still lively, noisy, and polluted. The taxi driver dropped me at the Minos Hotel, just off Omonia Square. On my way in I was propositioned by one of the many transvestite prostitutes in Athens. I listened intently to his pitch. I wasn't interested really, but I hate to turn down a bargain.

I was given a small room overlooking the square. It was a very humid night but the air conditioning made an awful racket. I lay under a thin sheet, the window open, mosquitoes and gasoline fumes pouring in. I dozed off thinking about Stassinopolos. Even had a little dream about him.

We were in the black magic chapel, just the two of us, and I was denying that he had magic powers.

"You're saying you don't believe me, Mr. Madrid?"

"That's right—though I'm willing to be convinced."

"How's this?" Stassinopolos said.

"Impressive," I said. My voice was a bit muffled, but then all my clothes were hanging down over my head as I hung upside down from the ceiling.

I was already awake when reception gave me an alarm call at six. The square had never really gone to sleep, but I'd been woken by the traffic when it started again in earnest, claxons and horns sounding, at around five.

I had a bowl of hot chocolate and a stale bread roll in a cafe on the square, my eyes already starting to sting from the pollution, then took the train from Omonia Square down to Piraeus Harbor. The ferry left Piraeus at seven thirty. I spent the journey sleeping on a bench on deck, in the shade of a tarpaulin awning. Twelve hours later, I was in Crete.

FOURTEEN

I phoned Ashcombe Manor from a phone kiosk on Hania Harbor. The quayside was busy. Tourists were coming out for dinner under the maroon awnings of the open-air restaurants all around me.

Moira Cassidy's voice sounded remarkably close.

"The body is gone but the spirit lingers on, eh, Mr. Madrid? Am I ever to be rid of you?"

"You'll regret saying that when I'm not around any more," I said, waiting for a response. None came.

"Hello?" I said.

"I'm waiting to hear the purpose of your call."

"Has Priya already left?"

"This morning. Shortly before the police came looking for you. Where are you, Mr. Madrid?"

"You're going to tell the police?"

"I think not."

"Where everybody else is headed."

"The yoga center Priya is coming to?"

"That bay, yes."

"I'm beginning to feel left out. Perhaps I've been underestimating you."

"Probably not."

"You'll let me know how it all turns out?"

"Of course I will. You can trust me—I'm a journalist."

She laughed her musical laugh.

"Perhaps I can at that. Be well, Mr. Madrid."

I'd only brought a couple of T-shirts and a pair of chinos with me so I spent the next half hour buying extra supplies. I also bought a snorkel, mask, and flippers.

The car hire firm only had Unos and Pandas left. At around nine, when it was already going dark, I squeezed into the Uno I'd rented and set off for the south of the island.

There aren't many roads on Crete, particularly going north-south, so traffic was initially heavy, even at that late time. It took me over an hour to get into the high, bleak mountains of central Crete and another hour to come down into Agios Pavlos Bay.

I'd phoned ahead to book a room at one of the taverns. They knew me there, so they had left the key in my room door and gone to bed. I dropped my things off and strode down the steep steps to the beach. The shingle crunched under my feet as I walked to the water's edge and clambered on to a large outcrop of rock—gingerly, for its broken edges were sharp.

The night was very still. Above me the huge dome of the sky was studded with stars. The gibbous moon shone its cold white light on the bay and the headlands. I was strongly aware of the tug of the tides as the silver specked water rushed and sucked at the rock I was perched upon.

I knew I was only a step away from the truth. The truth about Aleister Crowley and *The Key of Solomon.* The truth about who had murdered Miles and Edith Lyttle. But I didn't know how to take that next step. I also knew that somewhere close was a double murderer, someone who, I was sure, wouldn't hesitate to murder again if it meant possessing *The Key of Solomon.*

I looked up at the moon and remembered that first night— was it really less than a week ago? The procession of lights on the

Manor grounds. The procession of animal-headed humans silhouetted against the line of the Downs. The convoy of gypsy caravans. The sound of the car racing away from the pub at closing time. The body of Miles Lyttle hanging like a bat from a tree branch.

I woke next morning in a sweat, bad dreams and hot sunlight pouring in on me in bed. I'd forgotten to close the window shutters when I'd finally come back to my room last night.

I slid out of bed and opened the window. The sky was deep blue, the colors crisp in the bright morning light. Leaning on the windowsill I looked out over the clear, turquoise waters of the bay. A single fishing boat lay at anchor, over by the opposite headland, painted bright blue and yellow, an eye etched on the side of its high curved prow. On such a morning, it seemed hard to believe in the dangers hovering somewhere around.

Agios Pavlos comprised little more than the yoga center, half a dozen houses and five taverns, three of them on the rim of the horseshoe-shaped bay. The yoga center was high up on one headland, built into the rugged cliffs as protection from the fierce gales which blew here six months of the year.

On the terrace of the yoga center I could see a group of students doing their morning T'ai Chi practice.

I was staying in one of two taverns which were side by side almost in the center of the bay. A third, with a lovely terrace shaded by a line of pine trees, was off to the west. The other headland was undeveloped.

I showered in cold water—I wasn't being macho, that's all the water there was—slipped on trunks, shorts, and a T-shirt and walked out onto the tavern's terrace. No one here was stirring yet.

I took the steps down to the beach two at a time, stripped and dived into the water. I'm a strong swimmer and soon I was out almost between the two headlands.

Once, a couple of years ago, I'd swum all the way round from Agios Pavlos to the nudist beach. It had been further than I expected and the waves had been choppier, too. I kept close to the rocks all the way round the headland but I would never have been able to climb up on them.

They were jagged and forbidding and the waves pummelled them hard. Then I got to thinking about sharks and other things swimming deep below me. Creatures which might suddenly loom from the depths and nip a bit off me.

Now I floated on my back and closed my eyes against the sun. Then I felt something brush my leg. A moment later I felt a stinging pain. I jerked over on to my stomach and headed back towards the shore. Something else nudged against me. Another sting. I was being attacked.

By the time I got back to shore, my heart racing, I'd been stung a number of times. I'd finished my retreat like a cartoon character, almost running across the surface of the water. For by then I knew what my enemy was. I'd seen the horrible translucent sacs drifting beneath the surface of the water. Jellyfish. Dozens of jellyfish.

I dried myself off on my T-shirt then trudged up the slope on to the headland on the far side. It was slow-going, sliding back a step for every two I took. I paused to look back across the bay to the whitewashed buildings of the yoga center.

Ten minutes later I was standing on the ridge of the undeveloped headland, looking down on the waves crashing in on the beach below. That beach extended west in a long sweep, mile upon mile of it, stretching across to the distant headlands and soaring mountain ranges.

The next headland was some two miles away. I could just make out the pile of stones that, since the German occupation, was all that remained of the old Templar fort.

There was a figure moving along the beach below towards a

dry river bed which came down to the sea. I was too far away to be able to see a face but something about the gait, even on sand, was terribly familiar.

Henry.

I presumed he was heading for the fort. If I went the top way—following a path through the scrubland along the cliffs overlooking the beaches—I could get there well before him.

It was an easy walk. At every step, I brushed against wild-flowers and wild herbs, which released their pungent scents. I kept Henry in view at first but I soon left him behind.

I reached the fortress mid-morning. Stacks of stones, crumbling lines of old walls. Rough cut steps led down from the headland to the little bay where Priya and Chris had practiced their free diving.

I did a few calculations whilst waiting for Henry to appear. The sun was scorching now and I was grateful that I'd brought a hat.

Henry and I saw each other at almost the same time. He was red-faced and sweating, jabbing a long stick into the sand to help him make his way up the steep incline.

"You," he called when he was still some twenty yards away. "Here's a surprise."

"Not too much of one, surely. You must have worked out what an intrepid investigator I am."

"Intrepid?"

"The word was invented for me."

"Really? I can think of other words more apt that might have been invented for you."

"Here on holiday?" I said, grinning.

He was standing in front of me by now, staring at me boldly. He ran his eyes over the bright swellings on my legs and arms from the jellyfish stings, curled his mouth in a small sneer.

"Nobody likes a smart arse," he said.

"How did you know to come here? Was it in the vicar's diary?"

"Does no harm to tell you," he said. "According to the diary, Crowley told the vicar he visited Crete in May 1932. Met a Turkish merchant with an interest in the esoteric in some back street souk in Heraklion. Purchased *The Key of Solomon* along with some other ancient—and generally worthless—manuscripts and books.

"The manuscripts had been discovered in the cellars of a big old house in Heraklion—the old St. Catherine School. The merchant seemed to have no idea what it was he was selling. He knew that the diagrams in the manuscript must have some mystical meaning but that was all. Crowley realized what he had."

"So Crowley went to Crete and brought *The Key* back to Ashcombe Manor?" I said, though I knew the answer.

Henry smiled.

"So we presumed."

"But something in the vicar's diary gave you the clue that perhaps it never left Crete?"

Henry nodded.

"A casual remark in a conversation with the local vicar. When the vicar pointed out that witchcraft was illegal—the law wasn't repealed until 1951, you know—Crowley made some baiting remarks. On their own of little significance but put together with other things …"

"And you were working with Chris Ellington?"

"Lyttle had spilled the beans to him one night in the pub when he'd had too much to drink. And my meeting with Chris proved to be very fortuitous. The diary was somewhat vague about the whereabouts of the Templar castle. Chris knew it well. The irony for him is that he spent many hours on these ruins without realizing their significance."

"You were the one sending Lyttle the threatening e-mails?"

"I did not want other people to know about *The Key*. Oh not for magical reasons—I leave the mumbo jumbo to Chris. I am not interested in black magic, or spells, or stories to frighten children on dark nights." He paused and rummaged in his knapsack. He brought out a flask and took a sip from it. "However, I do like money."

"So you're hoping to sell *The Key?*"

"It is worth a great deal of money."

I looked at the staff he was holding firmly in his left hand.

"Enough to kill for?"

"You would have a very hard time even attempting to prove that I have killed anybody. My interest is entirely mercenary."

I looked around the ruined fort.

"But how are you going to find it? If Crowley did leave it here, the Germans surely would have found it during the war. And, given Hitler's interest in the occult, if they recognized it for what it was they would have sent it back to Berlin. If they didn't find it, I can't see that there's even a ghost of a chance that you will."

"Chris is planning a magical ceremony to help with its location. A ceremony in the spirit of Aleister Crowley. I think he has an appropriate assistant already marked out."

"Sex magic?" I suddenly thought of Julian's remark about adult virgins and black magic. Priya. "You believe in this ceremony?"

Henry shrugged.

"Well then, what do you hope to achieve here?" I said.

"I have time and patience. Eventually I will find the book."

"You're being naive."

"How so?"

"Because if you didn't kill Miles or Edith Lyttle then you're competing with someone who doesn't hesitate to kill to achieve their goals. And you know what that means?"

"Tell me," Henry said, though without his usual sneer.
"It means you could be next."

I could see a small village back in the hills, the blue dome of its church glinting in the sunlight. I left Henry at the ruin and walked over to the village, arriving in time for lunch. I tucked into squid and a Greek salad with a very salty feta cheese and strong olives. I washed it down with one of those pint bottles of viscid retsina. Well, yes, I do like the taste of turpentine.

I was sitting beneath a pine tree, enjoying the smell of the sap, when I heard a jeep arrive. It came to a halt with a great revving of its engine behind the tavern. A few moments later, Zane Pynchon, in shirt, tie, and a linen jacket, walked into the restaurant.

Seeing him was surprise enough. But when Julian walked out of the tavern you could have knocked me over with—well, with almost anything.

Julian looked embarrassed to see me but quickly covered himself.

"Nick, goddamm!" He flung himself down in the chair opposite me, pinched an olive from my salad bowl. "We'll have to stop eating like this."

Zane Pynchon stood over me and gave me a quizzical look. "So, Mr. Madrid, why are you here?"

"Yoga, what else? More to the point—what are you doing here?"

"Scouting locations."

"But why here?"

"Crowley lived here for a time, didn't you know?" Pynchon said.

I knew, but I wondered how he knew. Had Julian told him I was coming to Crete? Alarm bells started to chime in my brain.

"Could have saved myself a lot of time if I'd realized it when

I was here for the yoga," Julian said.

He looked at my almost empty bottle of retsina.

"That's for me. Zane?" Zane nodded. Julian got up and walked over to the counter. Pynchon sat down facing me.

"Why are you making this film?" I said.

He made a steeple of his hands underneath his chin.

"I've got several low budget, psychologically dark pictures I'm anxious to make," he said. "I'm the kind of guy will put 10 million dollars of my own money into a movie if I believe in it. Although I'm seen as a big-studio filmmaker, I always think more like an artist."

"So why Crowley?" I persisted.

"I'm interested in the power within us all," he said. "Crowley, I think, accessed that power."

"With the help of a little book of spells," I said. He didn't respond to that.

Instead he said: "See, I know about power. I had it in Hollywood for years. Too much power, too much money, too much freedom. For years I could do what I wanted. Hollywood is a town that allows as much eccentricity as you like—as long as the hits keep coming."

Years before, I knew, Zane had been fired as head of production at one of the big studios because his drug abuse was getting out of hand.

"There's probably a revelatory experience awaiting everyone that has to do with finding out who and what you are," Zane said. "And when that occurs, if it occurs, you reach Nirvana—heaven. And the degree to which you don't reach that place of realization, you're in eternal hell."

He'd lost me there.

"I'm just a rationalist," I said, smiling apologetically.

Julian brought three more retsina bottles and filled our glasses. Zane took a sip and spat it out.

"It's kind of an acquired taste, Zane," Julian said with a grin. Pynchon looked at him suspiciously over the rim of his glass.

"So do you believe in magic?" I said to Zane.

"Magic is—it makes for independent people. Crowley's magick develops self-knowledge. You know, all our arts came out of magic—the rituals that produced drama, music, dance, and art. Hell, magic made the European Renaissance possible. Could even say the movies too—they started with the magic lantern, you know."

He stopped speaking and stared into space. After a moment he walked over to the edge of the terrace. I looked at Julian. Julian shrugged.

"What the fuck are you doing here?" I said. "I told you what was going on."

Julian threw up his hands.

"What was I supposed to do? Zane insisted. But, listen, Nick, you're sure you're not getting a little paranoid here? Far as I can gather, Zane really just wants to scout locations. I've got in the script about Cefalu in Sicily, where he set up the Abbey of Thelma. But filming in Sicily is ... tricky, on account of their old style customs."

He rubbed his thumb and finger together in the gesture for corruption. "So we thought we might do both here. 'Cept there isn't much left of the fortress. I warned Zane but he insisted on coming."

Julian scratched his unshaven chin.

"And what about *The Key of Solomon?*"

"Probably lost forever," I said. "Though there's a guy here hoping to do a little abracadabra to find it."

"That so? But how come you're so much on the ball? Where are you getting your information from?"

As I started to speak, Pynchon turned and started back towards us.

"Pynchon wanting to come here is just too coincidental," I hissed. Julian frowned. "All I'm saying, Julian, is keep an eye out—for your own sake."

Priya was at the yoga center when I got back to the tavern. I could see her sitting on the terrace, straight-backed, wearing a lungi, her black hair plaited in a long tail down her back.

I wandered up there, said hello to some of the staff that I knew, and walked over to Priya. She put down her mint tea.

"Well," she said. "You are a man of surprises. Don't say you've come all this way just to apologize. Our date was two nights ago, in another country, you know?"

"Had a bit of a crisis," I said, bending to kiss her on the lips. She turned her head slightly so that my kiss landed on her cheek.

She was sitting with a man of indeterminate age, his dark hair close cropped. He was wearing shorts and a cheesecloth shirt.

Judging by the filthy look he gave me, I was interrupting something. I sat down anyway.

"My lady—my soulmate—is beautiful, compassionate, meditative, and visionary," he continued to Priya. "Her soul sparkles with an ancient wisdom. She has magic in her eyes, a playful heart, and yearns to touch the divine stillness within."

"How lovely," Priya said.

"We share the same interests and delights: nature, healing, finding a point of balance, empowerment, tantra, transformation, generosity of spirit, fun, movement, and moonbeams."

Priya sighed.

"What does she do?"

"She is a practitioner of the healing arts. A dancer. A light worker."

I didn't know whether to vomit or punch him—I could see what he was up to. Instead, I said: "Sounds quite a babe. When do we get to meet her?"

He gave me a frosty look.

"I haven't met her yet." He gazed at Priya. "I'm talking about my ideal lady."

Creep.

"Perhaps you'd like to run along and try to find her now," I said. "Only I need to have a private word with Priya."

Unwillingly, he got to his feet.

"Thank you for sharing these precious moments, lovely lady," he said to Priya, kissing her hand.

When he'd drifted away, Priya said: "See, Nick, that's how you should treat a woman. How did that make you feel?"

"Physically sick. What a geek."

"A geek?"

"Yeah, a geek. A Sad Sam. A nerd. A Willy Wet Leg. What does he do anyway?"

"He's a spiritual masseur."

"Whatever one of those is."

"What are you doing here, Nick?"

"Aren't you pleased to see me?"

"Sort of. But whatever happened between us was back there. This is my space—and you're in it."

"I'm here because of *The Key of Solomon.*"

"I don't want to know. I don't want anything more to do with black magic and the occult and Aleister Crowley. I want things that are life-affirming, not destructive."

"Yes, well, I don't want to alarm you, but you might not have any choice in the matter. Has Chris, your therapist friend, arrived yet?"

"I don't know. I haven't seen him. Why?"

"Does he know you're a virgin?"

"Please, ask me intimate questions, why don't you? As a matter of fact, he does. Why?"

"I think he's planning a little ritual magic to locate the Clavicle."

"So?"

"Sexual magic."

"So?"

"Particularly handy to have an adult virgin in the vicinity for that old virgin sacrifice."

"A magic ritual to deflower me?"

"Well, deflowering would come into it, but I think it would be worse than that."

"How much worse?"

"I think in the proper ceremony, when they've finished with you, they chop you up into seven pieces and toss you to the seven winds."

"That's quite a lot worse, isn't it?"

"As I said."

Priya laughed.

"Novel try, Nick."

"I'm serious!"

"How is he going to do these things against my will? I'm not exactly defenceless, as you may recall. And even if he were to overpower me, I know we're remote but we're not in the middle of nowhere. What can he do?"

"I only know that two people have been murdered on account of this bloody book."

She looked uneasy for a moment, then patted my arm.

"Well, I'm appointing you my bodyguard. If the bogeymen get me, you're the one I'm going to blame."

"Okay, great. So what are we going to do this afternoon?"

"I'm just going to chill. But, as I understand it, the Powers of Darkness only have their power in, er, the hours of darkness.

So I think I'll be fine in the daytime. And no, that doesn't mean you can spend the night with me."

She eventually agreed to meet me for dinner that evening at the tavern under the trees. When she went off, I decided to wait around for Chris to show. I went to my room and sat by the window. I looked down into the bay to see if Priya might be swimming with any passing dolphin. No sign of her.

I was impressed by her calmness. But then again, sitting here with the sun beating down it was hard to think of murder and mayhem. Such things seemed as alien as the jellyfish in the bay.

Crone is an evocative word. Down the centuries, it has conjured up the same image for each of us—a witch, hunched, wizened, and toothless, with mad eyes and talons for hands. The Great Crone. Terrifying. And here she was, in a black frock, taking our order.

Priya and I were sitting under the trees, a welcome breeze blowing in from the sea. A couple of bats were swooping and, well, flitting in the fading light. And here was this old, withered woman who looked like she had the Evil Eye, standing beside us.

"I know what he did with the book," I said, watching the woman cautiously as she hobbled away.

"Who?" Priya said.

"Aleister Crowley. Stassinopolos pointed me in the right direction."

"I told you I don't want to talk about all that negative stuff." She raised her voice theatrically. "Don't tell me any more about Aleister Crowley or Theodakis Stassinopolos!"

The crone heard. Her ears pricked up. Crone's ears are apparently prone to that. When she brought our meal, she hovered. I smiled politely. She said something unintelligible—to me, that is—with Stassinopolis's name embedded in it. I remembered him talking about his cousins owning taverns in the south.

"You know Theodakis?" I said politely, in my impeccable Greek. Sort of impeccable. Well, I try but then, hey, I'm a traveller not a tourist, right?

I mangled her language some more.

"The Great Beast," she said, more clearly than anyone could hope for.

I smiled and nodded as she bared her toothless gums.

"She could have a couple more teeth," I said to Priya. "So she didn't fill the stereotype so absolutely. I feel I'm in a Mel Brooks film."

The Greek woman hobbled away and I began my ritual struggle with the red mullet, trying to coerce flesh from between its powerful ribs.

A few minutes later I noticed the crone was standing nearby looking avidly at us. A young man was standing beside her. I smiled my best 'Yes, it's lovely now fuck off' smile but the young man misunderstood and came forward.

"My great aunt wishes to tell a story to the friends of my cousin, Theodakis Stassinopolos, if you will listen," he said. "He telephoned to tell us to expect the beautiful woman and her companion."

I pushed my plate to one side and invited them to join us. The young man brought a bottle of ouzo and four glasses. And there, in the silent grove of trees, the only other sound the chink of the cicadas, we heard the old crone's story of her encounter with Aleister Crowley.

Her name was Anna. She explained that she had been very beautiful when she was young. I was willing to believe her.

The castle on the hill had been a picturesque ruin for a hundred years when Aleister Crowley pitched up there.

He was with the latest in his long line of Scarlet Women, a skinny, diseased junky he'd picked up in Piraeus, and a ragged boy with almond eyes and a sullen demeanor.

Anna's family was very poor. She worked as Crowley's servant for the duration of his stay. Crowley had rigged up a canvas awning as a roof on the one part of the castle, which had walls in good repair.

Late at night the bay would echo to his hieratic cries. Crowley bought a couple of sheep and sacrificed them—except he couldn't bring himself to do it, so he delegated the act to the young boy.

This was the story I'd read in Crowley's notebook—although now I was hearing it unfiltered by his egotism.

Crowley used to eat in this tavern. He dressed in some peculiar mixture of clothes betokening English aristocrat and magician. He had the mop on his head.

Anna's parents were worried Crowley would try to take advantage of her. But he wasn't particularly interested. He was more interested in the almond-eyed boy, who buggered him senseless at every opportunity. The boy was servicing the Scarlet Woman, too.

Crowley seemed very depressed whilst he was there. The Scarlet Woman left with the almond-eyed boy. Crowley remained alone, using a drug I assumed was heroin, sitting on the cliff top watching the sun come down. After a couple of weeks of doing this he went away again.

"Did he have a book with him?" I said. "An old, handwritten manuscript?"

The young man translated. The woman nodded eagerly.

"And he threw the book in the sea?" I said.

The woman nodded again. I looked at Priya and grinned.

"Told you I knew what he'd done with it."

"Okay, clever clogs, how come?"

"Remembered my *Tempest*. At the end, Prospero chucks in the job with a grand gesture— 'This rough magic I here abjure—'"

"— 'I'll break my staff, bury it certain fathoms in the earth, and deeper than did ever plummet sound, I'll drown my book.' Yes!" Priya grinned, too.

"That's that then," she said.

"Not necessarily." I took my notes out of my pocket. "He did a Prospero. But just in case he changed his mind, he wrapped *The Key* in oilskin."

"You mean it's still down there?"

"You bet. And you can find it."

"I don't think so."

"Sure. Free diving—easy peasy. It's not very deep and the water is so clear you can see the bottom easily enough. He's indicated where he threw it in by landmarks on both headlands."

"After all these years the tides could have moved it anywhere."

"He will have thought of that. He will have weighted it down. I'm telling you."

"It's a waste of time. Besides, I don't want anything to do with black magic. It's bad karma."

"You're from Leytonstone, what do you know about karma?"

"I'm Indian, in't I? It's in me genes."

"Wish I was," I muttered.

"What?"

"Nothing. Look, why don't we just try for half a day? For fun."

"There's nothing fun about this. I've done underwater archaeology. We should do it properly."

"What does properly require?"

"We fly in a helicopter to do aerial surveillance, get a one-man sub, and go down there."

"What if we do it improperly?"

"Then a long length of rope and a big stone should do nicely."

FIFTEEN

Next morning the dozens of jellyfish had turned into an armada. Hundreds, maybe thousands, hanging in the water across the bay. Some as big as hubcaps, bobbing on the surface with the ebb and flow of the waves.

"No way am I going diving with them around," Priya said.

"It might not be the same in the other bay."

"Did you see those silent flashes of lightning in the night?" Priya said.

"I did." I looked at her. "Huddled alone in my little bed."

"It's character-building," she said. "Believe me, I know. The lightning portended a storm at sea, which is what drove the jellyfish inshore. They'll be in every bay and inlet along the south coast."

I took a sip of herb tea and grimaced. We were sitting on the terrace of the yoga center again. Different varieties of loose herbs were laid out in plastic bowls to make into infusions. I had no idea what any of them were, they all tasted foul, but I was sure I was doing myself good drinking them.

"*Portend?*" I said. "Nice word."

"It's the mention of *The Tempest*. Makes me all Shakespearean. Didn't that start with a storm at sea? Spooky or what?"

After I'd walked Priya back to the yoga center the previous night and locked her safely away, I'd reread the notes I'd made from Crowley's notebook. He had given exact coordinates for the spot at which he'd dropped *The Key of Solomon* into the sea.

If Crowley believed in the power attributed to *The Key,* he had made a grandiloquent gesture. There was nothing in the notebook to indicate why he had done it. His notes, insofar as I could decipher them, read as the ramblings of a drug-addled mind. Words of conjuration, boasting, attempts at poetry. He scattered repetitions of one line haphazardly throughout the text. "Ashes are no translation of fire."

I was conscious that we were in danger. I was suspicious of both Zane Pynchon and Chris Ellington, who had yet to make an appearance in the bay. As far as I was concerned, the sooner we could fish the book out of the sea the better.

I persuaded Priya to get her equipment ready just in case. The yoga center had a small fishing boat with an outboard motor. We loaded it with the few things needed for free diving, nudged through the jellyfish, and pootled around the headland, heading west. It took about half an hour to reach the Templar castle. Thankfully the sea was calm.

We couldn't see Henry anywhere when we came into the bay below the ruins. I'd been puzzling over how we could retrieve *The Key* from under his nose. I stopped the engine and let the boat drift. We peered into the water looking for jellyfish. Couldn't see any.

"So much for your theory," I said.

"I'm still not going in there," she said.

"The sting doesn't hurt much," I said.

"It's not the stinging I'm worried about—it's how they make you look."

"They don't look so bad," I said, glancing at the red welts on my legs and arms.

"That's what you think," she said.

I took my notes out of my pocket and looked around us.

Crowley's coordinates were the Templar fort on this headland; a gnarled and twisted tree—which I was relieved to see still stood—on the opposite headland; triangulated with the blue dome of the church in the hills behind us.

"It's somewhere over there," I said, pointing vaguely between the headlands. I looked down into the water. I'd been hoping we'd be able to see the bottom but below the surface the water was an opaque blue. "How deep do you think it is?"

"Deep enough, thanks. It shelves away steeply about twenty yards out."

"I've got a mask and snorkel in my room."

"I don't want to know about your sexual peculiarities," she said.

"Ha ha. So how do we do this dive?"

"How do *I* do this, you mean?"

"I'll be in the boat," I said indignantly.

"What—they also serve who sit and get a tan?" She squinted against the sun. "It's simple, really. We drop a weighted rope over the side of the boat and I use it as a guide to dive down until I reach the seabed."

"Wonder why the sea has a bed but the ocean has a floor?" I said.

"Focus, Nick, focus."

"Sorry. And you're sure you don't need oxygen tanks?"

"It's all done by breath control." She took a deep breath to demonstrate. Ouf. She exhaled. I lay back, trembling.

"I slow down my breathing and that slows down my pulse rate—which means I don't need as much oxygen."

I remember the Frenchman explaining, in very technical terms, what molecular changes went on as you went deeper to balance the external pressure on the body. I couldn't remember what they were but it meant that coming back up you didn't need to worry about the bends.

I'd long ago been convinced of the power of breathing. There's ample proof that Indian yogis by controlling their breathing could survive burial alive for hours on end. Why they should want to be buried alive in the first place—well, that was another matter entirely.

I knew that Tibetan yogis, wearing only thin cotton garments, thrived on icy winters at 18,000 feet by using a breathing technique, known as *tumo,* which created body heat. Ditto above question.

Harry Houdini, the escapologist, used yoga breathing for one of his most famous stunts—surviving for three hours trapped in a chained and padlocked casket, lowered to the bottom of a swimming pool in a posh Los Angeles hotel. He did it for the money.

Priya and I sat in the boat for a further ten minutes as it drifted towards the shore. She frowned and pointed into the water.

"Have you seen all these dead fish?"

It was true. In the shallows, we could see dozens of fish, floating on or just below the surface of the water.

"That's the next five years worth of red mullet taken care of," I said. "Must have been quite a storm."

There was a ring in the rock beside the steps down from the castle. We moored the boat.

"Early this evening for the dive?" I said.

"Maybe," she said.

We walked up to the tavern in the hills for lunch. Zane Pynchon was sitting at a table in the shade.

"Zane," I said, walking over and shaking his hand. "You're still here."

"Always state the obvious, do you, Nick?" he said with a little smile. He looked at Priya and I thought his shades were going to steam up. "D'you think that really was a Templar castle?" he said, when we had joined him.

"So they say," I said.

"Man, they were into some heavy stuff." He shook his head.

"So they say."

"Black magicians to a man," he said. "Worshipped a god called Baphomet. Supposed to have some link to Christ and Mary Magdalene, too—I passed on optioning a book about that once."

Was Zane the man behind it all? Why else was he still here? More to the point, how could I make him confess?

"You just got an academic interest in Crowley or are you into the magic too, Zane?" I said, bored with beating about the bush.

He took off his glasses. Bloodshot eyes gazed blearily at me, then at Priya. I wondered what drug he was taking too much of.

"Whatever it takes. You never want to break out of your skin? You never wanted to be able to do whatever your imagination suggests? That's where I'm coming from."

"How'd you know about Crowley's connection to this place?" I said.

"Don't recall. Julian told me?"

"When?"

He sat up straight.

"You interrogating me?" There was an edge to his voice.

"No, no," I said quickly. Typical craven journo. Our motto: when the going gets tough, we just go.

"Where is Julian?" I said.

"Gone over to Italy to check out Cefalu. Not too impressed by this place."

"And you're just chilling for a couple of days?"

"Right. I like the vibe. I'm leaving tonight though." He looked at Priya. "You want to be in the movies, honey?"

"Doesn't everybody?" she said, in a flat voice.

He dug a fat hand into the top pocket of his jacket. Pulled out an embossed business card. Pulled himself to his feet.

"Call me the next time you're in L.A.," he said, handing the card over to her.

He lumbered away and Priya and I looked at each other .

"He's one of my main suspects," I said. "I mean, why is he here? Really?"

Priya shrugged.

"Guy's an asshole—but that doesn't mean he's killed anybody. He's so fat—how would he do it?"

"He'd hire people. You remember those guys on the Palace Pier we sorted out? The ones who chased us on horseback?"

"*We* sorted out? I seem to recall I did most of the work."

"True—but it was my stick of rock."

"Ha."

"I could have done the same thing but in a different way."

"Like how?"

"I'd have made them eat the rock—do you know what kind of garbage rock is made of?"

"You'd have hit them with tooth decay? Novel idea—but a bit slow acting, don't you think?"

We wandered back down to the bay. Priya stood looking into the water.

"Oh fuck," she said. "Let's do it."

I started the motor and we chugged out to the center of my coordinates. Priya looked over the side.

"How deep do you reckon this is?"

"I should know? I know I can't see the bottom. Look, maybe we should get oxygen tanks."

"Stow that talk, Mr. Madrid. I've gone to sixteen meters on one breath."

"How did it feel when you got to the bottom?"

"I thought, this is interesting, here I am at the bottom and I have no air left. But you'll have that feeling."

I must have looked puzzled.

"You're coming with me."

It took ten minutes to uncoil the twenty-five meter length of rope and heave the iron weight over the side of the boat. I watched the rope snake over the side and skinned my palms slowing the progress of the weight.

"Do you think it has hit the bottom?" I said when all the rope had played out.

"No," she said.

Shit. Seventy-five feet in old money. The deepest I'd ever been was about fifteen.

Priya tossed me a wetsuit jacket, then handed me a weighted belt. I put both on then sat on the floor of the boat putting on flippers. She passed me a snorkel and facemask.

"Okay, this is how it goes," Priya said, all focus. "You take a dozen slow deep breaths, lasting about five seconds each, through your snorkel. That should slow your heart right down. Then you take one long breath at the end of it. That's the breath you're going to go down and come back up with. If we do it right it will be like a moving meditation. If we do it wrong—well, let's not think about that …"

She explained some more how it was going to work. I explained what we were looking for—some kind of parcel wrapped in oil-skin. We sat quietly doing our breathing. Then she passed me a powerful underwater torch and helped me over the side.

We went in on a duck dive. We dropped our bodies down, laid one leg back on the surface of the water and stuck the other leg up in the air behind us. Then we brought both legs together and scissored down.

I was surprised at how quickly and smoothly I descended. I lost sight of Priya almost immediately. I could see the rope in the light from my torch. The rope was intended only as a guide or point of reference, although if we got in trouble it was there to shin back up to the surface.

I used my flippers lazily—everything in free diving was about minimum effort—and felt myself slice through the water, heading down. I felt totally calm—the breathing—and slightly spaced out. The storm had thrown up lots of particles so that, after the first few feet, the turquoise waters gave way to cloudiness and limited vision.

Usually when I go snorkelling I get a bit panicky about what's behind me. The mask magnifies whatever you see—first time I saw my feet underwater, I freaked—and the sound of my own breathing always makes me think there's someone sneaking up on me.

But here I couldn't even see my feet and I wasn't taking a breath. I knew that I had a few inches of air trapped in my snorkel, but as I descended I had no sense of breathlessness. Priya had dinned into me that the fatal thing to do in free diving was to panic, especially about the small matter of running out of air. The lack of air was what caused the molecular changes which allowed the body to exist with much less oxygen than it usually required. If, that is, you stayed calm.

I felt calm as I continued to descend. I had no idea how far down I had come. Visibility was almost non-existent, the torch illuminating just a few inches around me. I was dimly aware of a pressure in my ears and on my chest, but I was more aware of the cold which ran along my body with the eddies of the water.

I had been descending for what seemed like an age, my breath still strong in my chest and abdomen, when I felt something brush against me. Lazily, I moved my head, expecting to see Priya. My mask had steamed up a little so visibility was only partial. In fact, I could see nothing at all.

I continued to drift down, hazily aware that my breath was depleted, but surprisingly unconcerned about it. Something brushed against me again.

Was I nudging the rope? I shone the torch down to see if

I could see the bottom. Or, for that matter, Priya. A niggling thought was in my head. I had been holding my breath longer than I think I had ever held my breath before. It was running out. And I was still descending.

The niggle started to blossom into alarm, the alarm into panic. I swivelled my head around for a sight of the rope, of Priya—of anything but the opaque waters which hemmed me in.

Well, not quite anything.

When the beam from my torch landed on Henry's grinning face I recoiled in shock and automatically sucked in air. It shot down my snorkel and a moment later my mouth was full of seawater.

I managed to stop myself sucking more water in. I held the seawater in my mouth and played my torch around me, feeling my heart thud but trying desperately to ignore it, to stay calm—but without attempting to draw breath.

My torch caught Henry in its beam again. He was rolling in the water, some kind of weight secured to his body by a twist of rope, a harpoon sticking out of his chest.

Priya saved my life.

At sight of Henry I lost it. Suddenly my mouth and nostrils were full of water and I had no air at all inside me. As I started to struggle and sink—and take in more water—Priya appeared at my side. She grasped me firmly and passed me her snorkel, with its precious few inches of air.

I sucked on it hungrily as she rummaged at my waist. I felt the weighted belt fall from me then I started to rise in the water. I looked and Priya had hold of the rope with one hand, my waist with the other. Effortlessly, smoothly, she led me upwards until, when I thought my lungs must burst, we broke the surface of the water.

The spiritual masseur was standing looking down at me.

"Where'd you spring from?" I heard Priya say.

"I walked across the headlands," he replied. "I was watching you from the tavern."

I was cool.

"Found your lady yet?" I snarled, then coughed up more water.

"You heard about the explosion?" he said to Priya, ignoring me.

"What explosion?" Priya said, sounding shaky.

"They think it was a German bomb from the Second World War. Went off in the night. In the bay here, by the Templar castle."

"Anybody hurt?" I heard Priya say.

"Only the fish," I said, cackling, remembering all the dead fish we had seen.

I drifted away again. The next I knew, I could hear the put-put of the engine and feel the boat rolling in a gentle swell. I propped myself up on my elbows.

"Did you see him?" I said, my voice a croak from the water I'd swallowed.

Priya, sitting by the rudder, nodded. She was pale under her beautiful brown skin.

"Henry," she said.

"Did you reach the bottom?" I said.

She shook her head.

"Interesting dive," I said and started to cackle again. A cackle that turned into a cough, expelling the seawater from me.

"I must admit the notion that there was a cache of German explosives just waiting to go off in the bay makes me feel exhilarated, too," Priya said.

"That's your would-be lover trying to worry you," I said.

"File under: nice but wacko," she said blankly.

I managed to sit up properly. We were out of the bay.

"Wonder why these explosives are just going off now?" Priya said. "If there is a cache of them down there, they've been there over fifty years. Why haven't they gone off sooner?"

"Probably have over the years," I said slowly. "Or more likely there's some cocktail of toxic gases been mixing that, now, finally, is ready."

"So what are we going to do about *The Key?*" Priya said.

I shrugged.

"Abandon it."

We chugged into the next bay. I was coming round but it was a hot afternoon and I didn't have my hat with me. The sun hit like a hammer. I looked at Priya, stripped down to a bikini top and shorts, sprawled on the seat at the front of the boat.

"You know we may be being watched," I said. I was thinking of Henry and my telling him that he might be next. "We need some time to think. Why don't we take the boat into the grotto?" I said.

"Sure." Her voice was flat.

We came to a series of broad, flat shelves of rock reaching out into the sea. The water was calmer here. Looking down into its turquoise opalescence I could see shoals of small fish.

"No jellyfish," I said.

"Yet," Priya said.

I steered towards a cave entrance at the bottom of a rugged cliff. The grotto. We could hear a dull booming. Over the centuries, the sea had hollowed out a tunnel in the rock. It went in to a depth of some twenty yards and at it furthest extreme there was a tiny sandy shelf, some twelve yards across by five yards deep. Sun splashed down on this beach through a funnel in the rock above it.

The acoustics were such that when the wind blew groans and strange noises issued forth. Local people and some of the more credulous visitors to the yoga center were convinced this was a supernatural manifestation. I knew that the Delphic oracle had been nothing more than a similar acoustic effect in an odd rock formation.

As we drew nearer, the booming of the water in the funnel grew louder. Priya slowed the boat right down as we approached the entrance to the cave.

"The little beach?" I said.

She nodded.

I cut the engine and the boat slid forward slowly into the tunnel. Reflections of the water swayed on the low roof.

As we neared the beach, illuminated by a beam of sunlight coming down through the funnel, I saw something that poured cold water on my slowly reviving spirits.

A body, lying face down, wearing a black diving suit and a bright blue oxygen tank.

Chris, the ponytailed psychotherapist, had finally turned up.

"Do you think it was the explosion?" Priya said, her voice reverberating oddly in the low chamber.

"Maybe." I peered over the prow of the boat at Chris's body. "He doesn't look to be banged up. Maybe the concussion of the explosion? But why would he be out in the middle of the night? He'd be able to see bugger all. And the explosion doesn't explain the harpoon through Henry back there in Templar Bay."

"What do we do?"

"Make sure he's dead, then get the police."

"There's no police within thirty miles," Priya said.

I shrugged and climbed over the side of the boat. The water came up to my thighs. It was very cold out of the sun. I pulled the boat up on to the shallow beach, then bent down beside Chris. Awkwardly, I rolled him over.

There was a huge stain of blood in the sand beneath his head. I looked away quickly when I realized that it had poured out of his neck when his throat had been cut.

Priya saw too and gave a little gasp, her hand to her mouth.

The great thing, usually, about Agios Pavlos was that it was virtually cut off from the rest of the world. Right now, I wished vehemently that we were in some busy city street, or anywhere where there were other people.

Perhaps it was a shadow falling across me, but something made me look up. I couldn't be sure, but it seemed as if a head had pulled back suddenly from the far end of the funnel.

"I think we have company," I said. I looked round in vain for a weapon. Priya turned towards the entrance.

A few minutes later a man in a wet suit appeared, silhouetted against the light. A ledge ran along one side of the grotto. It was narrow, but if you were careful you could use it to get to the little beach. He walked towards us. His face was hidden by a facemask. He held a harpoon gun, vaguely pointed in our direction.

When he got within five yards he pushed his mask up on to the top of his head and I sighed with relief when I saw who it was.

"God, you gave me a fright!"

"Mr. Madrid," he said, dropping down on to the beach. "You do pop up at the most inopportune moments." He pointed the harpoon gun at Priya, standing in the boat. "And the beautiful yoga teacher for whom he has pined in vain for so long." He grinned. "We've vaguely met but I don't think we've been formally introduced. Why don't you do the honors, Nick?"

I looked at him for a long moment. Then: "Priya, say hello to Julian Parkinson."

"Always wanted to change my consciousness," Julian was saying. "Change my relationship with the world around me. I started out on acid—wasn't hip at the time, it was before it came round again. Moved onto coke when I was in the ad industry—me and virtually everybody else."

Julian sniffed. "Then E, then back to acid. Tried crack. Heroin … . But you know none of it, none of it, is anything compared to the buzz you get from this fucking magic. And I've only glimpsed it. Teeny, teeny glimpse."

Priya and I were tied together, back to back, with the painter Julian had cut from the boat. He had held up the knife he was using on the rope, pointed it at Chris.

"Not bad for three quid from Heraklion market." As he'd tied us together, he'd chatted away as if we were down the pub. "One thing I do know about is knots," Julian said. "All this bonding on yachts you do with the Hollywood movers and shakers. But then you saw my work on Miles Lyttle. That took quite a bit of figuring out, I can tell you."

"But why, Julian," I said. "I don't understand? You're in cahoots with Zane Pynchon?"

"That asshole? Please. He thinks I'm in Sicily but I had to go to Heraklion—only place on this island you can buy a wetsuit. What do you think?" He did a quick pirouette. "Suit me?"

We were lying beside Chris's body.

"Why him?"

"Guy got ideas above his station. He was my sorcerer's apprentice. Looked very impressive as Anubis—that weren't just any old dog head in Novington, you know, he was supposed to be a real hound from hell. Wasted on you, of course. Sometimes I don't know why I bother."

Julian kicked at Chris's leg.

"Decided he wanted to be the big dog—no not Stacey's idea of one, Nick—oops, better not mention her in the present company, eh?" He kicked the leg more viciously. "But there can only be *one* big dog." He pointed to his chest. "Yours truly."

He chuckled.

"The sex magic. It's a real kicker. You know, man, sometimes I've been a goat, sometimes a god, but either way, the feeling you get, the feeling of *power*."

I realized that, although I'd spent quite a bit of time with this man, one way and another, I didn't know him at all.

"You gonna give me the whole story?"

"Sure." He sniggered. "What Nick, you think it's chance Marlowe dropped out of the film? I freaked him with some magical mumbo jumbo. Threatened his family. Anonymous, but it did the trick.

"See, the film was mine. I conceived it. I wrote it. Then Zane had my script rewritten, saddled me with a pile of garbage. Didn't matter. Those moron actors. Didn't matter. I was still doing the Crowley film, getting closer to what he was about.

"I went to Miles Lyttle for his professional advise about Crowley. We had a few drinks. He let slip about his book. What he was going to tell the world. Said it would start up a great hunt for it. Occultists from all over the world.

"Of course, I couldn't let it happen. See, I knew about *The Key,* from letters Crowley had sent to the OTO in Pasadena in the forties. I'd seen them and I was after *The Key.* I mean *The Key's* discovery at this juncture was clearly meant to be. At the new millennium, at the dawn of the new age. But not just anybody could discover it. It was reserved to me. I was chosen." He suddenly giggled. "I'm not saying I'm the anti-Christ. I'm not into devil worship. I just want the power."

"You tried to have me beaten up," I said.

He spread his hands.

"Actually, I tried to have you killed. What was I supposed to do? You were poking your nose in too much. Even someone as inept as you might have accidentally blundered on to something."

"Thanks a lot," I said.

"Some other time, you'll have to tell me how you got off the pier. My boys were a little bashful about that. And the cattle stampede—masterful. They almost got you in London, though, with something as simple as a glass of beer."

"Why string Lyttle up in such a perverse way?"

He shrugged.

"I'm an artist, man, what can I tell you? Can I help it if I have a strong visual sense? I didn't want anyone else to know about *The Key*. I wanted to find it for myself. I wanted to warn other Crowleyites off. Anybody who knew the Tarot would know I was threatening death by violence to anyone else trying to find the book."

"Why Henry?"

"I know—it's ridiculous, isn't it? I mean, where do you stop? Actually, I've quite got into the swing of it. I'm thinking of putting together a hit list of Hollywood producers who've fucked me over. Zane Pynchon would be at the top of it, of course." He grinned mirthlessly.

"Only joking. I didn't think I'd have to make a career of it."

"You're going to kill us, then," Priya said, with impressive calm.

Julian tutted.

"Bad manners to ask that kind of question in these circumstances. Besides, if I tell you, it takes away the suspense. I'm enjoying talking to you. And such a pleasure to meet you, the virginal Priya. What a gorgeous babe! So sorry I never got the chance to know you better, if you know what I mean. Don't look at me like that—rape's not my scene. I have some morality."

Priya looked at Chris.

"I noticed," she said.

"Sweetheart!" Julian adopted a hurt expression. He looked at me. "See, Nick—out of the mouths of babes, eh?"

"Why kill Edith?"

"Feisty old dame, I'll give her that. Thought the bitch would never stop struggling. I went round to see her about Lyttle's book. Just to make sure she hadn't got a disk tucked away somewhere. Turned out she had but she wouldn't let me have it. Guess we had a falling out. After I killed her I got to thinking. Maybe she'd posted it to you."

I remembered the mugged postman.

"Taking a risk spending so much time in the neighborhood weren't you?"

"You know it. But whenever I was around I wore a cloak of invisibility."

"They help," I said. A cloak of invisibility is one of the things magicians are supposed to be able to conjure up at will. Pull the other one, please.

His eyes burned. He suddenly hit me hard across the face.

"Worked, didn't it?"

I shook my head, tasting blood in my mouth.

"Guess it did. What about the hand?"

"The Hand of Glory? Lucky chance—I had it in the back of my car. Overly theatrical, I know, but what the hell. Looked pretty realistic, didn't it? Bet you heaved your guts at the sight of it."

"So what happened the night you killed Lyttle?"

"We arranged to meet in the churchyard. He was going to take me through the tunnel from the church to show me the black magic room. I got there early and I heard him mouthing off to Henry about the book. Couldn't afford to let that kind of thing happen."

"Where were you parked?"

"Pub car park. Made a bit of a racket when I finally left there. Was easy enough to truss him up—he didn't weigh much."

"And then?"

"And then I was no further forward finding where *The Key* was. Must admit it was hard to keep my mind on the filming, especially with Dennis playing up the way he was. The lunk here told me about Crete. But once I was here I still didn't really know where to look."

He reached over and took my notes out of my shirt pocket.

"Good luck for me that when I came back from Heraklion this morning I saw you in your boat in the bay there, referring to these very notes."

He frowned.

"Don't suppose these tell you what was going on in Crowley's head? Guy intrigues me. A lot of people think Crowley was a crank, a con man. And he was a showman, no doubt of it. He loved the theatricality. But one thing has always puzzled me. Why did he suddenly fade? He spent his last fifteen years doing nothing. Why? What happened to him? Especially as he had at his fingertips the most powerful magic the world has ever known."

"You gonna tell us, then?" Priya said, cockney creeping back into her speech.

"Supposing Crowley knew he was just a con man, didn't believe in any of this magic rigmarole, never really believed in it as a link to another world? Then he gets *The Key of Solomon* and it looks as if it might work. Saw the possibilities. The risks. Crowley was a blusterer and a coward. And he turned away because he got frightened.

"He gave up. Got further into his drugs. That was the end of his life really. Then couldn't live with himself. All that garbage he'd been spouting in over a hundred books. And now he had *The Key*. But he was too chicken to open the door.

"Well, I'm not chicken. I'm going to take your toy boat and go down and find the book that you've pinpointed so kindly."

"What about us?"

"Going to have to leave you trussed up, I'm afraid."

"You're not going to kill us?"

He took the oxygen tank from Chris's body and lowered it into the boat.

"Nick, you're my friend. Priya's beautiful. I couldn't sully my hands with your deaths."

"Thanks," I said, meaning it. I thought to warn him about the German explosives.

"Julian, watch out for—"

"Besides, you'll drown in here when the tide comes in." He clambered into the boat and pushed it off. "Can't stand around gassing all afternoon. I've got my destiny to fulfil." He looked down at me. "Watch out for what?"

I smiled at him.

"The jellyfish …"

The spiritual masseur was untying us when we heard the dull rumble of the explosion. We looked at each other in silence.

"That sounds like it's the last of the German bombs," the masseur eventually said—okay, okay, I do owe him, I can at least call him by his name—*Joseph* said. He'd been following us—well, Priya—on land when he saw Julian leave the grotto in our boat. He'd found us when he came down to investigate.

It took us almost an hour to get back to the Templar fort. The sea was calm. Wood from the boat was scattered like matchwood all across the bay. We were standing there when D. I. Bradley, he of the furry ears, walked up alongside us in bright green Bermuda shorts, long Pynchon socks, and brown, open-toed sandals.

"Spout of water thirty feet high when it went off," he said, gazing out to sea. "Straight up into the air. The boat just fragmented. Awesome."

"The diver?"

"Got here just as he was going over the side. Didn't see him come back up. Be scattered between here and the Peloponnesus by now." He scratched his chin. "I assume, Mr. Madrid, he was our *prime suspect*."

"I wonder if he found the book?" Priya said. "You know—actually got to touch it before he died? Though, of course, it may have been the book that killed him."

"Run that by me again?" I said, squinting into the sun as I looked up at her.

"If the book was what people have all been saying it was, perhaps his death was to do with the power of the book. Maybe the book destroyed him. He thought he was chosen. Maybe he wasn't." She looked at me. "Don't give me that expression. You don't know. And we'll never know."

"Actually, I think I do," I said.

"Go on."

"In Crowley's notes he repeated several times the sentence, 'Ashes are no translation of fire.'"

"So?"

"The guy in the British Museum told me that there were so many different versions of *The Key* because for it even to stand a chance of working the magician had to write it out for himself."

"You believe that?"

"I don't believe any of it. But Crowley believed it."

"So?"

"Suppose whatever power the spells had only resided in the original. Somehow latent in it? The original would be in Hebrew script."

Priya thought for a moment. Then: "Ah."

"Not Crowley's own language. He would have to translate it. And if he translated it, the paradox was that it would lose its power."

"Ashes are no translation of fire." She nodded. "So as far as he was concerned, it was no use to him. But why didn't he keep it—or sell it, if he was always so hard up?"

"Maybe he liked the big gesture."

We started to trudge back over the headland, heading for Agios Pavlos.

"Are you here to get me, D. I. Bradley?" I said.

"That was the original idea," he said. "Quite exciting really, getting to fly out after you. But now I'm not so sure. This is a little more complicated than I envisaged."

"Might have to postpone that retirement?"

Bradley took a deep, noisy breath and flashed his very white teeth.

"Oh, I do hope so," he said with feeling.

EPILOGUE

I was gazing into the fire in the lounge bar of The Full Moon when my mobile phone rang. I knew who it would be.

"So, Shagger, did you do finally do it with her?"

"Where are you? I phoned the magazine and they were very mysterious about your whereabouts."

"Buggers dumped me yesterday. Guess who they made editor? That little wanker Rufus. All that hard work he was doing, he was doing for himself."

"Bridget, I'm sorry."

"Don't be. The contract I negotiated meant I had a very nice pay-off. And I put your payments through before I left. Going to go on a long holiday. Didn't know if you fancied coming to South America with me. Assuming you're not going to end up in jail."

I smiled over at Kathleen behind the bar.

"No, I think the police believe me. I'll be coming back to London later today when I've said my goodbyes here. I'm having a drink with Moira Cassidy a bit later."

"Glad you're getting right back on the horse," Bridget said. "Or should that be right back in the saddle?"

"It's only a drink, for goodness' sake."

"Sorry you and Priya didn't work out," she said softly.

Priya had stayed on in Crete after I'd come back. So had that dickhead Joseph, the spiritual masseur, so God knows what was going on there. She liked me well enough, but I was far more stuck on her than she was on me.

"So *did* you shag?" Bridget said.

"No," I said.

"No?" she said, incredulous.

"We made love."

"Yeah, yeah. How was it?"

"Bridget, that's personal."

On that last morning, Priya and I had gone for a walk.

"Am I going to see you again?" I said.

"I'm sure we'll bump into each other from time to time."

"You know what I mean."

She squeezed my hand.

"No. But thanks. For, you know, the other night."

"No problemo," I said. "Any time."

"There only is the one time." She looked at me. "I'm glad it was you. I mean it. I really am. I give you roses, kisses, and sapphire showers."

"Thanks very much," I said.

"So did she say anything?" Bridget yelled in my ear. "She must have said something."

"She did, actually."

"Well?"

I preened.

"She said she was glad it was me for her first time."

"What a nice thing to say. Did she say why?"

I'd asked Priya the same thing.

"D'you mind if I ask why?" I said.

"Not at all," she said. She leaned over and put her lips to my ear. "It was mercifully brief."

AUTHOR'S NOTE

I used *The Book of Tarot* by Fred Gettings for information about The Hanged Man. John Symonds's *The Great Beast*, Colin Wilson's *Aleister Crowley: The Nature of the Beast,* and Colin Wilson's *The Occult* provided me with biographical information about Aleister Crowley. I have invented his stay at the fictional Ashcombe Manor, his possession of *The Key of Solomon,* and his visit to Crete.

All that I have written about *The Key of Solomon* is accurate, except that a Hebrew original has never been found. Yet. Theriomorphism is alive and wagging its tail somewhere near you. To my knowledge, there is no Templar castle in southern Crete, although there is an excellent yoga center at Agios Pavlos. It has all the good and none of the bad qualities of the fictional yoga center referred to in these pages.

No Laughing Matter

by Peter Guttridge

Tom Sharpe meets Raymond Chandler in *No Laughing Matter* a humorous and brilliant debut that will keep readers on a knife's edge of suspense until the bittersweet end.

When a naked woman flashes past Nick Madrid's hotel window, it's quite a surprise. For Madrid's room is on the fourteenth floor, and the hotel doesn't have an outside elevator. The management is horrified when Cissie Parker lands in the swimming pool—not only is she killed, but she makes a real mess of the shallow end.

In Montreal for the Just for Laughs festival, Madrid, a journalist who prefers practicing yoga to interviewing the stars, turns gumshoe to answer the question: Did she fall or was she pushed? The trail leads first to the mean streets of Edinburgh and then to Los Angeles, where the truth lurks among the dark secrets of Hollywood.

0-9725776-4-5

speck

Two to Tango

by Peter Guttridge

Journalist Nick Madrid finds himself up the proverbial creek—the Amazon—without a paddle when he's dispatched to South America to report on a Rock Against Drugs tour.

As if monstrous spiders, piranhas, kidnapping, and tiny, spiky fish that swim up a stream of urine to lodge where a man least wants a tiny, spiky fish to lodge aren't enough, Madrid is drawn into the mystery of who is trying to kill the tour's headlining larger-than-life, pain-in-the-posterior rock megastar Otis Barnes.

Madrid soon discovers that the murdering queue forms on the left for Mr. Barnes. Question is can he prevent Barnes' date with death at the final concert at Macchu Picchu?

"Brilliant one-liners, lightning action, lots of suspense, and very funny—self-deprecating Madrid is fast becoming my favorite hero."

—*Good Housekeeping* (UK)

1-933108-00-2

speck

Bullets

by Steve Brewer

When a contract killer bumps off a high roller in a Las Vegas casino, a tangle of romance, gambling, and gunplay follows. The killer, Lily Marsden, is a mysterious and cold woman who is a true professional. But soon, the casino owner, his henchmen, and the victim's two brothers are on Lily's trail.

Former Chicago cop Joe Riley is pursuing Lily, too. She cost him his job as a homicide investigator when suspicion of a bookie's murder fell on him. Joe is certain Lily killed the bookie, and he's tracked her across the country to Vegas.

Throw in some local cops, a playboy, a new widow, a rug merchant, a harridan, and a couple of idiot gamblers named Delbert and Mookie, and the mixture soon boils with intrigue and murder. Add a dash of romance as a strange magnetism develops between Lily and Joe, dust the whole concoction with Steve Brewer's trademark humor, and you end up with *Bullets*—a crime novel you won't soon forget.

0-9725776-7-X

speck

DeKok and the Geese of Death

by Baantjer

"Baantjer has created an odd police detective who roams Amsterdam interacting with the widest possible range of antisocial types. This series is the answer to an insomniac's worst fears."
—*The Boston Globe*

Renowned author Baantjer brings to life Inspector DeKok in another stirring potboiler full of suspenseful twists and unusual conclusions.

In *The Geese of Death*, DeKok takes on Igor Stablinsky, a man accused of bludgeoning a wealthy old man and his wife. To DeKok's unfailing eye the killing urge is visibly present in the suspect during questioning, but did he commit this particular crime?

All signs point to one of the few remaining estates in Holland. The answer lies within a strange family, suspicions of incest, deadly geese, and a horrifying mansion. Baantjer's perceptive style brings to light the essences of his characters, touching his audience with subtle wit and irony.

0-9725776-6-1

speck

For a complete catalog of *speck press* books please contact us at the following:

speck press
po box 102004
denver, co 80250, usa
e: books@speckpress.com
t: 800-996-9783
f: 303-756-8011
w: speckpress.com

All of our books are available through your local bookseller.